The Sea of Innocence

The Sea
of Innocence

KISHWAR DESAI

**SIMON &
SCHUSTER**

London · New York · Sydney · Toronto · New Delhi

A CBS COMPANY

First published in Great Britain by Simon & Schuster UK Ltd, 2013
A CBS COMPANY

1 3 5 7 9 10 8 6 4 2

Simon & Schuster UK Ltd
1st Floor
222 Gray's Inn Road
London
WC1X 8HB

www.simonandschuster.co.uk

Simon & Schuster Australia, Sydney
Simon & Schuster India, New Delhi

A CIP catalogue copy for this book is available
from the British Library.

HB ISBN: 978-1-47110-142-7
TPB ISBN: 978-1-47110-143-4
EBOOK ISBN: 978-1-47110-145-8

Typeset by Hewer Text UK Ltd, Edinburgh
Printed and bound by CPI Group (UK) Ltd, Croydon CR0 4YY

For Jyoti, Scarlett and the thousands of women
who have been raped and murdered in India – in
the hope that one day they will get justice

The Sea of Innocence

Chapter 1

The girl in the video did not look older than sixteen, a pale flame flickering amongst the four dark-skinned boys who crowded around her as she raised her hands and moved to the music. The boys merged together in the dim light as they tried to get close to her. They may have been older than her but since they were all dressed in t-shirts and bright shorts, and two of them had their hair tied in ponytails, they seemed young. The girl was tiny, in a yellow halter-neck top and short blue skirt, as they circled her, dancing with her eyes closed, mesmerized by the hypnotic beat.

A low ceiling was visible behind them, lit by a single bulb covered with a red scarf, the light spilling in splashes of blood onto the swaying figures. Curtains lined the wall, and in one corner a circular window was visible. Familiar-sounding trance music bound them into a robotic movement.

One of the boys suddenly said something vehemently to the girl. It was difficult to distinguish the expressions on the faces. The video was possibly shot on a mobile phone and the images were grainy. No effort was made to adjust the quality or to zoom in – and though the tone of his voice was sharp, the words were muffled by the music. From her relaxed manner, it seemed the girl knew him well. She shook her head and pushed him aside while he was trying to say something into her ear. It was obvious she was confident of herself. Without even opening her eyes, she carried on dancing.

The boy slipped his arm around the girl and cupped her left breast. The other boys stared and the dancing came to a standstill. Nervous laughter broke out as the girl slapped him and one of the boys blocked the camera-view momentarily, trying to stop the fight, perhaps. He was jostled by the boy next to him and, as though made aware of the camera, he looked over his shoulder and stepped alongside the girl. The girl threw her long curly hair back over her shoulder and struggled with the boy, who continued to grope her. He managed to untie her halter top, exposing her breasts.

The other boys became absolutely still.

She quickly pulled the two ends of the top behind her neck, retying them. And then she lunged at the boy to hit him. But he ducked and caught hold of her wrist. There was a momentary pause, as though the script had gone wrong and someone had given instructions to redirect the video.

'Oh, come on!' one of the boys said. This time both the words and their implication were clear.

'Shut up, you idiot,' the girl replied, and then giggled and added, 'Don't be stupid.' Oddly, she didn't sound angry.

The screen went dark. Then when the video started again three of the boys and the girl were on a bed. One of them was lying on his side, speaking to her.

'You promised. You can't be . . .'

The audio was once more slightly blurred, and even the little conversation which could be heard was jagged and unclear.

She was obviously immune to his persistent, persuasive tone. She lay flat on her back, still in her halter-neck top and short skirt, staring at the ceiling. Her legs were crossed but her feet were moving in time to the music.

The camera was jerkier than before. Earlier it might have been placed strategically on some table; now someone – perhaps the fourth boy? – was holding it.

'Come on . . .' The voice was aggressive and shrill. The girl looked directly into the lens, but her eyes were completely unfocused. She pushed herself up, moving slower than before, and slid back as though the effort was beyond her. Was she drunk? Why didn't she get up and leave?

'Just take off her skirt,' another voice said, even more loudly than the previous one, with a distinct Indian accent. I thought I heard a Goan lilt.

The lens moved closer to the bed and hovered over the girl, scanning up her pale legs, getting closer to the fabric

3

of her skirt, when there was a sudden flash of bare thighs and a triangle of blonde hair. Then the screen went blank again.

The video did not last more than three minutes.

I stared at the small dark screen of my mobile phone, still in a state of shock.

The clip had been sent to me by Amarjit, an old college friend of mine and a police officer presently based in Delhi (while recovering from a high-profile divorce).

It was accompanied by a message saying he wanted to speak to me. But after his ex-wife had threatened to name me as a co-respondent in their divorce, there was very little reason for me to communicate with him. In fact I had broken off all contact from him for the past three years.

So was this some kind of horrible joke? A schoolboy prank: a lewd video sent to intrigue me and break the ice instead of a bouquet of flowers? Hook me with a mysterious and very disturbing message, and then reel me in.

I wasn't going to fall into that trap again.

I answered politely, suggesting that he tie his feet to a 500-kilo weight and drown himself in the Arabian Sea.

But the video had an unsettling effect. Its very visible sexual overtones and the vulnerability of the girl upset me more than I had thought. I was also puzzled and angry that Amarjit had chosen to send me the video, and at this time.

As he probably knew, since he was still in touch with my mother, I had come to Goa for a holiday, to lounge on the fabulous beaches while the sun spread a golden glow on the water. Not for this. In fact I was still depressed after hearing about the horrific gang rape of a young paramedical student on a public bus in Delhi. No, I could not deal with this.

I sighed and, chucking the phone into my bag, which was already overcrowded with guidebooks and the sunscreens I had come to collect from our hotel room, made my way back to the beach. I wanted to join Durga, my 16-year-old daughter, as quickly as possible, nervous that she had been left alone even for a short time.

Durga, meanwhile, was sitting comfortably on the sand getting a henna tattoo of broken hearts in a daisy chain painted onto her arm.

'Too depressing. Why broken hearts?' I asked her briskly, deliberately not looking at her, unprepared for another argument, as we seemed to have had quite a few in the past few days, mostly over trivial things. Though we always made up, I didn't want to risk an all-out war, which was so easy on holiday, particularly when you're meant to be having a good time. 'Try something else.'

Maybe that's what 16-year-olds want? a voice retorted in my head, as I began to liberally lather on the sunscreen.

After all, I was thirty years older than Durga, and anything but trendy, even though I now lay next to her on a sunny beach, wearing a flimsy pink sarong over my daring black swimsuit, to hide any unseemly bulges.

5

Durga had insisted on wearing an old-fashioned swim-suit with a high neck and a little flared skirt. If she was so decorous, I should have definitely been wearing a burkini, at least! And yet, secretly, I was relieved at her choice. After what I had just seen on my mobile phone, I wouldn't have been able to deal with Durga's sexuality, even inci-dentally, on display.

I could just about handle her current passion for sad songs and heartbroken tattoos. What kind of a holiday was this going to be? Not very jolly, that was for sure.

The black nail polish she had applied this morning had been a bad omen, and should have warned me of worse to come. Was she turning into a goth? What if she wanted rings punched into her lips and safety pins in her belly button? And what if she insisted on being miserable? Despite my resolution that I wouldn't say anything, I felt my irritation rise.

'How about a string of paisleys around your arm . . . like this.' I tried to inject a happy note in my voice.

I waved my own plump arm with its intricate paisley henna tattoo (which looked quite nice, if you ignored the accompanying bingo wings – with only a touch of cellu-lite, mind you), while being observed keenly by Veeramma. She was the canny beach vendor who had painted the tattoo on me, and had subsequently attached herself to us for the past three days, showering us with endless compliments in fluent, if ungrammatical, English,

French and Russian – as well as her native Kannada. She sold everything from head massages to sarongs and all the while looking like she had just stepped out of a village in Karnataka. She was smarter than I could ever hope to be, proving the value of never stepping inside a school.

'Perhaps you should've got a dragon tattoo,' quipped Durga, as she presented her other arm to Veeramma. 'It's more suited to what you've been up to.' She was teasing me about my penchant for trying to solve difficult crime cases, even though my avowed profession was that of social worker. And there were many who described my voluntary work as annoying interference in matters that didn't concern me.

Determined not to be provoked, I laughed at Durga's little jibe and said 'Touche!', mindful of the fact that we still had a week left of our holiday. No point getting annoyed and ruining it.

Instead, I wondered how Veeramma and her gang of fellow beach gypsies had the energy to walk around all day, barefoot on the hot sand, with a swathe of elephant-print sarongs slung on one arm, a bundle of silver jewellery dangling from the other, and a patchwork embroidered bag over a shoulder. And she smiled and smiled, used to dealing with camera-clicking, sensation-hungry tourists from all over the world. In fact, it was probably some of those very tourists who had tutored her in multiple languages.

I had a feeling she was humouring us – sharing a wink and a smile with her sister vendors, gathered around us in a good-natured crowd. In India, a *tamasha* – a spectacle – could be created within minutes.

Right now I had drunk too much beer to bother about the women's obvious interest in us. I lit a cigarette, pleased for once at the slow pace of the Indian government, as the long-proposed ban on smoking on the beach still had to be implemented.

I blew smoke rings and watched Veeramma deftly dribble another thin line of black henna on Durga's arm. Obviously she knew who was more likely to win the battle of the broken hearts. I sighed and fell further back into the sand. Why argue when Durga wasn't going to listen anyway? I tried to synchronize my breath with the rise and fall of the waves.

Veeramma squatted comfortably on the sand next to us, while the other six vendors now edged closer to me and began complaining about their husbands and their mothers-in-law. They asked me, half-teasingly, to take them all, or at least one of them, back with me to Delhi, as they said they hated their lives, wandering around on the beaches all day. They longed to be inside a house, cooking and gossiping and squabbling like the overdressed house-wives in the TV soap operas they watched at night. They did not even mind being hired as domestic help. Anything, so long as they were not looking for customers, made objects of ridicule, treated almost like untouchables, shooed away from the shacks serving food and drink which lined the Goa beaches.

I glanced back towards the row of beach shacks: temporary thatch-roofed, sand, cement and wood structures. Barring a few, they would be removed every monsoon and then reconstructed in the holiday season, the licences given to them providing an additional income to the government *babus* who carefully priced every stamp of approval for these coveted allocations. The shacks created their own economic and social environment and life (or, very occasionally, death) on the beach depended on which shack you attached yourself to.

'Bastards no let us come up to deckchairs, still taking *hafta*,' Veeramma grumbled under her breath.

I had already learnt that the cops who gave them permission to sell their wares took a cut from their earnings. In the few days that Durga and I had been in Goa, we had realized that a well-oiled, systematic food chain existed. The tragedy was that no matter who postured as the biggest fish, there were others still larger than them.

Reluctant to get up, I gestured to the waiter near my erstwhile deckchair to bring my beer over, as it seemed too far away to reach in my flip-flops.

In my present cautious mood, I especially did not want to leave Durga alone with the gossiping women. What if they asked her something awkward?

They might want to know about the men in our lives and ask where my 'husband' (and presumably Durga's father) was. Having revealed so much about their own lives, wouldn't they be eager to know about ours?

These were always difficult questions for an adopted child such as Durga to answer.

Of course, she and I had discussed what she should say when asked. As rehearsed, she should mention that she lived in Delhi with her grandmother and me and that her father had died some years earlier. All of this was technically correct. There was no reason to reveal that her father had no connection with me. Or that he had been murdered. Nor should she discuss the tragic circumstances under which I had adopted her.

And if after this brief introduction she withdrew into silence, hopefully any further queries would be stalled. I knew it was difficult and unfair to ask a young girl to keep so much to herself, but thankfully she had never been very loquacious and the last few years in the Delhi school had trained her well.

The sand was soothingly warm against my back and I lay back, relaxing while Durga's tattoo was completed.

Slowly I became aware that Veeramma's hypnotic movements over Durga's arm had stalled as she stared towards the sea, her eyes glued to a young woman in a bikini running past us, her blonde hair bouncing behind her.

I felt my stomach knot in tension. She reminded me far too much of the girl I had seen in the video less than an hour ago.

Veeramma said something to one of her friends, who was also closely watching the girl. I couldn't follow her comment, but both of them burst out laughing. Puzzled, I watched the girl speed over the sand, lightfooted like a gazelle. She seemed no different from all the other tourists who crowded the beach and were swimming in the water. Why had she caught Veeramma's eye?

'What's so funny?' I asked her.

Veeramma shook her head.

'Nothing. She new catch, I think.'

'Caught by whom?' I asked.

A silence followed. Durga moved uncomfortably, as Veeramma's grip on her arm tightened slightly. Then Veeramma looked up and smiled. But the smile did not reach her eyes.

'Some beach boys like fish.'

The woman sitting beside her cut in swiftly, 'They sell in market!'

Another added, 'And making tasty curry.'

'No. Masala fry! Chop chop! *Bon appétit!*' giggled the woman next to her, saying the last few words in a perfect French accent, bowing slightly towards me and presenting her palm as though serving a culinary treat, while the other arm looped the air. Where had she learnt that astonishing perfection? Could just mixing with a few international tourists give these women this accent and style? Or was there some other secret behind their multilingual skills?

As she stopped for applause, I thought the divergence between her words and light-hearted gestures was not only macabre, it was frightening as well.

Watching her, all the women laughed out loud. Yet there was nothing funny about the implication of young men snaring women like fish and then selling them or slicing them up.

Almost by a hidden signal the women started gathering their things, and stood up to leave.

'What do you mean?' asked Durga, her eyes darkening. In her own childhood she had seen and understood, far too early, about cruelty. She knew immediately that something wasn't quite right. She might have also felt my unease.

'Forget it, madam. Enjoy holiday. Many things on beach you don't want to know.'

'*Goa, Goa . . . Goa, Goa.*' Another woman swung her hips in time to the chant, as she pirouetted on one heel.

Veeramma poured a bit of oil on Durga's henna hearts, and told her, 'Don't rub off now. Leave thirty minutes then tattoo will stay for few weeks.'

I handed her the payment, but couldn't help asking, 'And how do you know that girl?'

'I did tattoo, madam,' she said, suddenly looking shy. 'But private place.' She quickly placed her hand just below her belly button and darted a look at Durga, who was listening fascinated.

'Not you, baby. Shut eyes, ears,' she added. Even though Durga was as old as the teenager who had just run past on the beach, Veeramma made the classic blunder of thinking that, being an Indian adolescent, she would be more innocent.

A cold shiver ran through me while I remembered the permanent tattoo that Durga had once had on her arm. We had later had the design erased, at her request. Little did Veeramma know what Durga had been through in her young life.

Perhaps I shouldn't have brought her here, a place that might unleash difficult memories that had thus far been assiduously contained. The carefree feeling which had been somewhat dented by the morning's video suffered further erosion. After all, it was only a few years ago when Durga had come into my life as a traumatized teenager, unfairly accused of murder. I had managed to get her out of jail and adopt her. But I couldn't protect her from the unexpected. My foolish assumption had been that Goan beaches would be safer than the streets of Delhi for women and young girls.

In the past few days I had realized that the naivety which once existed on Goa's beaches had disappeared long ago. There was an uncomfortable and very apparent dichotomy between life on the beach and the rest of Goa. The sandy rim of the sea seemed almost like another country, which was, for some, ruled by its own laws of behaviour. Even though the beaches looked serenely cosmopolitan on the surface and offered a variety of sea sports and other innocent pleasures, there was a looming darkness around the edges. Like a hungry nocturnal sea animal it padded through the sand, seeking victims. Shades of it had been apparent in what Veeramma said about the girl, but a suspicion of it was in the dead eyes of some of the beach boys, and the cynicism with which they looked at the near-naked bodies strewn on the beach. Not everyone on the beach was here for a good time. Or perhaps everyone had a different description of what a 'good time' was.

In contrast to the beaches, mainland Goa seemed almost puritanical, despite the proliferation of the liquor shops and bars. The interior was where much of the history and culture lay. But right now it seemed too much of an effort to explore it.

Durga smiled back at Veeramma.

'So why do you think she had the tattoo done down there?' Durga asked, trying to look as though she hadn't understood. 'No one would ever see it.'

'Only fish in sea,' Veeramma quipped.

Many days later I would remember our laughter and realize how eerily accurate Veeramma's answer had been.

'She's quite clever, isn't she?' said Durga, looking towards Veeramma as she picked up her bags and joined her friends.

'You have to be, I suppose, if you want to survive on this beach,' I replied. 'Veeramma's quip about the beach boys made me think of the men in the video. Could it have been shot around here, and did the clue to their identity lie in their casual attire, the shorts and t-shirts that everyone wore around Goa? The fact that Amarjit had sent it to me while I was here might not be purely coincidental. But why, after all these years, would he want to get in touch with me, and in such a strange manner? Was it something to do with the girls that Veeramma had spoken about?

Almost guessing my thoughts, Durga asked, 'I wonder who that blonde girl was,' as we trudged back to the restaurant under the thatched roof, on the higher ground. Dusting out our towels, we settled back into our deckchairs.

I shrugged. I had already been worried that our holiday would get ruined by our occasional squabbles, and now I had another reason to be concerned.

Urging her to order some king prawns I lit a cigarette and asked for another bottle of chilled beer.

I decided that I would erase all memory of that girl in the video, and stop worrying about what happened to her. I would also ignore Amarjit's attempts to get back into my life. This was not my problem. I was here just to holiday with Durga.

Famous last words, as they say.

Chapter 2

Much to my annoyance and despite the increasingly rude messages I had sent to dissuade him the previous evening, Amarjit decided to show up, in person, at the hotel at 8 a.m. the next day. Which made me realize that he must have actually arrived in Goa yesterday, or even earlier, and then sent that video. He might have even seen me on the beach. What the hell did he want? Why was he being so persistent?

I hated being stalked like this.

Meeting former boyfriends is difficult enough for me when they drop in unannounced. But more so after I have been dealt with rather vigorously by a masseur and my hair is standing on end.

Quite apart from the fact that the massage had given me an oily sheen that made me resemble a gold-plated Rolls Royce (I probably looked as large too, in my crumpled kaftan), I simply didn't want to meet Amarjit. He had already wrecked my stay in Goa with that video. It was hardly the sort of thing to send to someone holidaying with her 16-year-old daughter and it had depressed me more than I'd realized.

16

I hadn't been able to push those depressing images out of my mind. It was especially curious that the girl seemed to have willingly put herself in such a risky situation. Even if she had misunderstood the intentions of the young men, she surely knew that being alone with them, given the fact she was a foreigner, could lead to some rather serious consequences. What puzzled me was that, after the boy molested her in front of the others, she had laughed, and even lay down next to him. Despite the peculiar circumstances, she seemed, at least to me, to be an ordinary middle-class girl just having a good time. So why then was she alone in a room full of men, who were probably filming her with them? And why didn't she walk away from that highly insecure situation?

Unfortunately, despite my determination not to think about her, when we got back from the beach, I continued to do so till late at night. Obviously I couldn't discuss the video with Durga for fear of disturbing her fragile calm. I knew that showing her the images or sharing my worry over this young girl would remind her of how vulnerable and alone she had once been. It might even bring back the nightmares that had finally stopped haunting her. Nor could I talk about it with anyone else, because I had no idea why Amarjit had sent the video to me, whether it was a recent incident, or part of some ongoing investigation.

As a result, I hadn't been able to sleep and had booked

17

myself for a massage at the crack of dawn, before Durga woke up and found me restless and anxious.

And now Amarjit stood before me, with that familiar half-smile. It seemed he had completely forgotten what I had said to him when we had last met, years ago, as well as the messages I had sent yesterday.

But to be honest, every time we met, I too tended to lapse into an easy familiarity, without even realizing it. Besides, his recent divorce made me a little more sympathetic towards him. Life was never going to be easy when your wife had cleaned you out and walked off with a younger man.

Instinctively I smiled back and then quickly looked away, changing that expression into a frown.

It was a struggle.

I wished I could hurt him and tell him to go away, but all the moments we had shared held me back. Former lovers (of which I have quite a few, I'm afraid) always have a peculiar impact on me. Perhaps I am one of those incorrigible romantics who live in hope that the good times will come back again. Though I doubted if Amarjit and I would ever make the Mandovi River sizzle. There was too much unfinished business between us, and I was sure he was still too cut up over the way his wife had left him.

Yet we did have a relationship which went back a quarter of a century, and much of that history was dotted with pleasurable moments. Barring the last few years . . .

Luckily Durga was still asleep upstairs in the hotel room and Amarjit and I could speak frankly. It was important she didn't know that he had come to visit us this morning. At the time when she had been kept in judicial custody it was Amarjit, a supposedly close friend of her father's, and a senior police officer, who had failed to protect her over and over again. Seeing him she would immediately sense bad news. And might even guess that our holiday was irrevocably wrecked.

It was now clear to me that my mother must have told him everything, including where we were in Goa, banking on our old friendship to make it a less acrimonious meeting. I also thought that she still harboured a hope (which she had hinted at earlier, on hearing about his divorce) that we would suddenly fall in love, again, if we met in the salubrious climes of Goa.

'Don't you have anything better to do than to hound me like this? It's just about eight in the morning. This is Goa, for God's sake! And I'm on a holiday!' I said as grumpily as I could manage, cutting through the smile he had pasted on his face.

I noticed that he had come to meet me minus the usual paraphernalia of police uniform, medals and fancy car topped with a red light and a flag. He was in a loose kurta and jeans and I hadn't seen him like that since our days together in St Stephen's College in Delhi. Mufti? Had he

19

forgotten who, and how important, he was? That would take a volcanic explosion, wouldn't it?

'Have they finally thrown you out?' I asked bitterly.

Amarjit raised his eyebrows, looking as though I had paid him a compliment. Apart from a guarded 'hello' he hadn't said a word thus far, allowing me to get all my angst out.

'Though,' I continued dryly, 'if you send sex videos to people, I wouldn't be surprised if they have.'

He waited for me to stop spluttering. And then paused for another beat.

I remembered this tactic only too well. The silences that could wear you down; and then, like a common criminal, you would be forced to grovel and confess – *Yes, yes; I did it. The fault was mine. All mine. I'm guilty.*

'Have you quite finished?' His voice was annoyingly amused.

We were still in the lobby of the hotel and so I turned around and marched to the coffee shop, sitting down without bothering to hide my irritation. I beckoned a waiter, and ordered black coffees for both of us. I was damned if I was going to offer him any breakfast.

I tried to forget that oil was dripping down my back, and in the mirror opposite I saw that strands of my hair were bunched together as though I had applied gel to them. Not a great way to look at all.

Perhaps concerned about who was likely to see him, he

looked around the room before sliding into the chair opposite. He sat with his back to the wall, half turned towards the entrance. It was the posture of a man ready to run, if required. Why was he so tense?

'Is Durga here with you?' he asked.

'Yes,' I muttered to the tablecloth.

What gave him the right to ask me anything?

'Is it possible for you to send her back to Delhi?' he asked. 'I need your help, and it might be a little dangerous if she's around.'

Affronted, I stared at him. He had just made my daughter sound like a piece of luggage! Send her off, indeed! My temper rose even higher.

Realizing that we were in the smokers' section, I deliberately and slowly pulled out a cigarette from my handbag, and placed it between my lips. I knew my smoking annoyed him, ever since the day he had given up and assumed I would follow suit.

But apart from watching me carefully as I lit the cigarette – almost as though I was indulging in some pagan rite – he did not rebuke me.

I slowly blew out smoke, making him wait for my answer. When I spoke my tone was, I hoped, annoyingly languorous.

'Let me explain this to you: I am here on a holiday with my daughter. We plan to stay here for at least ten days. We've barely been here for three. Why would I want her to leave? Since when are you my holiday planner? And, after the last time, why the hell would I want to help you?'

His ears turned red. A sure sign that he was starting to get angry. Good!

He ignored my words, and lowered his voice. 'It's not safe for Durga. Especially if you get involved in the case I've come to talk to you about. She's a very pretty girl and I don't want her to attract any attention.'

'I have already told you that I am not interested in the video, or in this case, or in fact in anything to do with you. Nor am I prepared to tell Durga to drape a dupatta over her head. She's sixteen years old. Get a life, Amarjit! Besides—'

I was about to remind him about his childless status. But knowing it was something he was extremely sensitive about, I bit my tongue. I could be mean, perhaps, but not cruel. Besides he could always make a similar remark about me. I had never borne a child, though at least I had managed to become a mother.

'What were your thoughts about the video I sent you?' he asked, looking around once again, as though he thought someone might be listening.

His obvious tension was giving me a headache.

I gave him a sweet smile.

'Oh dear, I think I forgot to thank you. Very entertaining. I had no idea you dealt in soft porn. And so, tell me: did they screw her in the end?'

There was a silence and I looked up to see, for the first and probably the last time in my life, Amarjit frowning, looking as though my question had physically hurt him. And because it was a crude question, and one I should never have asked, I, too, wished I could withdraw it. Even as the words had escaped my lips, I knew how unfair they were.

I just wanted him to feel as ashamed and awkward as he had once made me.

But he said nothing, and continued to stare back at me. So I took a deep breath and tried again, this time maintaining a gentler note.

'Alright. I give up. What's the story? I mean of that girl in the video?' I asked.

Was my reluctant interest responsible for his obvious relief? He quickly lowered his gaze to the coffee cup. Yet when he looked up he seemed uneasy. Was he hiding something from me?

'They probably did molest her . . . and rape her. But I have no proof of it.'

'So where is she?'

He spread his hands and shrugged.

'Your guess is as good as mine.'

'When did this happen?'

'It could be weeks or just days, or months. I have no idea. Now she's gone and all we have is that video. It was found on a mobile phone last week near a shack on the beach. There is no SIM card within, and no traceable number. The same video was also sent out to various people in the government and the police. We don't know who sent it or why. Perhaps it was just to warn us that this was happening to the girl. She vanished some time back, I've been told.'

'So who complained about the fact that she was missing?'

'Her sister. They are . . . were . . . both in Goa on a holiday. The video was probably shot somewhere around here.'

'In a house with round windows,' I said, thinking back to the video.

'What?' Amarjit looked startled.

'Nothing.' I shook my head, determined not to be the least bit intrigued by this case.

We stared out through the veranda, shrouded in greenery, at the calm blue sea outside. It was a picture-postcard scene, with the first few swimmers bobbing among the waves. The fishing boats were further out in the water and I could see their sails, like the closed wings of butterflies resting on a blue garden. The water was peaceful, gentled by waves which were spreading themselves in welcoming smiles on the sand.

How could one even imagine this to be a scene of violence?

And yet I had sensed it lurked beneath, yesterday.

I wondered if this was my cue to abandon Amarjit and ask Durga to go down to the beach with me before I was dragged any deeper into this. But the thought of waking a sleeping teenager was daunting.

Besides, I was curious why he was so keen to find out more about the missing girl. Hundreds of Indians and scores of foreigners went missing every year. Few were ever found and it was very rare for a senior police officer to take any interest in their disappearance. What could have possibly upset him? And why had he come all the way to Goa? Even though the video had upset me a great deal, I covered up my unease, and began to demolish his argument that a rape had occurred.

'That girl seems a survivor. She looked like she knew those boys quite well,' I said thoughtfully. 'Are we then worrying without a cause? Yes, they were trying to feel her up and get her to strip, but it might have been consensual. Like a game. She didn't make an effort to leave, and it was obvious that they all knew that a video was being shot. Even this scuffle between them may have been part of a prepared script. Are you sure this wasn't staged, and that they weren't actually shooting a movie? Maybe even porn?'

Amarjit looked as if he was about to say something that would possibly persuade me to the contrary, but I carried on determinedly.

'Look, she's a young woman, in a strange country.

25

Why would she agree to go into a room with four – or was it five? – Indian men to dance, or whatever it was they were doing . . . And then why would she agree to lie down next to them on a bed? Why didn't she try to get away from them even after one of them touched her breasts? My hunch is that she knew exactly what she was getting into.'

Amarjit looked around again, as though worried that someone would hear us. But we were in a corner of the coffee shop, with a row of plants screening us from the rest of the restaurant, a safe distance from the nearest table.

I knew I had said some very politically incorrect things, but then I had heard the local Goans complain more than once about some of the female tourists and their behaviour. The insinuation was that these women were trying to seduce the local men. I did not subscribe to this point of view, but right now I felt we must at least consider it.

It was difficult to tell if this was just a clash of cultures. After all, the women could equally complain that the men who 'succumbed' to their charms were looking for sex and a foreign passport.

Was it a larger problem that an apparently modernizing India did not know how to deal with female sexuality, and assumed that normal, friendly behaviour and western clothes meant that the women were available?

Some Indian village *panchayats* in a northern state had recently reacted badly to Indian girls wearing jeans and carrying mobile phones, and had banned both: jeans and mobile phones. Goans would not hold such extreme views, surely, but I felt that in recent years the constant presence of tourists in this small state might have had an adverse impact. Especially since many of the locals veered towards a fairly conservative lifestyle while life on the beach was anything but that.

Just because the girl might have consented to being alone with these boys for a 'dance', was it presumed that she would willingly take her clothes off and sleep with them, I wondered. Or, as I had suggested, had she known what was going to happen and wanted to be there?

'Don't look so shocked, Amarjit. You think if I question what the girl was doing with four or five boys in a room alone it will sound like an antifeminist view. *How can Simran say this?!* But, to me, this girl looked like she had a choice. While I don't think that foreigners who come here must behave like vestal virgins, it would surprise me hugely if they are so very blasé about everything. How could she go into a situation like this and not expect something sexual to happen, damn it?! And then the whole thing is being filmed! Come on. She looked at least fifteen or sixteen years old. Most western girls have been on dates by then, have had sex and so on. She knew what she was in for . . . and I am sure it did not end in . . .'

I stopped because I noticed how increasingly grim Amarjit had become.

He completed my sentence, pushing his coffee cup away as though the brew was not distilled from the best coffee crop from Chile, as the menu claimed, but from hemlock.

'In rape. Or murder. Or both. And now we don't know where she is. Which is why I had to come down, and try to talk to you.'

Provoked, at last, I thought he might tell me the truth behind his interest. I couldn't believe he had come down to examine the single case of one allegedly missing girl. Why do that when he had so many lackeys who could do it for him?

'It's a long way to come when you're not even based here. That's strange.'

'Someone has asked for my help, and that's why I'm here. Please don't try to grill me on who it could be. Suffice it to say that the government is very worried about incidents like this is Goa. They've happened a few times in the past, and we've received complaints that the local police just hush it up. This time we want to investigate the system, see if anything is going wrong. And also check if any of these complaints, especially by foreign nationals, are true. Now that this girl has vanished, we need to know if this is also part of the same conspiracy of silence.'

'And so you've been sent here to do some firefighting?'

'Just to get a proper investigation going. I can't

announce it to my local colleagues here because the state government will object if I interfere. But everyone is upset because these cases can become very high profile, hurt the image of the country, and even affect tourism.'

I was startled by his last words. *Affect tourism?* I thought he was here because he was worried about the girl.

'And of course, then the economy gets hit as well,' he went on.

'Which part of the world is she from?'

'She's British.'

So it wasn't just the problem about this missing girl, but now the larger economic and foreign-policy implications which were worrying the mandarins in Delhi. All because a young British girl had disappeared.

'Have there been many more cases like this? I only know of two cases so far: this girl, and that other girl, also from the UK. I can't remember her name.'

Amarjit hesitated. 'Scarlett Keeling.'

As soon as he said the name, it all flooded back. Because of the publicity it had generated I had followed the case quite closely for a while.

That name had been in the headlines non-stop for almost five years, while Scarlett's mother had fought for justice over her daughter's brutal murder in this part of Goa. Initially the police had simply said that the 15-year-old had drowned while out swimming at night, and rushed to close the case. But the mother, Fiona MacKeown, had found too many loopholes in their investigation, including the fact that the girl had been naked except for a brassiere dangling from one shoulder, when her bruised and battered body had been found one morning, on the beach. Three days after her daughter's death, she stumbled upon the clothes her daughter had been wearing on the night she died: the shorts, t-shirt and underwear stuffed behind a shack close to where Scarlett's body had been discovered. The police, apparently, had not even bothered to hunt for her missing clothes.

I remembered that she alleged that Scarlett had probably been given drugs, raped and then murdered. Fortunately, one witness, a British national, stepped forward. He claimed he had seen her being sexually assaulted by a barman of the Luis shack at Anjuna beach (not far from my hotel) early in the morning. Even though the girl had been somewhere on the beach or in the vicinity from 12.30 at night till her death sometime around five or six in the morning, no one could explain how she died.

Two men were eventually arrested: the barman accused of the rape, and an alleged drug dealer who was also at the shack that night. Scarlett had been seen snorting some of the cocaine he had spread out on the shack's kitchen table.

But Fiona accused powerful people in the government, including a minister's son, of a deliberate attempt to obliterate the evidence. It could have been due to the alleged involvement of government officials and their families, or to the normal procedural judicial delay in India, but the case dragged on, and only very recently had the girl been buried back home in Devon. Nothing had been proven conclusively and the hearings were tangled in legal knots. The accused were out on bail and for the past few years had been leading normal lives.

Very little had gone well in the Keeling case. Nor did the investigative agencies apparently behave in an exemplary fashion. The forensic department completely failed to provide any conclusive evidence. And after the girl's recent burial no one knew, as governments changed and ministers were reappointed, whether anything would ever be resolved. No wonder Amarjit was hesitant as he reminded me about it.

'So do you think this is very like the Keeling case? Was there any suggestion she, too, could have been gang raped?'

He nodded slowly.

'We don't want this to hijack the headlines. As I said, Goa is opening up. Lots of investment is flowing in, we don't want it to look unsafe.'

I raised my eyebrows at that. He had the grace to look sheepish, at least, as we were both reminded of the recent rape of a young girl on Delhi bus. *What about her?* I wanted to ask.

'And why are you worried about this girl in particular?'

31

He knew what I meant.

He paused again.

'It's actually her sister who is worried. She is threatening to go to the British High Commission and the media and create a stink. She says she can't just allow her sister's disappearance to be forgotten like this. Her story is that they were last together at a shack on this beach. Drinking with some friends. She claims their drinks were spiked and when she woke up the next morning, she was alone in the guest house she'd been sharing with her sister, Liza. No one has any idea where she could be. Frankly I don't have all the details, but I thought if you could speak to her and others on the beach, discreetly of course, and find out more . . . When it happened, etcetera, etcetera. Especially since this video has surfaced. It's been sent to a lot of fairly important people and we're worried.'

'Any idea who could have sent it?'

'None. But it was sent from a computer that's difficult to trace. We're working on it.'

'Not from the mobile phone on which it was found?'

'No – that doesn't seem to match.'

'Did you ask the sister?'

'I don't think she knows about the video. I haven't mentioned it to her either. And right now it would be best to keep quiet about it, as she might give a copy to the wrong people.'

'You mean the media?'

He nodded.

'That's why it has to be kept very confidential. Please don't talk about it to anyone. Especially not the press or the police out here.'

I didn't like the sound of this at all.

'Surely you have more details about it?'

I didn't think Amarjit would come to Goa without being armed with everything he could find out.

He still looked a little evasive. 'The reason I want to involve you is that you could give us a fresh insight. You see, I'm not quite certain about what exactly happened to the girl, or if she's still alive.'

But he displayed an air of helplessness that made me furious.

'What's the problem? Don't the highly efficient Goan cops have enough ideas about where she could be, Amarjit?'

I fixed a steely gaze on him and slammed my coffee cup on the table. It was time to show him that I didn't believe a word of what he had just told me.

'Why the fuck are you here to ruin my holiday? Tell me the truth. You know I don't buy this story. It's too . . . too glib. Girl vanishes and the cops have no clue what happened. And suddenly you are motivated to fly out to Goa to find out what happened. Complete crap. If there is a cover-up tell me who is involved and why. There must be someone important behind this, there usually is.

Was she someone's girlfriend, someone's mistress? Wasn't that what was suspected in the Scarlett Keeling case, too? That some minister's son had raped her? And if that's what you're worried about, what can I do about it anyway?'

'Help me find her,' Amarjit said quietly.

'Look at me. I have a young daughter to look after, who, thanks to you, went through a huge amount of trauma a few years ago. I need to spend time with her. I will not dash off looking for a missing girl on some whim of yours—'

'I don't want to wreck your holiday, for God's sake,' he cut in, trying to calm me down, using blatant flattery as a weapon: 'I just need someone like you to handle this. You have this way of speaking to people, getting them to open up. It's a fabulous coincidence that you were here just when this video turned up. I can't trust anyone else, because I don't want the press to know that this girl Liza Kay has disappeared. And if the cops know we are looking for her, she's dead anyway.'

It was strange to hear a police officer say that, but it was true. If someone had kidnapped her or had hidden her and knew that the police were on their trail, they would kill her even quicker. Assuming she was still alive.

'All it means is asking around a little, since no one connects you with any of this. You've been here with your daughter, you don't look like you're involved in the drug mafia or any of the usual suspects! You don't look like a cop either. Just keep a lookout for information, for any clues. All these beaches in North Goa are very closely linked to each other, and you're sharp. You'll be able to pick up something very quickly—'

Despite his overwhelming and somewhat false flattery, my attention was diverted by something he had said.

'Did you say the *drug mafia* . . .?'

Amarjit looked slightly uneasy.

'All I meant was that you seem like a normal tourist and so people will talk to you.'

'And you're sure you can't trust your own cops?'

Amarjit nodded reluctantly while I lit another cigarette. This time I didn't do it to irritate him, but needed time to think this through.

The answer came before I could take a second drag of my cigarette.

My mobile rang. Durga had woken up and wanted to go to the beach for a late breakfast and a swim.

I shook my head at Amarjit, inwardly relieved. I needed a way out desperately, and now I had my answer. I simply did not think I could handle such a complicated case when I had promised my daughter a holiday. And I wanted her to stay for at least as long as we had planned. All of ten days.

Putting away the mobile in my handbag, I said, 'Nice

try, but I'm afraid Durga comes first. She's the reason I came here, not you, or this case.'

I got up.

'Goodbye, Amarjit. Let's meet in Delhi over a drink and talk about something more pleasant, perhaps?'

I put it as gently as I could, extinguished my cigarette and walked away before he could stop me.

But I knew the expression on his face only too well. There had been many moments when he had looked at me like that. Puzzled, rueful, hurt.

And all too often, feeling guilty over something I was not responsible for, I had changed my mind. Instead I marched briskly up to our room and, mentally pushing Amarjit back to the bottom of the ocean where I had consigned him earlier, helped Durga pack a beach bag for the day.

Beer bottles beckoned and so did the sea.

Chapter 3

Even though the day passed without any incident and Durga swam and ate another lazy lunch of grilled butter prawns, I did keep a lookout for Amarjit. To reduce Durga's annoyance over my inattention, I explained to her that he had asked me for help. I could see that she, too, hoped that he wouldn't sabotage our holiday.

From my past experience I knew he wasn't someone to give up easily. So I had been sure he would try harder to persuade me. And I have to admit that I was a little disappointed when he didn't even contact us on the beach.

Later I glimpsed him walking at a distance with two men. They were silhouetted against the sea, standing out because they all wore trousers and shirts on a beach where everyone else was almost naked. He looked in my direction, but even as I lifted my hand to wave, he left. Obviously I had upset him more than I had meant to. Or he hadn't seen me.

And so when Durga suggested that we attend a party that evening at our favourite shack, Bambino's, I thought it was a brilliant idea. Perhaps the depression I was

sinking into, just thinking about rape and its consequences, would lift.

The colourful posters promised a 'DJ from Mumbai',
and though normally I could not bear loud music, at least
Durga would get to meet other teenagers, and be spared
my rather unexciting company for this evening. In fact we
had planned our Goan holiday with the knowledge that
some of her school friends would be here at the same
time. A large group of them were staying at a guest house
close to our Hotel Delite but we were only expecting two
of them this evening.

Getting into the cotton dresses we had bought that
morning from a roadside shop near the hotel (I had
completely abandoned wearing sarees in Goa), we were
at Bambino's at around eight at night to find that the place
was already crowded. This was the run-up to Christmas,
when the place was popular with both foreign and Indian
tourists. Multicoloured neon lights blinked at the entrance
and neat rows of paper stars shone brightly down on us
inside.

We pushed our way inside to a table and grabbed four
chairs.

Near the bar I thought I recognized the two men
Amarjit had been speaking to earlier. They glanced at me,
perhaps because I was staring at them, but showed no
interest. I looked away quickly before they jumped to the
wrong conclusion about me.

Since they were slightly closer than they had been when I'd seen them on the beach, I noticed how similar in appearance they were. Perhaps they were brothers. Both were tall and well-built, and in their grey trousers and dark t-shirts, they certainly stood apart from the holiday crowd. Curious, I decided to keep an eye on them.

Later, I saw a pretty Indian girl join them briefly. As she spoke to them and looked around the shack, I wondered if she was looking in my direction a little too often. Had Amarjit said anything to them about me?

It was beginning to bother me that he seemed to have left without even saying goodbye. And because I didn't want him to get the impression that I was considering his plea to help find the girl, I refused to call him to find out where he was.

As the crowd filled almost every available crevice in the shack, and the music decibels increased, I determinedly shrugged off my apprehensions. If I kept worrying about Amarjit, I thought, I might as well go out there and hunt for the missing girl.

Soon all seats were taken. Tourism seemed to be doing well. No wonder Amarjit was worried about the case becoming media fodder. The rape of another beautiful foreign girl in Goa would be the lead story in every newspaper and on each television channel all over the world.

A makeshift stage had been set up at one end of the

39

shack and it trembled uncertainly with the collective stamping of feet.

Durga stood up to clap and sway, along with her two school friends, Siddharth and Renu, whom she'd somehow found in the crush of dancers. All three of them then eventually negotiated their way to the bar to collect their glasses of fresh juice. Still under the legal age for alcohol, they were all actually teetotallers, much to my relief. Despite my own unabashed urge to drink, Durga hadn't (as yet) shown any desire for it.

Meanwhile, I ordered another beer, attracting unwanted attention from a group of Indian men at a nearby table, who looked like junior executives in a bank or a call centre enjoying a bonus holiday. Perhaps it was my off-the-shoulder cotton dress and the fact that I was sitting alone.

Disconcertingly, I realized it was actually the second time that I had encountered them. They were obviously here for 'fun and frolic', as advertised by the local low-cost hotels. In recent years Goa had begun to attract budget Indian tourists in large numbers, many of whom were men.

Which was not always a good thing, because now Goa was overrun by Indian men who regarded it as one large beach party, overflowing with bikini-clad women.

It was an image of the state that I knew many Goans disliked and resisted. Disturbed, they tried to project a more noble, holistic Goan identity, delving into the past to resurrect a rich, syncretic and spiritual culture. But, alas, commerce always won, and it was debatable whether many tourists were attracted to Goa for its heritage, though some did explore its old churches and temples, as part of their package tours.

So did this mean Goa was abandoning some of its cosmopolitanism? Just this morning I, too, had wanted to censure at least one of these Indian male tourists. And now the same man was amongst the group at the adjoining table, raising his beer glass in a silent but deeply offensive toast. Clearly, either my annoyance earlier in the day had not been communicated, or the Indian male was developing an extremely thick skin.

In the forenoon when I had waded into the sea, happily paddling around, this same portly gentleman in his late twenties, with thinning hair plastered on his forehead, had risen out of the sea, a very unlikely Venus, and said, 'Madam, can you teach me how to swim?'

If he hadn't sounded so salacious, I might have laughed.

Both because I am of a certain age and because swimming is obviously not among my better-known skills, it seemed like nothing more than a cheap pick-up line. Moreover, while there were better swimmers than me in the sea, I had been floating about on the waves or sleepily collecting shells. There was absolutely no swimming expertise on display.

His fraudulent appeal made me furious. But present-day India offers little room for arguments on the street, and even less on the beach, especially for single women. I had no illusions about knights in shining swimming trunks springing up to defend me from this watery intrusion. And even if anyone were to prevent a woman from being harassed, the outcome could be fatal. I remembered the recent case of a boy stabbed to death, right next to a police station, protecting an unknown woman on the street of a small Indian town. And even in high-profile Mumbai, two young men had been murderously attacked and killed by goons who had tried to molest their women friends.

Similarly, in the recent gang rape on the Delhi bus, the young man accompanying the rape victim that night had also been brutally beaten up and stripped naked before he was thrown from the bus. The girl, whose intestines had been ripped out with an iron rod, lay unconscious on the street, and the young man lay bleeding next to her for a long time without anyone responding to his cries for help.

Thus, sadly enough, it was better for a woman alone to beat a hasty retreat.

And even more so if she was in a swimsuit.

I had looked around for an escape route and found that Durga had already spotted the danger signals and was swimming towards me with short, powerful strokes. There was little doubt who would have been better at giving swimming lessons.

But at that moment I was glad it had not been her that this man had surfaced next to. Being young, she would have retorted in anger – and then who knew what would have happened?

As she came closer, trying to protect me, I was amused at the reversal of roles.

But I didn't want her to say or do anything. In fact, at that moment, I was more troubled about her than myself. I started paddling (as best I could) towards her and both of us swiftly and simultaneously got out of the water. We didn't exchange a single word with the man, who fell about in the water, gesticulating frantically to his friends to come to his rescue, feebly flapping his arms, buffeted by the waves.

We gratefully scrambled over to the deckchairs and to safety.

The incident also reminded me, once again, how unfair and flawed my argument about that girl in the video had been. It was not necessary for a woman to deliberately place herself in a vulnerable situation to be attacked or harassed. It did not matter whether she was clothed from head to toe or was naked, nor did it make a difference if she was stoned, or drunk or sober. Or whether she was a prostitute. She could be attacked at any time and for no reason whatsoever. Once more I regretted what I had said to Amarjit.

The morning's experience also reminded me how much

Goa had changed since I had first come here twenty years ago. At that time women on the beach hardly attracted a second look. And so I had imagined that this state continued to be an oasis of safety. In fact, at the time of my previous visit, flower-children from all over the world were still here. Everyone was relaxed about what they wore or what they did not wear. Even the nudists had been left alone, whereas now, to my embarrassment, I saw groups of men, sometimes individuals, ogling at western women, photographing their bodies. Who knew which website this material would surface on! Some of the women protested, but not everyone was quick enough to object. Many did not even notice that their privacy was being intruded upon.

Pushing these upsetting thoughts out of my mind, I focused on the music which was perceptibly louder since the 'DJ from Mumbai' had arrived. Durga and her friends were now on the dance floor, and I watched them with a rare pleasure. I loved seeing Durga in this avatar, a carefree teenager.

As I turned my back firmly on the annoying man at the next table, I found myself staring at a young woman, who was leaning across, waving 'hello'.

She looked familiar with her dangling earrings, long blonde hair and the ubiquitous short kaftan, but I wasn't sure if I had met her before. I guessed she was probably British, because different beaches of Goa attracted different nationalities, and there was a large British community on this one.

Certainly the Israelis and the Russians went elsewhere. Everyone preferred to be insulated in a bubble, with their own language and culture. Even the menus and the names of the beach restaurants were in Hebrew or Russian or German or English, depending on which part of Goa you were at. As part of the legacy of the hippie movement that had made its home in Goa in the sixties and seventies, the state had been thoroughly colonized by international travellers in post-independence India. It has been to the credit of the local Goans that they have accepted the changing nature of their state, looking upon it as an irrevocable by-product of being an attractive destination, perhaps.

This inclusiveness had some positive results as well: Goa was now a tiny microcosm of the world, well reflected in the number of languages spoken by Veeramma the beach vendor. Not everything was dire.

'May I sit here with you?' the girl across the table asked, and then as I nodded assent, she sat down without further ado. I assumed she had chosen my table because of the three free seats I was keeping for Durga and her friends. There was no room left in the shack, but as Durga was still on the dance floor I didn't bother to refuse.

She reached over the table, straining to be heard over the music.

'Sorry to barge in like this. I'm Marian.'

She held out a beringed hand. I noticed that her neck was covered with large and small beads of every variety. A good customer for Veeramma?

I shook her hand.

'Simran Singh.'

'Are you in Goa for a few days?' It was definitely a British accent, though over the music it was difficult to make out anything at all.

'That's right.' I nodded.

'Having a good time?'

I shrugged. 'My daughter and I are on holiday. Some of her school friends are also here and we all love the beach.'

'I love it here, too, though lately it's been a bit difficult.' I thought I saw a glint of tears in her eyes.

'Oh dear,' I said, remembering my own day, and then to cheer her up, added, 'Would you like to share a beer with me?'

'Why not?' she said, blinking furiously, as though to stop those tears from spilling over. I gave what I hoped was an understanding look and she smiled back reluctantly.

I gestured to the waiter for another glass and then for a while we sat silently drinking and listening to the music, occasionally smiling at each other and keeping time to the beat, if a familiar song came on. Frankly, a conversation conducted through shouting was impossible.

After we had shared a second beer, I leant forward to ask, 'So, what happened to you? You seem quite upset.'

'It's a long story,' she said. She looked over her shoulder at the increasingly noisy crowd and then continued: 'Do you smoke? Would you like to step outside?'

'It takes one to know one,' I said happily. I caught Durga's eye, beckoning her to come back and sit down in my chair as I got up. *Keep the table*, I mouthed across to her, and she reluctantly abandoned the dance floor to walk back towards us, accompanied by her friends.

Outside, the sea roared and whispered, stretching out in dark silky seductive ripples, as we reached its edge struggling to light a match against the warm breeze which blew through our hair. As I inhaled I could taste the salt in the air and on my lips. The foam felt cool as it licked our ankles.

We found a flat, well-compacted knoll of sand which dipped into the water, and sat down, listening to the hypnotic rhythm of the incoming tide. The moon shone down with a watchful gaze. It was an evening full of possibilities.

'She disappeared on a night like this.' The words just seemed to slip out of Marian's mouth, as though it was something she had been longing to say.

I didn't have to ask who she was talking about.

The pattern to this evening suddenly seemed all too predictable. Why hadn't I guessed it earlier?

I sighed.

'How long have you known Amarjit?' I asked her. I should have realized he would have had another plan to surprise me with.

She looked at me apologetically.

'It was very obvious, wasn't it? . . . Just a few days. He said not to tell you, or you wouldn't speak to me.'

'But he knows how to use a remote control.'

'How much has he told you about me and Liza?'

I remembered he had said that Liza was the name of the missing girl.

So Marian was probably the sister he had mentioned. Even though she did not look like the girl in the video at all, there was something in the shape of the mouth and the large eyes which reminded me of Liza. No wonder I had thought Marian looked familiar.

'Just that you're worried because she's been missing.'

Since Amarjit had said she hadn't seen the video, I couldn't mention it. But I was curious. How much did she know about Liza's disappearance?

'So what do you think happened to her?'

'I have no idea,' she said quietly. 'It's all very strange.'

'Tell me about yourself, then. When did you and Liza come here?'

Marian spoke slowly, choosing each word with care. Obviously this was very difficult for her. I decided I wouldn't ask too many tough questions or get involved in

48

too many details as I was still uncertain if I could handle this case and enjoy my holiday with Durga at the same time.

'We came down from London a while ago. Liza had dropped out of school because she wanted to be a hairdresser and was taking some time off. I had just quit my job and decided to go back to university. But I wanted to travel and, like you, Liza loves the beach, so we came here because we could have a cheap holiday. To start with it was fantastic.'

Every now and then Marian would pause and smoke silently, and then without further prompting, continue. She had obviously thought about it all many times, perhaps even the style of the narration. What to reveal and what to conceal. A deliberate vagueness that could be irritating but I refused to let it get under my skin.

'She made a few friends on the beach, in the shacks, and seemed very busy with them. At one stage I actually thought she was going to get some sort of job here. In a hotel or a travel agency; something to do with tourism. One of her ideas was to explore India more thoroughly. She stopped talking about hairdressing and told me about this very interesting person she had met who was going to employ her. I didn't really interfere with her plans because she's been brought up to be very independent. She could be very headstrong – but I must point out that she's quite an innocent thing, fairly gullible. I did try to guide her as much as I could. But because everyone here is so friendly, I let her be, and do her own thing. Perhaps it might have gone too far, she had too much freedom . . . I don't know.'

With a sense of resignation I decided to remain courteous and let her tell me the whole story. In her own way.

It was not her fault that Amarjit could be so devious.

'And was there a special group with which both of you were involved?' I asked, trying to understand what their life had been like. 'Or any place where you liked to go regularly?'

'Not so much me as her.' Marian paused, remembering. 'There's a shack called Fernando's. She used to hang out there in the evenings.'

'Drugs?'

She shook her head quickly. Perhaps too quickly.

'Never. I'm just about to go to Oxford University – managed to get in – and I'm not going to wreck it. I don't think Liza takes anything, either, except that night when I suspect those guys put something in our drinks—'

'Which guys and where? Were you together at the time?'

Even in the dull moonlight a shadow passed across Marian's face. Was she telling me the truth? She seemed to become even more tense. She lit another cigarette.

'It was the night that Liza disappeared. We were at Fernando's, and, yes, we were together. But I don't know any of the people who were there; I met them for the first time.'

'So why were you there at all?'

'I know it sounds odd, but these were mostly Liza's friends. I went along because she had asked me to. I hadn't seen any of them before. But I don't think even she knew the guys who gave us the spiked drinks—'

'Hang on. First you went with your sister to a restaurant where you didn't know anyone. And then both of you were given spiked drinks – spiked with drugs, I presume – by total strangers?'

She nodded, looking, to be fair to her, quite embarrassed.

'If they were strangers, why did they offer you a drink, and why did you accept it? Did they force you?'

My incredulous tone made her pause, as though she was trying to remember every detail.

'No. What happened, as I said, was that there was a comfort level, because we were with people Liza knew quite well. Fernando, the owner of the shack, was with us and a few others. One of them was a friend of hers called Curtis. He was quite helpful to me . . . afterwards . . . you know, when I couldn't find Liza.' She stopped again, now taking nervous drags of her cigarette before throwing it into the sea.

'Then there was a government chap; a minister, I think. We all sat upstairs in a secluded area on the first floor.

What makes me feel really terrible is that we were actually having a good time. Liza was keen on staying on, because she had been told that her job was going to be finalized that evening. And that night she would meet some of the people she would be working with in the future.

'That was when the waiter brought drinks for Liza and me. He said they were from a secret admirer . . . Everyone found it funny and laughed, so I thought it would be stupid to act suspicious. It looked like juice and tasted slightly bitter. But the fact is that, after I drank it, everything began to get fuzzy.'

'And what did you think it was?' I asked her.

'I really thought it was fruit juice with vodka. We had maybe two or three of those and then Liza said she wanted some fresh air. She went out and that's the last time I saw her. I lost consciousness and when I woke up I was back in my room. And Liza was missing.'

I had heard stories like this far too often. A little too glib, as Amarjit's had been. No one knew anything, and meanwhile a catastrophe had occurred. And then someone else would come in and clean up the mess.

But I kept quiet.

I looked at the dark shape of the beach. We were not very far from the neighbouring beach of Anjuna, where Scarlett Keeling's almost-naked body had been found in shallow water when the tide had gone out. Perhaps her murderers had thrown her in the sea not realizing that the waves would bring the body right back.

But, ironically for them, there was a low tide that morning. And the National Institute of Oceanography was to later point out, in response to a query, that when 'between 0250 and 0750 the . . . waves started moving towards the sea . . . no article lying on the beach would go out with the sea water, with the waves'. Instead, it was noted that, at this time and in these conditions, the sea would have deposited most material within it on the beach. I remembered reading that report. So if Liza had also been murdered in the early hours of the morning, in this area her body might have surfaced later the same morning.

Obviously, since there was no trace of her, it may have given Marian hope she was still alive.

I wondered if Marian knew about the Scarlett Keeling case, but decided not to say anything. It was frightening enough to be in a strange country trying to find a lost sister.

I now had a strong feeling that she actually hadn't seen the video, because her tone wouldn't have been as calm. Did she suspect anyone? I decided to test the water.

'The cops? What do they say?'

'I only spoke to one person, who is a friend. He's related to a police officer. He warned me to keep it quiet. He said if we make too much of a fuss it might put her in some kind of danger. And then out of the blue I got a call from

Amarjit, whom I have been told is looking at similar cases in Delhi. My friend had told him about Liza. Incidentally, Amarjit also thinks that there may be nothing to worry about and that she might be travelling with a friend, or might have run away just to have some fun. It's very possible, because she was very adventurous and did have a lot of friends around the beach. I hardly spent any time with her, to be quite honest.

'I, too, didn't want to make a fuss and then end up looking like a fool. I knew she wanted to travel around India, and that's why I didn't say anything to anyone for quite some time.'

'So why now?'

'Well, she's been spotted around Goa recently and, though I haven't seen it, someone told me there is a video with her in it. I just find it strange that she hasn't got in touch with me if she's around. So I want to know what's going on.'

Amarjit hadn't told me that she had been seen in Goa recently. That was odd, because he suspected that she had been raped and then possibly killed and, even though he did not quite say so, he had given me the impression that there was only the slightest hope that she might still be alive.

I decided not to say anything just yet to Marian, either, as I wasn't even sure I wanted to be involved in this case.

'Was she likely to appear and disappear, just like that?'

'Well, she's quite headstrong. Led her own life, even though she's only sixteen.'

Marian was remarkably stoic and I admired her for her fortitude. Her voice shook only a little as she spoke. But she looked like she was about to start crying again.

'What have you told your parents?'

'They don't know. I didn't want to worry them, especially my mother, who hasn't been very well lately. Instead I've told them that Liza is on a tour of Goa and the phones here don't work very well. Luckily I have lots of photographs of us on the beach and so I send those to my mother once in a while, to reassure her.'

'But she's only been gone for a few days, isn't it?' I interrupted.

Marian seemed puzzled at my remark, a little hesitant as she replied.

'Not exactly, it's been much longer than that.'

I noticed how she quickly batted away the answer to that. She was very good at the non-specifics.

'Besides, my mother is quite a worrier. She expects an email update regularly. I have to send her something at least once a week . . .'

'And what about Liza's friends, did Fernando and Curtis say anything? Do you think they could have been involved?'

'They seem to have a cast-iron alibi, because once she

walked out of the shack, some eyewitnesses, as well as the waiters in the shack, said that both of them looked after me, after I blacked out. They took me back to my room. That's what I was told when I woke up.'

'And hopefully you were safe?'

She nodded. 'I think so. I don't think I was messed about with, and for that I am very relieved. Except that . . . poor Liza. I wish I had known that . . .'

But then she covered her eyes and her shoulders slumped with grief.

'I feel so guilty, so terrible that we did what everyone tells you not to do. After all, she was my younger sister and I should have looked after her. At my age I should have known better – you are always warned not to accept drinks from strangers. And Liza . . . I'd feel responsible if anything has happened to her. I only hope and pray that she is safe.'

She rubbed her eyes, wiping away tears.

'How do you think I can help with all this?'

'Amarjit is full of praise. He says you've helped him crack some cases before – that you're sympathetic, you're interested, you're—'

'Nosy and quite opinionated, not an easy person to like. I've taken some rather tough decisions in the past and had some squabbles with Amarjit, so be prepared—'

Suddenly I realized that we had been away from the party at Bambino's for quite a while, and Durga must be wondering where I had gone. I began to worry about having left her alone.

'We should go back. Let me think about what you've told me and see what's possible.' I leapt to my feet.

Damn you, Amarjit! was my last thought, as I went back to the party and then to the room with Durga, who was understandably irritated with me for going away for so long. As soon as we returned, her friends, Siddharth and Renu, decided to walk back to their own guest house.

When we got back to our room, Durga threw her handbag onto the bed and flung herself into a chair. 'There's no point coming on a holiday with you,' she said angrily. 'You just left us there and disappeared. I was dying to dance some more but I had to sit there and guard that stupid table.'

For once her words did not cut deep – I was just enormously relieved that no one had misbehaved with her while I was away. The more I learnt about Liza, the less secure I felt about Durga. I also continued to wonder about Marian's composure. She was definitely sad, but her lack of agitation made me wonder if there was something she knew, which she was keeping from me? And why hadn't Amarjit told me that Liza had been seen around Goa recently?

Chapter 4

The next morning, as I had expected, a message arrived from Amarjit saying that he would like to meet me before he left town.

He had presumed, after my meeting with Marian, that I had already agreed to help. It annoyed me immensely, but the fact that he often took my support for granted was the reason why we had remained (sort of) friends, even through the years when he, his wife and I had formed an uneasy triangle.

She had come and gone through his life, usually creating turmoil. And I had flattered myself that he came to me, again and again, not because he wanted help with one case or another, but because he could not forget what we had once shared. It was another form of self-deception on my part, I suppose.

Amarjit waited in the cafeteria of the hotel, in the same place as the day before, and with the same cautious look on his face. Once again he kept an eye on the door, one leg impatiently stretched out. Who did he expect might suddenly ambush him?

He came straight to the point.

'Did Marian explain what had happened?'

'Not the details, just the broad picture. She was quite evasive about the time line and so on. I'll meet her again and find out the rest. But Amarjit, you must realize that I can't help on any of this immediately. It will take time, as Durga is already annoyed that I am not spending enough time with her. Perhaps after she leaves, in the next ten days or so . . . after the New Year's Eve celebrations. And frankly, I need to think if I want to do this at all.'

An irritated look crossed his face. But, to his credit, he quickly hid it behind a smile.

'And besides, you didn't tell me Liza had been seen around here recently.' My tone was also a little tetchy, and this was clearly not what he wanted to hear, having (supposedly) brainwashed me yesterday. So he would now have to recalculate his moves.

'I didn't mention it because while we are hoping she is alive, these sightings might just be a case of mistaken identity. After all, Marian says she hasn't seen her either. She's only heard about her reappearance. All of this makes our search for her really, really urgent,' he said gently.

Just then our attention was distracted by a commotion at the entrance of the cafeteria, voices raised in argument. I spun around and found the two men I had seen walking alongside Amarjit on the beach, and who had also been at the party last night, speaking to the cafeteria manager with more than a little roughness. I could only catch the occasional word, as the latter threw up his hands help-lessly. They gave a swift glance around the cafeteria, obvi-ously looking for someone.

To my surprise, Amarjit did not react at all. That was odd, and I was about to comment on his silence when the men looked around the room once again and left. Their eyes skimmed over Amarjit without recognition. So I too said nothing, storing up the information for further thought. Meanwhile, Amarjit was carefully typing on his mobile phone. Was the men's lack of interest deliberate? Had he already sent them a message not to approach him?

Ignoring the incident, I asked, 'Is there anything further I should know about Liza? And by the way, Marian said she knew there was a video, though she hadn't seen it. Have you shared anything about it with her since we last met?'

'Not as yet. We still think that some of the boys in the film might be local, so she could be in danger if she mentions it to anyone. Which is why I wish you could take up this case as soon as possible.'

That meant that if I was going to be persuaded to help, I couldn't delete the video clip from my phone as yet. Since the images were tiny on my mobile, I planned to transfer them onto my laptop, so that I had a better chance of identifying the boys if I saw them anywhere around the beach.

In the meantime, I was worried that Durga might

accidentally see the video. Its unpleasantness and sexual overtones would definitely disturb her. Uneasily, I realized I had left my phone in my room before I had gone for my massage, once again, earlier this morning. I hoped she was still asleep.

'Do you think it's a genuine video? These days it's easy to fake video footage,' I said.

'It looks authentic and it will be interesting to find out where it was shot. Just to warn you – it seems there is a healthy trade in pornographic material around here. In a few cases we know it's not been staged with the participants' knowledge, I'm afraid, and unsuspecting people get caught. A lot of honeymooning couples come to Goa, for instance. As do others who could be simply having a good time, such as you. All it takes is a hidden camera! So be careful.'

Seeing my concerned look, Amarjit smiled and gave what I assumed was meant to be a reassuring pat on my hand. Though his words were anything but that.

'Don't worry. It's not just in Goa. This can happen anywhere in the world today, because the technology is so easy to use.'

I knew what he meant, because I myself had surreptitiously collected visual evidence on a mobile phone for a particularly difficult case.

But the papers were also full of incidents where the technology had been misused. In one case I had read about, the warden at a girls' hostel in Haryana had been accused of making secret, indecent films of the residents. Elsewhere, a man had been nabbed for uploading a video of his wife having a bath. And then some British schools had reportedly installed CCTV in washrooms because they wanted to monitor the children. Whether it was justified or not, this technology was simple and people often did not realize the consequences of sharing the material, which was equally easy to do . . .

Would we, from now on, have to scour each hotel room for hidden cameras and mobile phones? Fortunately, with my fear of flying, I rarely travelled and so was unlikely to be filmed in too many hotels.

I wondered if cameras were recording us even as we sat here. As I looked around, to my surprise, I saw Durga, Siddharth and Renu coming up to our table. All three, strangely, seemed quite tense and upset.

As they reached our table, I caught a glimpse of fear on Durga's face, as she was confronted by the man who had let her down so badly three years ago. Even though I had warned her about his presence nothing could have prepared her for this sudden meeting. Before I could say anything, Amarjit was on his feet, and put an arm around Durga. Thankfully the man had not lost all his good sense. After all, he had seen her grow up, and initially, it was he who had brought me into her life. Perhaps she remembered all that, while he hugged her.

As she looked at me over his shoulder I smiled at her with as much reassurance as I could manage.

'Your mother told me you were here, but we thought we shouldn't disturb you since you would still be fast asleep! I hope you don't mind my wanting to catch up with the two of you. I happened to be on holiday here, and couldn't resist meeting you.'

His voice was steady and his words plausible. But Durga was still quiet, not exposing the fact that she knew why he was really there. She quickly stepped away from him. There was a momentary, awkward silence.

I cleared my throat and added, 'He's here just as a friend, Durga. There is nothing to worry about, darling. And how nice to see Renu and Siddharth so early in the morning.'

The colour had begun to return to Durga's face. But obviously something more than this unexpected meeting was upsetting her. Her friends, usually very forthcoming, were equally quiet, and hung back, visibly disturbed.

Alarmed at their depressed demeanour, I drew up more chairs and made them sit down.

'All of you are very quiet. I've never seen the three of you so out of sorts. What's wrong?'

Durga obviously decided to forget past issues with Amarjit and focus on her friends instead.

'Renu and Siddharth had a bad encounter with some men last night, and they . . . they don't want to stay on,' she said in a hushed tone.

Her friends certainly looked as though they hadn't slept at all. Durga frowned worriedly as she put an arm around Renu, who kept wiping away her tears.

Trying to calm them down – after all, these were just three schoolchildren, supposedly on a holiday – I ordered breakfast for them.

'I'm sure we'll deal with whatever is bothering you,' I said, trying to sound cheerful and confident.

At the same time, I found I couldn't bear to look at Amarjit directly. Would there be a triumphant glint in his eyes? Was he, quite unexpectedly, being handed a big prize: Durga's departure?

'This is quite serious, Ma,' said Durga, grimly. 'Siddharth, why don't you tell her what happened?'

Looking a little embarrassed, she said, 'We really had a great time at the party, but as we were going back to our guest house afterwards, two men came up and started walking alongside us. In fact, I think I'd seen them at the party. They seemed nice, said they were living close by and began chatting. Initially it all seemed harmless.'

'Only two of them?' I asked, wondering if they were part of the group of voyeuristic junior executives who had been staring at me rather rudely the night before. I looked at Renu, adding, 'And I hope they didn't misbehave with you?'

Both Renu and Siddharth were just turning eighteen, slightly older than Durga. They were capable of looking after themselves, and holidaying without parental guidance, but being accosted by strangers at night couldn't have been pleasant at all.

'They didn't *misbehave*,' said Renu. 'But they were very intimidating. There was something very odd about them. We thought they may have been local, because they spoke to each other in Konkani. And yes, certainly only two came up to us. If there were others we didn't see them. We tried to ignore them but they just wouldn't leave. It's like they had been given an agenda. They said they just wanted to talk to us, and—' She stopped abruptly as fresh tears rushed into her eyes. She brushed them away equally swiftly.

I was relieved. At least there had been no physical assault or sexual harassment of any kind. That had been my main fear.

Siddharth added slowly, 'That's right. They were very strange, as Renu said. Because we didn't know them, but they wanted to know everything about us. And yet, when they started talking, we realized that they *already* knew quite a lot about us. At one point they even spoke about you and Durga. And then they asked about how long you were planning to stay, and so on. Renu and I thought it was as though they wanted information about you from us.'

'Or,' I said slowly, 'they wanted to let you know they were keeping an eye on us. Particularly me.'

Amarjit leant forward, and for once he looked genuinely sympathetic.

'And what did you tell them?'

'I thought they would go away if I gave some noncommittal answers, but they were very persistent. I think we told them too much about all of us . . . I'm really sorry. But both of us got a little scared. It was dark and . . .' Siddharth looked at us, obviously mortified. Had the men said or done anything else to frighten these children? If so, Renu and Siddharth obviously didn't want to disclose it. They were far too crushed to say more, thinking they had unwittingly endangered the four of us.

But then the thought struck me: could we have been targeted not for some prurient reason but for my recent interest in Liza's disappearance?

'I don't think we should stay here any more. We should all go home. They know our hotel room numbers, which beach we go to, our plans for today,' Renu said.

'Even the school we study in,' Siddharth added. 'When we reached the hotel we simply ran in – and this morning we quickly packed and left, because I thought they might come back.'

'Can you describe them?'

'Neither of us got a good look, because they met us at that patch between the guest house and the beach where there's no light at all. I think they were almost identically dressed . . .'

Could it have been the two men who had been at Bambino's and who had come to the cafeteria? Could they have followed Renu and Siddharth out here just now? While the two had gone upstairs to our room, to meet Durga, had the men barged in here looking for them? But in that case, was Amarjit part of this plot as well?

But before I could ask anything more, Amarjit spoke up quickly. 'Do you want to register a complaint with the police?'

'No!' Durga and I spoke up simultaneously. There was little doubt in our minds (even though we were sitting with a police officer) that problems always began to multiply when you entered a police station.

He frowned, disappointed, and his keenness to register a complaint made me think he might not be involved in this, after all.

'So,' I said, trying to look at the positive side – and relieved that it was only the two over-inquisitive unknown men that had caused the panic, and nothing else. 'What would you like to do about it?'

'If ... if you don't mind, I think Renu and I would rather go back to Delhi. As I said, we've already checked out of our hotel, and left the luggage at the lobby here. We'll just stay here for a while, till we get our flight tickets confirmed. As soon as we talked to Durga, we made the calls to the airline from your room. All this has made us both feel uncomfortable; it was quite scary. I don't know why those people asked so many questions. And I really do apologize, because I think we might have given too much information about us all to them. Believe me, these were not nice people. I certainly don't want to run into them again. We both spoke to our parents and they would like us to return.'

Durga sighed. 'Ma, I think I'd like to leave with them.' There was a note of determination in her voice. I knew that once she made up her mind, it was difficult to dissuade her.

I wasn't sure if I wanted to make her stay under these circumstances.

I felt a wave of sadness overwhelm me. I had really wanted a holiday with her.

'Who could they be?' I wondered aloud. The thought that our holiday was being so swiftly curtailed changed my sorrow to anger.

I contemplated briefly whether Amarjit was devious enough to have set it up. After all, just a while ago he had asked me to send Durga away. This was very convenient for him, wasn't it? Right now, though, he still had a concerned and sympathetic expression on his face.

'Well, I'm leaving for Delhi by the afternoon flight, and if you want to leave or want help with the tickets let me know. I could even take you with me to the airport,' he said, a little too swiftly, perhaps, and then getting up, turned to me: 'Simran, can I have a word with you?'

We walked a few steps away from the teenagers. At that point I was completely unsure whether I should also leave Goa or stay on for the case. Or whether I should let Durga go under pressure. I hated having decisions forced upon me.

Amarjit looked at me carefully, and kept his voice very low, so he couldn't be overheard. 'Take that suspicious look off your face. I swear I have no idea about any of this. All I know is that this disappearance has worried a lot of people. Seeing you with Marian might have made them wonder who you are and why you're here. But I would really urge you to stay on, and help us find her. This is our only chance.'

He sounded sincere. But I wasn't convinced – these recent events appeared to be too much of a coincidence. If so, I wondered whether I could subvert his plans.

Looking as noncommittal as I could, I went back to the table, where Durga appeared a little less unhappy, as were her friends. The thought of going back might have brought some comfort. In my present contrarian mood, I couldn't resist one last try at keeping them all here and rescuing what was left of our holiday.

'Perhaps,' I said thoughtfully, 'Durga and I could move to another hotel. We could even stay some place with a more private or secluded beach. And in case both of you – Renu and Sid – would like to stay on as well, I'll see if we can manage a booking. That might make you feel secure. It's also possible that there is nothing suspicious about all of this and that these two men had got information about us from the hotel or elsewhere. I know that Maggie, the receptionist here, is very chatty, always trying to find out more about us, but I've never given it a second thought. Next time anyone asks us anything we can always give innocuous replies!'

My deliberately light and jocular tone did little to allay their fears.

To my dismay, Durga seemed completely disenchanted with my suggestion. She looked at the other two who also shook their heads. It was obvious that they had discussed the possibility of staying on but the incident had really unsettled them.

'I'd rather go back. We've had three-four days of fun, Ma, but I'm not feeling very happy about any of this.'

Her tone made me wonder if something had happened to her too? Something she wasn't telling me? The other possibility was that she had seen that dreadful video on my phone. Perhaps I should have told her more about Liza and Marian, after all. Events were moving far too quickly for my liking.

Amarjit looked directly at me, using words whose real meaning only he and I would understand. 'Now you know why I said what I did. It might be a random case, but we need to know what lay behind last night's incident for sure. I don't want to scare you – but perhaps the children should leave. But you could have a small holiday anyway. Why waste all the money spent on bookings? Meanwhile I'll check up on those two men who approached the kids last night.'

Irritated with his not-so-subtle attempt at getting me to stay on, I said as firmly as I could manage, 'Let me discuss this with Durga in our room, since she may yet change her mind. But just in case all three of them want to leave can I call to ask you to pick them up from here a little later?'

Amarjit made his exit. Leaving Renu and Siddharth at the table, finishing breakfast, Durga and I walked slowly up one flight of stairs to our room. To our surprise we found the door to our room was slightly ajar.

'I shut it,' whispered Durga, before I could say anything.

Pressing my ear to the door, I heard a murmur of voices inside. I knew it couldn't be the hotel staff as they cleaned the rooms in the afternoon. Perhaps it was the recent events which had put me on edge, but my instinct told me something was not quite right.

I raised a finger to my lips, wondering if the men had now broken into our room.

For a moment, I wanted to back away and leave. What if they had a gun, and ambushed us? But then, I thought logically, they would have shut the door and hidden within.

Prepared for the worst, my heart racing, I shoved the door wide open. My breath was stuck in my throat and I could feel Durga's fingers pressing into my arm while she followed close behind.

As we entered, two figures swung around, surprised. But they were not who we had expected at all.

Silhouetted against the window was Maggie, the receptionist whom I had just accused of taking too much interest in us. Half bent over the desk, a man was seemingly repairing the Wi-Fi socket to which my laptop was connected. The blood was still pounding in my head as they both looked towards us.

I waited for them to speak. Why were they here? And what was the man doing with my laptop? I noticed that it was in the process of shutting down.

Durga's hand fell away from my arm and I heard her sharp intake of breath. I did not blame her; even if they were not whom we had feared we would find in our room, this was a strange couple.

One side of the man's face had been ravaged in some kind of accident: it was completely scarred, and there seemed to be fresh bruises on it, as well. It was difficult to look at him, but when he got to his feet and wished us 'good morning' in a soft voice, I couldn't help feeling sorry for him.

'Wh— what are you doing here? You gave us such a shock!' I asked Maggie, who looked as nervous as we did.

To calm myself down I picked up a glass of water and drank it quickly. The morning had been full of twists, I thought, glaring at the duo. The man now was swiftly picking up his tools and closing his bag.

'I hope you don't mind. I didn't get any response from the room, and so I thought you may have left for the day,' said Maggie in a pert and friendly way, belying my suspicions. 'Someone complained about the Internet not functioning too well on this floor, and so I just wanted Vishnu to check if all the connections here were alright. He's brilliant about all this. I apologize that we put your laptop on to check if the Internet was connecting.'

'I finished, madam,' said Vishnu. 'One wire loose so repaired.'

I nodded grudgingly, trying to show my appreciation, wondering why I hadn't noticed any problems with the Internet. It had seemed fine to me last night when I had used it. Perhaps the problem had occurred early in the morning, after I had left the room.

'Thank you,' I responded automatically, still a little puzzled.

We waited for them to leave and then I sat down on the bed, patting it so Durga came and sat next to me. Now that the fright was over, I felt a huge sense of relief. But there were still problems I needed to sort out with Durga.

'Why did you sound so upset downstairs, when Sid

and Renu told us their story? Is anything worrying you apart from what happened with those kids? Did those men bother you as well?' I asked the last question with trepidation.

'No, I never met them . . .' Durga said, sighing again. 'I don't know. It's all freaking me out. I think it began that day when Veeramma and those women told us about the beach boys who treat the girls like fish, remember? And then, yesterday while you were swimming, Veeramma spoke about some girl who's disappeared. I guess it's the same one that Amarjit wants you to find. And then this happens with Sid and Renu.'

From what she had said, it was obvious that she might have seen some of the messages Amarjit had sent me. And the video. I didn't want to ask her about that, though, as it might lead to too many other worries for her.

I quickly picked up my phone from the desk and slipped it into my handbag.

Out of everything that Durga said, one name jumped out at me. Veeramma.

I wasn't pleased that she had added to Durga's present stress.

However, that meant she might also be a possible source of information.

Vendors like her were on the beach for a long time every day and knew everybody who came and left. I wondered if Liza had also been a 'fish', like the other girl we had seen on the beach. How much did Veeramma know about her?

But I still had to try to change Durga's mind, one last time.

'Look, we can shift out, go to a hotel where you don't even have to go down to the beach. A hotel with a swimming pool – how about that?'

Durga sighed.

'Apart from this thing that happened to Sid and Renu, I know it's better I go home, because you're going to try to find this girl, anyway. If anyone can do it you can, and so it will be good if you are left alone to pursue it. I'll feel bad if you don't do this because I'm around.'

I hugged her for her thoughtfulness. And I was moved by her faith in me.

I also felt guilty that I could not protect her from the world as well as I wanted to.

'Besides,' she said with a rueful smile, 'Amarjit will haunt you till you agree. And, ultimately, you will.'

She knew me too well.

Can I really do this? I thought, as we called Amarjit and told him to pick up Durga and her friends from our hotel.

After they left, I felt depressed and wanted to get away from the beach, which was taking on an increasingly sinister hue.

I took a taxi to Old Goa and for a while walked around

the ruins of the old sixteenth-century churches to calm down and remember that Goa had a history and a past which had seen many upheavals.

This present world – a world of probable rape and murder – that I was being thrust into was only a minuscule part of Goa's history of dramatic social change. Probably no one would even remember this contemporary episode, and it would not even be a footnote. Why did it upset me so much, then? Why did I feel so devastated when I thought of what was happening in this beautiful part of the country?

So much of Goa was hidden from view, I thought. What I remembered from twenty years ago was not the Goa I saw today. And yet possibly it still existed somewhere, just as these churches spoke of a strong Catholic past, which was alive in many homes and villages. Alongside the beaches with their tourists, the drugs and the rave parties.

On the surface the state seemed so peaceful. But from all accounts it too was torn between the ghosts of its Hindu, Muslim and Catholic history and the dreams of the future.

It was apparent that the inhabitants of this richly resourced state often blamed all its ills on the foreigners and outsiders who, they alleged, had stolen their identity and wrecked their culture. And had done so for hundreds of years, even before the adventurer Alfonso de Albuquerque landed here.

Yet the wonderful thing was that it had remained one of the most assimilative and secular states in India. The food, the clothes, the music – even the siesta in the afternoon – was more European than strictly Indian. But modernization had not been kind to Goa, and some of the evils of development visible everywhere in India – the slums, the garbage heaps and the haphazard growth – had also begun to stealthily mushroom here, even on the beaches.

Along with rapid urbanization had arrived the desire for wealth and white-collar employment, especially among the youth, many of whom had found job opportunities abroad. The ones who were left behind flocked to the beaches to make their fortune, and also to have some fun. Their upbringing might have been strictly traditional, linked to the churches, the temples and the mosques, but their interaction with the outside world would change them. The holiday atmosphere of the beach, with its indolent and relaxed ambience, created a false image of life as it should be. And quite soon this indolence became the aspiration.

Everything cannot be blamed on the outsider – and yet it is . . .

Was the rape and murder of girls like Scarlett Keeling – as well as the vanishing of Liza – somehow linked to the volatile nature of the state? Or was life on the beach completely separate and distinct from that elsewhere in

Goa – with its own rules and regulations, on account of the rumoured accessibility of drugs and the mafia associated with it?

I also wondered if there would be any real sympathy towards Liza, if she had actually been killed. Or would she become just another young girl who died looking for the good life in Goa?

Of course there were many young women who came to the beaches and survived. Some even stayed on; a few married the beach boys, setting up businesses and sometimes even taking the boys back to foreign shores. And who was I to be cynical about these relationships? If only I could find some love myself – that would make my mother happy, in any case.

Though I hardly ever pray, I found my steps meandering till I had joined the group at the entrance of the church commemorating Goa's most famous saint, St Francis Xavier, waiting to go in. I didn't know what I was looking for, but I wanted to find some solace in the high arches of this church. And I wanted to light a candle for Liza.

Chapter 5

On my return to the hotel, I was relieved that there was one less worry on my mind: the fear that something would happen to Durga had receded, as soon as she had got into the car with Amarjit.

Whatever else our relationship was about, I knew he would see her safely home. I had asked her to call when she reached Delhi.

It was early evening by now, and I decided to make my way down to the beach and meet up with Marian. I called on the number she had texted me, but there was no response, so, thinking she might be busy, I sent her a message asking her to meet me.

I decided to look out for Veeramma and her group as well. They usually came around to the beach at about midday and stayed on till evening, as that was the period during which most tourists were likely to be on their deckchairs or in the sea. These were the best hours to convince them about the importance of a henna tattoo or a sarong or a piece of jewellery.

I spotted the women fairly soon. They had surrounded a couple whose skin was slowly turning red in the hot sun, and were squatting on the sand around them, Veeramma in the lead as always. I smiled at the concerted attack under which any resistance from the two salmon-tinted bodies was visibly vanishing.

I waved to get Veeramma's attention and she waved back but made no effort to get up. She had new clients to seduce with her bantering and bargaining skills. I was history and unlikely to part with more money, so would have to wait.

I walked up to the group and spoke to the woman closest to me, who was distractedly listening to Veeramma's stories as she wooed the couple.

'Tell Veeramma I want to speak to her when she is finished,' I said.

'Even speaking has cost, madam. This business-time,' the young woman, obviously well tutored by Veeramma, replied with a wink.

'You want talk, you pay!' said another one, squinting into the sun, looking at me, and rubbing her thumb and forefinger together in an easily understandable gesture.

I was astounded at the impudence but then simmered down rapidly. I needed information and it was true that while talking to me they would lose work and by implication money. So the best would be for me to buy Veeramma's time.

I raised a finger. 'One hour. How much?'

The second woman raised a matching finger. 'One thousand rupees.'

I didn't bother to argue. The beach was an intensely well-connected microcosm. It was possible that bits of information had already gone out and some people were aware I was interested in Liza. It was also possible that Veeramma had some valuable information; after all, she had mentioned the missing girl to Durga. It might have been a deliberate attempt to lure me over.

Other things might have been noticed as well: for instance, my meeting last night with Marian. Or Amarjit's arrival and departure, even though he had taken care not to appear in uniform. He had been so tense each time we met that I had wondered if he thought someone would recognize him, or overhear us.

Last night, Marian and I had also agreed that though we might informally ask about Liza, we should not speak about her disappearance to anyone, as it might endanger her life, wherever she might be. Since I now suspected that people were also interested in me as well, it could be riskier than I had imagined. I would have to be even more careful about what I said and to whom.

'Tell Veeramma to meet me at the last shack at the other end of the beach. In around thirty minutes. She can send a message to me when she gets there, or call me.'

I handed over my number on a piece of paper to the woman, knowing it would be better to meet as far away from my hotel as possible.

'Yankee Doodle, madam?'

For a moment I was startled by the strange question, and then realized that she meant the name of the shack.

'That's right. At Yankee Doodle.'

As casually as I could, I took a few photographs of the beach, and of Veeramma's group, just in case I later needed to locate them again. Given the animosity between the beach-shack owners, the police and the beach vendors over their weekly collections or *hafta*, it might not always be easy to track down the group if I ever needed them.

When I aimed the phone lens towards them, the women struck poses with their wares. Even the German couple who were being tattooed each put one arm around the woman closest to them, and gave a thumbs-up sign with the other.

Looking at the smiling group, I battled sadness. Partly because I was missing Durga, and partly because I was searching for a young girl who should have been enjoying herself on the beach like the rest of the tourists. I just hoped she was safe. I thought of the sentimental candle I had lit inside the church a few hours earlier. Who could have ever imagined that I could get so maudlin?

Trying not to get too depressed, I rolled up my trousers and walked briskly near the edge of the waves, skipping over sandcastles, enjoying the feel of the sand between my toes, before going to the shack. Just as I sat down at Yankee Doodle and ordered a beer, I received a message from Marian, at last saying she was on the beach, looking for me.

'Yankee Doodle,' I announced, calling her back, sipping my chilled beer. 'That's the place to be.'

Within ten minutes I saw her swing into sight, her long blonde hair down, her eyes hidden behind dark glasses. For the first time, I realized (last night it had been too dark) that she was actually terribly thin. The short dress she wore today made it more obvious. Her bones stuck out everywhere and it was worrisome to see her knobbly knees, her almost painfully sticklike arms. Her neck looked like it might snap if she turned around too suddenly.

We decided to share the beer and I called for another glass, making a mental note to ensure she ate and drank well whenever we met. She would look far better if she gained a bit of weight.

'Have you heard anything more about your sister?'

'Well, this keeps happening. I get all excited when I hear something about her and it usually is just a red herring. I just met someone who said he had spotted her at the Panjim market a few hours ago. Liza got onto a motorcycle with a guy he didn't recognize and drove off before he could ask her anything. But . . . who knows? It may just have been any other blonde girl with curly hair. From a distance we all look the same, don't we?'

Panjim was only about half an hour away from our beach. But I wondered over the lack of excitement in

83

Marian's voice. She sounded tired, or was it the anxiety that had exhausted her? I tried to strike a positive note.

'That's really wonderful to hear! And how did she seem to them? Did she look happy or sad . . . or scared?'

'They said she didn't seem to be scared or in a bad shape but I find it all very odd. If she's okay, why doesn't she call or get in touch, with my parents or with me?'

'Did you have a fight of any kind before she left?'

Marian paused and took a large swallow of her beer, leaving a faint foam on her upper lip.

'We didn't exactly have a fight.' She took off her dark glasses, and looked at me with her large kohl-lined blue eyes, which had more than a hint of sadness in them. 'Though we did disagree on whether we needed to go to that party on the night she disappeared. I wasn't really interested, but as I might have mentioned earlier, for her it was work-related. Liza said her future boss was going to be there. He had promised her a job in a travel agency. Some clients and the guys who owned the agency were going to be there, as well.'

'You mentioned Fernando being there, as well as a guy called Curtis, and some minister. Who was he? Can you try to remember?'

She hesitated before replying. It could be either that she had forgotten the events of that night, and she was genuinely trying to remember – or that she regretted having mentioned the politician, knowing that to have done so

84

could be dangerous. Or like yesterday, this cautious manner of speaking might help her not to answer anything with precision.

'She had told me that she had met some pretty powerful people. I remember there was someone connected to a ministry that night, though I can't recollect his name. But I later found out that, because a part of Fernando's is quite secluded, well-known people who don't want to be recognized can come from the back entrance, and leave that way as well. I had never met this man before. He seemed alright to me. Much older than I expected, and they said he had a stake in a casino. You know those offshore boats on the Mandovi? Liza sat by his side, and he held her a little too close and kept, you know, touching her everywhere. It was very sleazy. I tried to stop her from sitting near him, but she got angry so I shut up.'

An older man. Obviously not anyone I had seen in the video.

'And this man was going to give her a job in a travel agency?'

'That's what she said.'

'I thought you mentioned she wanted to be a hairdresser?'

'She'd just turned sixteen. Who knows what she wanted? She had just wanted to enjoy herself and get a good job, make some money.'

85

I wondered if she realized that she was speaking in the past tense. Perhaps it was just the stress.

It was becoming more and more apparent to me that even though Liza was her sister, Marian seemed to know very little about her. It was not surprising: teenagers, I had found over the years, could lead a double life without anyone finding out.

'So did Liza get the job? Was there any discussion about it?'

'This guy did mention that he had arranged for her to fly to Europe and learn more about the work quite soon, but then, as I told you, after some time the evening became a bit of a blur.'

'Now when you look back was there anything at all that evening which would have worried you? Perhaps if you had been completely sober?'

'I was later told that most of the people at the table were also taking some drugs in the kitchen. Cocaine and so on. Everyone would go inside and come back after a bit. I thought they were just checking the food-and-drink order, because we were seated apart from the other guests in the shack, within a private party space. But I've now been told that drugs on the beach are quite common, and that probably people were snorting cocaine.'

'Did you know anything about Fernando's before you went there?'

'Not much. I think you must have guessed by now that my sister and I led fairly separate lives in Goa. Most people wouldn't even be able to tell that we're sisters because we have such different interests.'

She paused and lit a cigarette, passing me one as well. Even though I normally prefer smoking my own local (and cheaper) brand, I took one from her.

She continued. 'You may wonder that I didn't spend too much time with Liza . . . but I am more into spiritual stuff and yoga, while Liza was into parties and generally having a good time. We're very different and she's much younger than me – seven years. And even now, because I haven't made a fuss over her disappearance, only a hand-ful of people know that we're related.'

It was distressing that they were not close, but not improbable.

'Amarjit sent me a picture of Liza.' I took out my mobile phone and went through the images till I found the one I was looking for. I handed the phone over to her.

It showed a much younger girl than the one sitting oppo-site me. She had a big smile on her lips and her hair flowed over her shoulders and over her forehead in a curly fringe. The kind of girl you immediately warmed to. Apart from the blonde hair, blue eyes and the full pouting mouth, there was little resemblance between the pleasantly plump girl in the photograph and the woman sitting opposite me. Yes, it was true – few people would be able to guess that they were sisters.

As if she had read my mind, Marian gave the phone back to me with a slight smile. 'She still looks like a child. And of course, I look exactly like my mother.'

She opened her handbag and took out a frayed wallet, which contained a photograph of a woman who bore a striking resemblance to her.

'That's Mum.'

There was almost a tone of pride in her voice.

'Where is she?

'A busy woman. Works in a bank in London. I haven't seen her for a long time, but we are in touch constantly thanks to the Internet.'

I handed her wallet back to her and a card fell out on the table.

It said 'Astrologer Anne'. She reached out for it quickly but I picked it up before she could and turned it over. A glowing galaxy with a central meteor slashing across was printed on one side, with the slogan 'Unlocking the secrets of your life: past, present and future.'

For a minute I was surprised, and then realized that Marian was probably turning to the stars for an answer. Nothing wrong with that, except that very often vulnerable people like her, who obviously needed help, spent their whole lives between all kinds of astrologers, numerologists and face-readers. I was reminded of a friend whose son had disappeared, and who now spent all his time and considerable fortune on astrologers and palm-readers. He even had tried the Ouija board, talking to spirits he hoped would help him locate the missing boy.

Feeling even more sorry for her, I returned the card and she quickly put it inside the wallet, her face flushing a deep red.

'I guess you want to try everything,' I told her sympathetically.

She shot me a worried look. 'What do you mean?'

I injected a gentle note into my voice, trying not to sound too critical. 'I mean, you obviously would like to find out anything that you possibly can about your sister, by whatever means. I don't believe in astrology myself, but I know that in some parts of the world even the police use mystics once in a while.'

'And so they should, because often people don't tell you the truth. You need to go behind the obvious.'

It was an emotional moment and I found myself agreeing with her.

But before I could say anything further, over her shoulder I saw Veeramma coming over with her troupe of women. For some reason she hadn't called me.

Reaching the absolute limit of how close she could come to the shack, she stood at a discreet distance, raising her hand to peer inside, till she located me. No overt gestures were permitted, as the owner of Yankee Doodle would take offence at the slightest transgression.

Large notices had been put about, warning tourists from mingling with or encouraging the beach vendors. I wondered what had happened in the past that had forced such a harsh decision. Rumours had always been afloat of these vendors harassing tourists, and even the over-friendly Maggie at the hotel had warned me about them. But I doubted if someone like Veeramma would risk her livelihood and reputation by doing something under-handed. Besides, she had a whole group of women to look after. Once blacklisted, I imagined it would be diffi-cult for any of them to return to the beach.

I explained to Marian that I needed to speak to some-one urgently, and as she turned around to look at who it was, to my surprise I saw Veeramma pointedly swing upon her heel and turn her back on us. In fact she imme-diately walked a fair distance, followed by her friends, till she was near the sea and sat down on the sand, spreading her colourful cotton saree around her.

Leaving Marian to munch her way through the fish and chips that I had ordered, I trudged towards Veeramma, who was determined not to look towards us or face the shack. She seemed angry with me, which was surprising, as we had parted on very good terms a few days earlier.

She said something brusquely to the group. They glanced at me curiously and headed away from the beach. None of the happy smiles I normally associated with them were visible. I was a little hurt by this cold treatment, since I had promised to pay for her time. Even a thousand rupees were obviously not enough to merit a cheerful look today.

Thinking she might be offended because I had kept her waiting, I held the promised money out to her, and sat down next to her, staring out to the sea, which seemed a little rough.

'For the conversation we are about to have.'

She took the money, and put it inside her bag, but her expression did not alter. The corners of her mouth remained turned down.

'I'm looking for a girl called Liza,' I began abruptly.

She looked wary, drawing patterns on the sand with a twig she had picked up.

'Who?'

I took out the phone and showed her the photograph.

'Have you ever seen her?'

She peered at Liza's smiling face and almost disinterestedly shook her head.

'No, no.'

'But she must have come to the beach.'

'What you do with her, madam? Why you want mess? Ask police,' she said in an irritated tone.

I didn't like the sound of that.

'I'm trying to help her sister find her.'

'Her sister? If she her sister, she look after her, no? Why you care?'

It was irrefutable logic. I knew already that Marian, far from looking after her young sister, had allowed her to spend time with all sorts of men about whom she herself knew little.

It was not a good record.

Veeramma got up, using unnecessary vigour to dust the sand off her saree.

'Hang on. You told Durga that something happened to this girl.'

Veeramma hauled her bag onto her shoulder. 'Where your daughter, madam?'

'She's gone back to Delhi.'

I was puzzled at Veeramma's attitude. There was no desire in her to help me. It was a complete change from the charm she had previously demonstrated.

'That good, madam. And you go too.'

I quickly scrambled to my feet.

'Veeramma, I need your help. You obviously know something. You told Durga that a girl had disappeared. Where did you last see her?'

Reluctantly, Veeramma whispered, 'No remember. Too long ago.'

Too long ago? What could it possibly mean?

Turning around, she started walking away briskly. I was forced to half-run alongside, feeling like a fool. Usually vendors were the ones who pestered you. Today I was behaving like one of them.

'Please at least think about it and give me any information you might have. I tell you what, give me your phone number. You have mine already. Just in case. Please.'

I folded my hands together, prayerfully, as I knew that I needed her every step of the way. She was the eyes and ears of this beach.

As a reconciliatory gesture she called out to a woman standing at a distance, selling coconut water. She said something to her, and the woman quickly chopped off the top of a coconut, and sticking a straw into it, gave it to me.

'From me, madam. I your friend,' said Veeramma. 'But I no like your question. Big danger for you. Buy coconut, buy tattoo, but don't ask for Liza.'

Obviously she did not want us to part in bad blood, and though I was puzzled by her quickly changing moods, I drank the coconut water, handing the empty shell, along with some money, back to the woman who had given it to me. Keeping up the pretence that this was a 'gift', I did not pay the exact price, but twice the amount. These gestures, especially monetary transactions, could be an important part of building trust between Veeramma and me. Indeed, everything, even friendships, had a price here.

Looking somewhat mollified, Veeramma whispered her mobile number as though I had asked for a state secret. I immediately took out my phone and dialled it to make sure there were no mistakes.

As soon as her phone rang I hung up and put mine back in my handbag, and she began edging away from me.

'Shall I call you tomorrow? Please check with your friends. They might know something,' I said, still with that pleading note in my voice.

'Madam, I do tattoo for girl. That all I know.'

Firmly turning on her heel, as though it was her last word, she walked away.

More disappointed than I could have imagined, I returned to the shack. I had been so sure that Veeramma would tell me something about Liza; something about her attitude, and her reluctance to speak, clearly indicated she knew more than she had admitted.

Back at the table, to my amazement, I found that Marian had left as well. I had a feeling that she was as averse to Veeramma as the latter seemed towards her.

There was a note from her, however, which had a fairly friendly tone.

'Thank you, Simran. I have a lot of hope that you will find Liza. Let's meet tomorrow on the beach again and I will take you to the guest house where we used to stay. Have to rush.'

With a sigh I sat down. Apart from being a fairly complicated case, it was likely to be a very slow investigation, especially if Marian came and left as though we could afford to spend months, or perhaps years, searching for her sister. She appeared anxious but had parted with very little information so far. What was she trying to do? If I hadn't seen that frightening video I would have abandoned this case right now. But I felt I owed it to Liza to continue, and it was very possible that Marian, like Veeramma, knew more than she was prepared to tell me.

Was she trying to hide something about the timing of Liza's disappearance? Veeramma had said it was 'too long ago'. And her behaviour had been very strange.

It was possible that both women had been threatened. Perhaps by the same two men who had frightened the children into leaving?

I called home and learnt that Durga had arrived safely and that she and my mother were planning to join the protests at India Gate against the government apathy towards the Delhi gang rape survivor. The case was extremely tragic but as it made news all over the world it forced attention on the increasing incidence of sexual violence against women and the almost institutionalized indifference to the suffering of victims. Right from the police stations to the hospitals to the courts (if at all a case was registered).

I did not tell my mother about Liza as she would get worried. I smiled ruefully, thinking that Marian hadn't told her own mother that Liza was missing either. It was through these little omissions that we protected our families, I suppose. Or hoped that we were protecting them from painful reality.

But I did tell my mother that it might be a while before I came home and asked the travel agent to book me a return train ticket for two weeks' time. My fear of flying kept me from catching a quick flight back, so I had to ensure an escape route was available at a later date. If no evidence turned up in a couple of weeks, we could assume, sadly, that whoever had organized Liza's disappearance might have also engineered her death.

Feeling depressed and helpless I pondered whether to send Amarjit a message about the hurdles suddenly in front of me. I nibbled at the remainder of the fish and chips, and finished the beer which was tasting rather odd and flat. Lighting a cigarette, I tried to chalk out a plan for the rest of the evening.

Obviously I couldn't really relax or enjoy the seascape because I felt I had to expedite the investigation. I made a list of people I could speak to who might know about Liza's disappearance – along the beach and in the shacks, the staff of the guest house where she had stayed, and so on. The problem, of course, was what I could ask them that would not reveal I was hunting information on her? An impossible task.

I wondered if I should go to Fernando's on my own. It was just on the next beach down the coast. Why wait for

Marian, who was turning out to be a little too preoccupied with her own affairs?

I decided to go back to the room, change my beachwear for something more sober, and then set out again.

I had barely reached my room, when the familiar ping on my mobile phone told me a message had come through.

But I wasn't prepared for what I saw.

It was another video. Much worse than the first.

This time it came from an anonymous source, and the screen read 'number withheld'. The image was not as blurred as the first video, even though it was shot at night with little light.

The girl, with her distinctive curly golden hair, was walking, or rather stumbling, along a beach.

The video-maker must have been at a distance, as she showed no signs of even noticing him or her. There was an occasional blur of a pillar or the base of a palm tree, as though the videographer was trying to shoot from behind some kind of cover.

As the camera zoomed in, I noticed that her clothes were torn, and a streak of something dark, perhaps blood, was visible on one leg. She could have been drugged or drunk, it was difficult to say. Though it was dark, her blonde hair and slightly plump, full figure now seemed familiar to me.

'Liza,' I whispered, and then spoke her name out aloud again, as though she could hear me.

She staggered along the sand, falling down and then getting up again. The person shooting the video made no attempt to go closer or help her. Though the sea was not quite visible in the dark, the steady roar of the waves as they hit against the shore and the hiss with which they receded was audible.

Suddenly a man appeared from the side and put his arms around her. He was formally dressed in a shirt and trousers and his back was towards the camera. She struggled as he tried to kiss her and then fell down once more. Again she pushed herself up and somehow kept walking. But then he caught her and half carried and half dragged her to a row of deckchairs. Her hands moved feebly in the air as she tried to resist and she moaned as he roughly pushed her onto one of the chairs.

He pulled her legs up towards him and pushed his hand between them. In pain she screamed, 'No, no . . . don't!' But then her voice was muffled, as another man joined the first and covered her mouth with one hand, pulling her arms over her head with the other. Though she struggled to get free, it was obvious that she had been overwhelmed.

The second man seemed to be inserting his fingers into her mouth enjoying her helplessness as she turned her head this way and that. Even though he was facing the camera, the light was behind him and so it was difficult to make out what he looked like. He was dressed more casually, in a t-shirt and boxer shorts. He seemed taller and better built than the other man. He kept merging into the darkness behind. I was reminded of the other video.

'Come on, come on, baby. You know you want it.'

The words were distant, broken, but easily heard in the silence of the night, carried on the breeze.

The first man had now dropped his trousers and thrust himself upon her.

As he pumped harder and harder, the girl's legs twitched. Her body twisted and turned, though any movement from her was now barely visible.

She began to go limp, but as soon as the first man finished, the other one walked around and lifted her legs. Even before he pushed into her, her head fell to one side, and her arms flopped down like that of a rag doll. This time she did not scream. She had probably lost consciousness. The man did not stop raping her.

The screen went blank again.

My head began to pound. Who could have sent this to me?

It was a much more frightening video than the first. The first one, though sinister, might have been a bunch of delinquent kids just fooling around. This footage was extremely brutal and explicit.

The phone slipped through my hand onto the rug as I fell back on the bed and stared at the ceiling. I felt sick and nauseous, as though it was I who had been molested.

So she had been attacked twice but this time it was far, far worse. Now I genuinely began to fear for her. Could she have really survived this ghastly rape, in silence and secrecy, especially since there was no record of it anywhere? In the press or otherwise.

And, yet, quite to the contrary, Marian had told me that Liza had been spotted in Panjim, earlier today, looking fine.

Could she have been sexually assaulted, and yet appear again as though nothing had happened?

I got up and took out a bottle of whisky, which I kept hidden among the clothes in my suitcase. Right now I needed to get back my equilibrium any way possible. I poured a stiff shot into a glass and then knocked it back.

As the familiar heat ran down my throat, my mind began to function again.

There were at least three points which puzzled me.

Firstly, it was now certain that someone knew I was looking for Liza, despite the secrecy that Amarjit had wanted to maintain.

Secondly, the video came from an anonymous source, so someone wanted to either tip me off, or scare me away.

Thirdly, Amarjit was unaware of this video, or else I would have heard from him, I was certain of that. So I would have to send it to him straightaway, and ask him to urgently email me all the information he had about this case.

I looked outside; the light was rapidly fading along the

beach, as the sun sank into the sea. My enthusiasm for going alone to Fernando's was also diminishing. I was completely shaken up by this latest development.

Perhaps that was the sender's intention.

But now I was even more determined not to give up.

This video made it clear that Durga had been right. I had to find Liza somehow.

Chapter 6

The news from Delhi was not good at all.

The young woman who had been brutally raped in a moving bus by six drunken men was sinking. More details emerged of her deteriorating condition. All her reproductive organs had been ruptured and her intestines pulled out by one of the rapists with his bare hands, after he had inserted an iron rod inside her. In the multiple surgeries that followed only five per cent of her intestines were retained. People around the country were praying for her survival, and poignantly, she, too, had told her mother 'I want to live'.

It was a horrific case, made more macabre by the fact that the rapists seemingly had no fear of being caught by the police, even though the bus was driven through various checkpoints in the city for two and a half hours while they were assaulting her. Had there not been pressure from the media and from women's groups, it was thought unlikely that the men who had allegedly committed such bestial acts would ever have been caught.

It reinforced my fears about what had happened with Liza. And I was puzzled by the secrecy around it all. Why did Amarjit want to prevent the story from coming out in the media?

According to published records, more than eighty women were raped in the country every day. Would Liza's case create such an international storm that it was best hushed up? Why was Amarjit delaying the arrest of those young men in the video, especially as some of them could have been identified by now? Why had he asked me to conduct an informal investigation? Could it be that the drug mafia was involved in her rape and subsequent disappearance? Or was it someone even more powerful?

My suspicions were being raised because the morning newspapers contained equally grim editorials about discussions taking place in the Goa parliament on all these subjects. While one minister feared that Goa was becoming the rape capital of the world, another member of parliament had spoken of how, in a period of three years, almost every week there had been at least one death of a foreigner in Goa. The highest number of victims were British, followed by Russians. While many of the deaths were assumed to be accidental, it was also suggested that at least some could have been drug related. And it was pointed out that many of those who died were young.

So it was not surprising, another editorial noted, that when the Central Bureau of Investigation was called in to consider the Scarlett Keeling case, they found LSD and cocaine were openly and easily available on Anjuna beach, where the 15-year-old had spent much of her time. In fact, in one of the shacks, cocaine was kept under the plastic tablecloth on the kitchen table. Lines were cut and doled out from there, and on the night that poor Scarlett stumbled into the shack at around 4 a.m., reportedly quite intoxicated, an eyewitness recounted her being offered even more coke.

A helper at the shack allegedly confessed to the team that he used to chop lines every night, to be snorted by guests as well as other staff members – everybody from the cook to the barman to the shack manager. And around Christmas and New Year, extra cocaine would be brought in to fuel the parties. All of this would be hidden away in the kitchen, and taken out as required. It seemed to be a time-worn tradition.

So, I thought back to Scarlett's mother's allegations. She had said that there was an open drug trade in Goa, in which politicians, the police and the shack owners had all colluded. She had accused them of forcing Scarlett into taking hard drugs. But later the din caused by these accusations died away.

Perhaps it was inevitable. The situation turned into a farce when the then Home Minister of Goa claimed that all the allegations were lies and Goa was actually a drug-free zone.

But off the record everyone accepted that there might be some truth in the accusations made by Fiona MacKeown.

I wondered if anything had changed at all in the last five years.

Trudging along the smaller Vagator beach, I knew it would be another harrowing day. Yesterday's video kept playing in my mind over and over again. I heard Liza's voice in a non-stop loop in my head, begging the man to stop, and wished I could erase the sound from my thoughts, but it just got louder and louder. The mobile phone bearing the video weighed like a ton of bricks in my handbag.

And when I shut my eyes, I could hear the screams of the girl in the Delhi bus. Why had these young girls become the innocent targets of such bizarre violence?

I watched a young fair-skinned girl build a sandcastle near the sea. She was dressed like a tiny Barbie doll, with her matching yellow bikini top and bottom. Very sweet and innocent, but how long would it last? And at what stage would she be converted into a plaything, a sexual object? Just a few years ago, a 9-year-old Russian girl had been raped while playing on these very public beaches.

No matter what our daughters eventually became, it was the rapidity of their sexualization that was troubling. I thought of all the victims of violence that I had met over the years. Their bodies were never seen as their own. It seemed almost as though girls today were caught between peer pressure, commerce and tradition, depending on which part of the world they grew up in. At one end, extremely liberal attitudes could be responsible for their sexual exploitation, and at the other, they lost their childhood due to ironclad tradition.

Either way they would be victimized by their own culture. Young girls in the US and UK had been known to have sex and even babies as young as eleven, while in some parts of India little girls were forced into child marriage when they should have been at play or in school.

I wondered whether we could really protect them from growing up too fast? Or was it, as I had found in Durga's case, a constant negotiation with societal norms?

My mind kept going back to the story of Scarlett Keeling.

According to her diaries and emails later published in newspapers, she had been sexually active for a few years before she died. But how much of this apparent seeking out of sex was actually voluntary? She admitted in one of her emails that her Goan boyfriend treated her as though she were only interested in him for the 'sex or the money'. For a pretty and sensitive 15-year-old to be made to feel so mercenary and manipulative would have been frightening. She was, after all, still a child, who needed emotional reassurance.

Just a few nights before she was killed, an email she sent out read:

I wen to a beach party . . . last night took sum md an lsd and xstasy I was soooo fuked man an the police raided it an . . . I got dragged away by some weird man an everyone else had legged it an I was fukin buzzin man so I got a taxi back [to a shack she used to go to with her family] and slept ther but the boys showed me some hardcore porn movis on a phone then they all took it in turns tryin 2 rape me an I feel so shit right now . . .

It was the story of a young girl leading an artificial and very adult life, where she was seemingly pushed frenetically into one disturbing situation after another.

My gloomy thoughts persisted, so I went to my favourite shack where I could get a good view of the sea and ordered some scrambled eggs and a bottle of beer. It was still early in the morning but I needed to either be more optimistic or become completely numb to everything happening around me. I sent a message to Marian to tell her I was back at the cheerfully named Yankee Doodle.

My reverie was broken by a sudden blast of a Bollywood track played loudly on a mobile phone. It came from a group of Indian college students who were sitting close by. Equally suddenly, a boy and a girl leapt up and began dancing, complete with suggestive pelvic and bust movements, as per Hindi films.

Their spontaneity was the perfect example of another glaring hypocrisy, or at least, that is how I felt. The girl who was dancing with abandon expressed a freedom which probably did not really exist for many like her.

Because – while girls were allowed freedom up to a point, their sexuality was still something which the family controlled. And any transgression could mean the severest of punishments, even death.

Had both Scarlett and Liza – and now this poor Indian girl in Delhi – become victims of this fatal perception of what girls should and should not do? Or was there something deeper, larger and much more dangerous and organized, which made Liza's case different, as Amarjit had hinted?

While I tried to sort out my thoughts, Marian arrived.

I insisted she shared my scrambled eggs and beer, as usual overcome with pity when I looked at her skeletal frame. No doubt she felt equally sorry for my rather generously proportioned figure, which could politely be called voluptuous. She took a tiny bit of toast and egg onto a plate, pushing it around without permitting a morsel to actually reach her lips.

This morning she seemed fairly distracted, opening and shutting her handbag and smoking far more than she should have, even by my standards.

She looked more and more worn out. In a few days she would, no doubt, disappear in a puff of smoke. She was barely twenty-four, but seemed much older. Her sister's disappearance really seemed to be taking a toll. There was no doubt that her apparent vulnerability prevented me from asking the really tough questions, Indeed, I felt at a distinct disadvantage trying to cross-examine someone so frail and despairing.

I also felt frustrated, since I couldn't tell her about the latest video, or the previous one. I was still waiting for clearance from Amarjit.

He would have seen the beach video by now but there was no response so far. I imagined he might have also been puzzled about when and where the video had been shot – and crucially who had shot it? That person, after all, could be very valuable for us and an important eyewitness.

Marian's uneasiness had been transmitted to me, and I too began to feel a little queasy. Excusing myself, I went out of the shack to still my anxiety and to try to call Amarjit, but there was no answer.

Giving up, I joined Marian once more. After eating our breakfast, we walked together along the beach towards Fernando's.

On the way she suggested we should take a small detour and climb up the densely forested hill, just bordering the shacks. Perhaps, she said, I should also look around the small guest house in which she had shared a room with Liza. However, she cautioned me that people might not be very helpful and that I shouldn't feel disheartened if no one parted with any information.

'There is a general desire to avoid trouble. Everyone here is closely connected to each other; you may have noticed that – especially the beach boys, the police, the shack owners and many of the workers. Some of the politicians in Goa were beach boys once upon a time, or have connections here, too, so they have their own compulsions. They have all grown up in the same village and gone to the same school. And now they work for each other. Doing the good stuff and the bad stuff together. And because it's their own bad stuff, we, as outsiders, can't criticize anyone.'

Obviously since she had stayed here with her sister; her sadness was very apparent today.

'And so while things are going well, they all become your best friends. But when things go wrong, they simply forget about you, and you are blamed for everything. Particularly when you need their help. That's when most of them develop amnesia.' She sounded very bitter.

When we reached the guest house, up a tiny winding path, she said she would prefer not to enter, and would wait for me outside.

Almost hidden beneath her large straw hat, she wandered down to a nearby grotto containing a statue of Mother Mary, and sat on the cement bench in front of it. The grotto had been painted a dazzling white, and the sculpture itself, set in the recess, was colourful, dressed in blue robes, cradling a plump baby Jesus. As with most Christian icons in this part of the world, the colour of the skin and hair was much darker, the cheeks were highlighted in an unnaturally healthy red, while the baby Jesus had a shining halo of bright gold. Someone had taken a lot of care over the upkeep of the grotto. It had been built just last year, according to the blue plaque.

Marian's hands were clasped together as though in prayer. Still feeling a little unwell myself, I couldn't prevent a surge of sympathy.

I could understand how Goa could make one turn to religion. Yesterday even I, a strong atheist, could not resist lighting a candle inside a church. My mother would be thrilled at my foray into spirituality, though she might not be very happy if I became a Roman Catholic.

I noticed another sign that stated the grotto had been donated to the area 'By the kindness of Mr Victor D'Silva, MLA'. It was a name that cropped up quite frequently in the local papers. I made a mental note to find out more about him and why he had chosen this slightly rocky outcrop for a grotto. It was an odd location.

I walked up to the optimistically named Cozee Home, a gravity-defying, steeply built set of rooms painted in lurid blue. The complex was screened by a thick cluster of palm trees, so that it wasn't easily visible till you were upon it. The entrance was decorated with bright orange plastic marigolds, and a large wooden cross.

Two very svelte-looking women in skimpy bikinis, with beach bags and dark glasses, brushed past me on their way out of Cozee Home, but for once I wasn't envious of their figures. I was just worried about them. I hoped they would have a safe and happy day on the beach.

Obviously nothing would alleviate my morose mood today, not even the colourful sarongs and fish keychains dangling on one side of the desk. Usually I was attracted to kitsch like a magpie towards a shiny coin, but it had little effect on me today. Rows of lights twinkled over a framed poster of Jesus Christ looking heavenwards on the wall behind the reception desk. The owner of Cozee Home seemed determined to emphasize his Catholic roots.

As my eyes adjusted to the dim light, I saw that just to the side of the reception was a yellow cement staircase which probably led up to the rooms. Marian had said they had stayed just one flight up and I wondered if I should take a chance and quickly make a dash upstairs. But what if someone objected?

Just as I put a foot on the first step a voice boomed out behind me.

'Looking for someone, madam?'

I jumped around and found myself staring at a smooth hairless face, attached to a large, muscular body. The man had shaved his head and so the impression was rather like encountering a brown balloon bearing diamond studs. He was chewing gum, and wore fashionably torn jeans and a red Lacoste t-shirt.

'I was actually looking for a young girl called Liza,' I said innocently. 'I met her on the beach some time ago and she gave me this address.'

His eyes narrowed slightly, but his expression barely changed as he swung around the reception desk and opened his bookings register.

'Liza? Any idea what was her full name?' He spoke as we all did here, in lilting Goanese English. I found it very catching.

'Liza Kay – slightly plump girl, very pretty, with blonde curly hair.'

He shook his head, shutting the register.

'You sure she said here?'

'That's right, first floor. She shared it with her sister.'

'First floor we have only single rooms, madam. She must have told you someplace else.'

I decided to insist. Surely Marian couldn't have brought me to the wrong place? She would know where they had stayed!

'No, I'm sure it was here. Please can you check again?'

He ran his finger through the register once more and then shut it firmly.

'Nothing. Sometimes, madam, these girls are so spaced out they don't know who they are, let alone where they're staying.'

I wondered how I could persuade him to let me go upstairs. There could be a very good – though unpleasant

– reason why he had decided to forget Liza. Besides, why would I trust him either? After all, any man could have been one of her rapists that night at the beach.

On the other hand, I wondered if it would be alright to show him Liza's photograph.

Just as I was deciding what to do, another man, in his early twenties, came down the steps, and the breath stopped in my throat.

I remembered the video of Liza on the bed in an unidentifiable room with only a black and gold headboard behind her. Three men lay next to her. One of them had raised himself on an elbow and stared at her while she gazed blankly up at the camera lens.

This man coming down the steps bore a strong resemblance to the one who had been lying next to her on that bed, who had also grabbed her breast so brutally while they were dancing before. His curly black hair tied behind his head, and that thick-lipped mouth with a gap-toothed smile, made him more recognizable than the others (at one stage the camera had come quite close to Liza and to him). Perhaps it was the ponytail or the slight swagger. I couldn't tell for sure – and I could not have identified him conclusively in a police line-up – but I knew in my gut that it was him. And it could have been him who had raped her on the beach as well. I wished I could have taken out my phone and made a comparison with his image, or even taken his photograph; however, that would have been not only dangerous, but foolhardy. After all, as far as I knew, no one had been accused of her rape so far, even though Liza had been attacked at least twice.

Since neither of the videos carried a date, I couldn't tell which had been shot first.

Was this man the reason Marian had brought me here? I was puzzled, but determined to find out more.

'Hi,' I said brightly thrusting out my hand to him as he swung by, and trying as unobtrusively as possible to block his way.

Taken aback, he looked down at my hand and then shook it, grinning. While I inwardly cringed at his touch, he seemed delighted that his charm made even middle-aged women swoop down on him in the corridors of shady hotels.

'I – I'm Simran Singh. I was looking for a friend. A girl called Liza Kay.'

'Liza? Blonde girl with curly hair? Oh, wow. I'd forgotten about her. She hasn't been back for ages. Been at least a year now.'

'A year? But I met her a few days back,' I said quickly, though I couldn't be sure if it was the right thing to say. Perhaps he was mixing her up with someone else?

Now it was his expression which changed – to one of surprise and wariness, as he looked at me. But then he smiled again and said breezily, 'Really? That's very nice

115

for you, because she hasn't been in touch with me for a long time. You're the lucky one!'

Exchanging a high five with the man behind the reception desk, he said, 'If you see her, give her my love. It's nice to hear about old friends.' He paused and looked back at me, adding, 'What exactly do you want to meet her for?'

I felt my face flush a little. This encounter was so unexpected that I hadn't really thought it through. It was best to keep the reason as trivial as possible.

'I . . . oh, nothing important. I thought we could have dinner together sometime.'

His lips stretched in what I thought was a sardonic smile.

'That's very kind of you. But you see, she doesn't stay here any more, so I would suggest you don't waste your time here.' He looked from me towards the receptionist. 'But a friend of Liza's is a friend of mine. Melvyn, since this lady has come all this way, why don't you look after her a little. Something cold to drink? A glass of wine, some fresh juice? I wish I could join you but I have some urgent work. All I can say is she really broke my heart by going away. Do ask her, if you see her, why she left so suddenly. Never even said goodbye.'

With a friendly wave, he began heading for the door.

Feeling a little sick again, I tried to keep the quiver from my voice, saying, 'I'll certainly ask her, but I don't know your name?'

'Curtis D'Silva,' he threw over his shoulder. Obviously

he was related to the MLA on the sign outside. I should have guessed.

Curtis. I had heard the name before. I thought it was Marian who had mentioned him. He was Liza's friend who was at Fernando's the night she disappeared. It was extremely odd that she hadn't warned me he might be here.

He certainly wasn't trying to hide who he was or the fact he knew Liza. And yet he had knowingly been filmed, in a very disturbing manner, with her. Was she still around somewhere in this guest house? It would be a perfect place to hide her.

Perhaps he was trying to throw me off the track by saying that he hadn't seen her for a year. His words were confusing. I realized that the fault was mine. I had simply assumed that Liza had come to Goa recently, and for the first time. She might have come here more than once or she might have been here longer than I thought. I also recollected that Marian had been evasive about the time line. I felt a sense of danger, wondering if I had been set up.

'Is he related to the MLA, D'Silva who built the grotto outside?' I asked Melvyn.

'That's his dad. Made it last year. In thanksgiving.'

'What for? Anything to do with the son?'

Melvyn shrugged, saying nothing. Nor did he deny it.

'Was he in trouble over Liza?'

'No idea, madam. I said I didn't know her. Only the boss said he did. Now what juice do I give you?'

I wondered at his reticence; I wasn't going to let him go just yet . . .

'So his dad is the local politician?'

'That's right,' said the man, giving me a curious look, probably wondering why I was asking so many questions.

'And what does Curtis do?' I persisted, hoping he wouldn't get too suspicious, yet unwilling to give up a good opportunity to find out more about this Curtis D'Silva, who had known Liza so well that she had broken his heart. Had he raped her in revenge?

'Does he run this place?'

'He owns it. But he's a DJ at one of the casino ships. Just for fun. You should go there.' The receptionist looked at me and winked. 'You'll enjoy. You know my meaning.'

'Which casino?' I asked, still trying to look casual, even though I realized I was sweating from the tension.

'It's called the *Tempest*. Quite fancy – lots of people go there for the gambling and for Curtis's music. He sings as well. Now, madam, let me get you something to drink, like Curtis said. Just wait here. Glass of juice, wine or beer?'

He dragged a chair near the desk for me to sit down while I waited.

Asking for a glass of red wine, I settled down, still

upset that I had not been able to have a more detailed conversation with Curtis or learn anything really meaningful about him and Liza. I would have to find a way of meeting him again, somehow. So I was grateful for this chance to prolong the conversation with Melvyn, and hoped Marian wouldn't mind waiting a little longer.

As soon as he left through a side door, I dragged the reception register closer to me and flipped through it. As far as I could make out, he was telling the truth; there was no mention of either Liza or Marian Kay in the last six months or so.

I quickly pushed it away and shut it when I heard Melvyn's footsteps approaching.

He handed me a glass of wine, saying, 'You really look messed up. Next time you should stay here.'

I ignored his slightly rude remark about my appearance, which I knew was a little dishevelled, as I was feeling increasingly unwell.

'So how does one get onto the casino ship?' I asked, sipping the wine slowly.

'It's very simple. Go to Panjim to get the boat, and pay the entry fee. Thanks to Curtis I've been a few times; best fun is after nine.' He handed me a brochure which showed a ship festooned with lights on which glamorous people gambled, looking happier than I had ever seen punters look before.

Goa had recently allowed off-shore casinos, which were moored on the Mandovi River. It was a controversial move, as gambling was illegal in many parts of the country. So while initially the clientele had been mostly foreigners, now it had become de rigueur for Indians too. It was a fashionable step up for the newly rich middle class to be seen there.

Having elicited the details about the ship, which would help in my next meeting with Curtis, I decided to leave before Melvyn got the wrong idea. I wouldn't blame him if he did – after all, I seemed to be desperately interested in all the men I had met at Cozee Home! I had stopped one on his way out and had chatted up the other quite relentlessly.

'Though I hate gambling,' I said, 'I must visit this casino.'

Melvyn nodded enthusiastically.

I thanked him and then headed out for the grotto where I had left Marian. To my surprise, Melvyn followed me to the door and stood there looking at me curiously, as I walked towards the grotto.

Marian, however, was nowhere to be seen. Maybe it was my fault; I should have expected it, after yesterday. She was turning out to be quite unreliable.

For a moment I worried whether Curtis's exit from the hotel had anything to do with her departure. Surely she wasn't worried about him, because I remember she said he had been very helpful, and had even brought her home safely. She had clearly indicated he had a cast-iron alibi. Presumably she hadn't seen the video and so, unlike me, had little to be suspicious about. So why, when she had brought me here, would she have fled? Or had she left with him?

I walked around the grotto impatiently, trying to ignore Melvyn, who was still standing at the entrance of the hotel, and now talking to someone on his mobile phone. I knew he was still watching me.

Where the hell was Marian?

In a burst of anger I wondered if I was wasting my time with her: she had said she would take me to all the places she associated with Liza, and yet every day, after a fairly cursory conversation, she decided to vanish. Didn't she realize that I had stayed behind in Goa only to help her find her sister? Perhaps Veeramma's warning was correct and I should abandon this case, after all.

My headache, which had somewhat receded for a while, now returned; for a minute I felt the whole land-scape shift in front of me. With irritation I realized that I was getting some kind of heatstroke. Involuntarily, I felt a sudden chill as well.

My discomfort grew and so I sat down on a bench near the grotto, taking deep breaths to steady my sudden trembling. As soon as my hands stopped shaking, which had never happened to me before, I composed an angry text message to Amarjit on my phone, saying that Marian's involvement was actually slowing down the investigation.

Just as I sent it off with a sigh of relief, I heard a familiar ping.

A message had arrived from Marian, and my temper cooled as quickly as it had shot up.

'*Sorry to rush away,*' she wrote. '*Was told L was spotted again, this time near Fernando's. Am going there, taking the shortcut through the rocks. If you turn to your left at the end of the beach, cross over to Anjuna, you will reach Fernando's. 15 mins max! See you soon, but be careful.*'

Interesting. And there was no mention of Curtis.

So had she left before she had a chance to see him? I wasn't sure, but I decided to go to Fernando's anyway, as she had suggested. I could feel Melvyn still looking at me, as I walked down to the beach, but when I turned around to check, as I reached the bottom of the hill, he wasn't there. In any case the palm trees in between prevented a clear view of Cozee Home.

The sun was high up in the sky and I was beginning to feel more and more giddy. Perhaps it was the beer I had drunk that morning. Or something wrong with the scrambled eggs? I shouldn't have had the wine, I realized, when I was already unwell.

I paused to breathe deeply and fight the nausea. After sweating from the uncomfortable heat, I was now shivering violently from the inexplicable cold. A severe pain spread through my neck and shoulders. Because I occasionally do get spasms from spondylosis, I assumed that this was a return of the old problem, and tried to shift the weight of my rather large and heavy handbag from my shoulder onto my arm.

The sickness worsened and confusion descended. I found myself meandering down to the rocks which separated the small beach from Anjuna, to reach Fernando's. Puzzled, I tried to recall the route Marian had suggested and wondered if this could be it, because the dark rocks stretched unevenly in front of me, clumps of jagged, dark laterite looming out of the sea. But feeling a little dazed by the shimmering sea and the sharp sunshine, I told myself that they would become easier to negotiate the closer I got to them. They were still partly hidden by the hill dividing the two beaches.

Approaching the rocks, I tried to concentrate on where to put my feet on the slippery, wet surface, but my brain felt like cotton wool. What was going on? Could I have come the wrong way?

At every step the rocks in front of me expanded and contracted, the spaces between them becoming impossibly far and wide. I felt compelled to carry on, since going back looked even more dangerous, as I feared sliding into the sea which was grabbing me with hungry fingers. From the way the waves were crashing on the rocks, it was obvious the current around here was really strong. By now my head was spinning so much that I had to sit down and almost crawl from one rock to the other, occasionally getting scraped from the sharp surfaces. Part of me kept saying I was being stupid and I should turn back, but it was a small ineffectual voice. Because I felt that I had to reach Fernando's urgently. Marian was there and possibly Liza as well.

Fortunately I was wearing my jeans and so the scratches did not cut too deep, and my skin was peculiarly anaesthetized anyway. The waves of sickness were rising so fast that for a while I simply couldn't get up. After some time, which could have been three minutes or thirty, I couldn't tell, I thought I would shout for help, but my voice was hopelessly stuck in my throat. This must be a nightmare, I thought. Perhaps I'll wake up soon enough.

Some vendors selling all kinds of goods appeared and disappeared, growing eerily large then receding, sliding down from the hillside onto the rocks; but none of them came near me or even offered to assist. Totally disoriented, I once more got to my feet, unsteadily stumbling along, unable to decide at what point I should abandon the rocks and go onto the much less dangerous-looking hill track and catch a cab from the top, as I had done in the past. The angry sea snaking beneath my unsteady feet looked very rough indeed. Yet as I faltered I found myself unable to control my mind or my body. What I clearly remember is that, by now, I had absolutely no sense of the immense danger I was in.

I was concentrating so hard on reaching the beach at

the other end that I didn't think how strange I must have looked, as I slid and slithered precariously, increasingly sure I would never be able to reach Fernando's, but less and less concerned about it. I couldn't even remember why I wanted to go there and it all seemed so pointless anyway. I thought I saw Melvyn's face float into view, but I didn't want him to know that I was feeling so sick. He too drifted by, while I sat down and waited for the world to straighten itself out again.

I finally decided to give up all attempts and was on the verge of allowing myself the comfort of falling into the sea, when I felt a hand on my shoulder.

Turning around, I saw Veeramma, and shut my eyes again thinking she must be a mirage. But she didn't disappear when I opened my eyes. Sinking in and out of a black hole, I clung to what I thought was her hand on my shoulder.

'I have to go to Fernando's,' I told her, my tongue feeling like molten rubber, while the rocks around exploded into orange. The whole area took on a volcanic hue.

I was not sure if she understood me; she simply stood there becoming larger and smaller, in turns. It all was very funny, but I found it impossible to laugh. I hung on to her, thinking that she might fly away if I didn't anchor her. Though neither my mind nor my body was functioning properly, some primal survival instinct told me that unless I asked her for help, I would slide into the water.

Her hands remained steady, while the spray that splashed me from the sea felt hot enough to burn.

I was probably half lying on the rocks by now, and I struggled upright. But my legs were refusing to move forward, locked by some invisible key.

'Hold my hand.' Veeramma's voice sounded far away, and her shape changed and grew into a garuda, the great mythological bird. I blinked at her as I tried to move and found that I was completely frozen.

Somehow she dragged me across what seemed a long line of sharp rocks. I couldn't be sure of anything. I was in agony. Was I holding her hands or the garuda's claws? Was the pain I felt from the outside or from inside my skin? Were my eyes open or closed?

'Keep moving,' said another voice, very, very close to me. Melvyn? But I shook my head and slid immediately into the waves, which were still leaping out to get me. My arms and legs were being pulled out of their sockets; I felt like a rag doll, bumped along, pushed and pulled.

Veeramma's voice grew fainter and fainter and the water entered my lungs and I, thankfully, stopped breathing.

Chapter 7

I woke up in my room, with my head still throbbing, and with Veeramma by my bedside. She sat on the floor, her forehead knotted with worry lines. Her colourful beads and fake-silver ornaments were spread around her as she sorted them out.

I tried to sit up, but though the room still spun, I didn't feel as bewildered as I had been. I was reminded of when I was seventeen and had announced that I was going to get very, very drunk to my college friends – and proceeded to do just that. I had passed out and it took me a week to recover.

'You stupid or what?' Veeramma said so firmly and abruptly that I did not mistake her meaning.

An array of medicines was on my bedside table. On closer examination most of them seemed to be anti-nausea pills and vitamin-B tablets, with a few strips of paracetamol. Nothing serious, then. Obviously I hadn't died as yet. And was not likely to do so anytime soon.

'What happened?'

'You been sick all day all night,' she said grimly. 'The doctor said you drugged.'

'Drugs? I've never taken them in my life. I don't even know what they look like.'

The fact that I could have been slipped a drug made me remember what had happened with Liza and Marian. To say that I felt foolish would be an understatement. I remembered how I had taken a high moral ground, mentally castigating Marian for leading her sister astray and accepting drinks from complete strangers. What had I done that was any different?

Someone was definitely keeping an eye on me. Having successfully forced Durga and her friends to go back to Delhi, they were now trying to force me to do the same.

I had very hazy memories of what happened to me yesterday, and my attempt to cross over the rocks to Anjuna while obviously flying as high as a kite. Ridiculous! I had done many crazy things in my life, but this was probably the most embarrassing of them all.

I closed my eyes in despair, recollecting that at one stage I had crawled on my hands and knees, not caring who was watching. Obviously I hadn't been given a very high-quality drug – instead of being enjoyable, the experience had been a nightmare coupled with extreme pain.

I was lucky to be alive, since the slightest stumble would have seen me smashed against the rocks.

So, as I had suspected while talking to the two men at Cozee Home, the whole thing had been a complete set-up. I had been lured there – and given a dose of what Liza had got. Except that Curtis was not interested enough to have raped me.

Whose side was Marian on? And why had she taken me there, in the first place? Surely she knew I would meet Curtis, and why would she do something so brazen in which she was bound to be caught?

Yet, puzzlingly, she had spent the longest time with me, had taken me to Cozee Home. And, in between, I had been slipped those drugs.

Why would she do this? After all, I was trying to help her find her sister. It made no sense at all.

'I been sitting long,' Veeramma volunteered. She had stopped sorting out her wares, and was now staring at me unabashedly.

I was touched by her care. It was much more than any stranger was likely to give me. Especially after the way I had apparently behaved yesterday. I must have been frighteningly out of control.

'Cost me a lot of money then, since you charge by the hour,' I joked. But there was not a glimmer of a smile on Veeramma's face.

I picked up the prescription for the doctor's phone number, calling from the landline in my room. I needed to find out what happened to me. I didn't care even if that nosy receptionist was listening in.

Dr Sunny Diaz told me in no uncertain terms that he had to caution me about taking drugs which did not suit me. There was a lot of chemical cosh on the beach, mostly coming from Pune. And that at my age I should be careful.

I cleared my throat. 'Doctor, could it have been just food poisoning?'

There was a silence at the other end.

'Miss Simran, you are a tourist here. And you must be careful with what you eat or drink. If you prefer to call it food poisoning then I will let you do that. Though rarely do people hallucinate with an upset stomach.'

I was puzzled (and even more embarrassed) by his insinuation.

I thought back to the various possibilities. The most probable way in which the drug could have been given to me was in the wine at Cozee Home. But then I remembered that I had felt a mild discomfort all morning, as well, especially after sharing my breakfast with Marian. Thus had she given me a dose in the morning and had Curtis D'Silva unleashed his peculiar brand of hospitality on me and spiked the wine later too? More importantly, had Marian warned him that I would be coming to the hotel? Looking back, his appearance – almost as though on cue – to instruct Melvyn to give me a drink was suspect. Of course, I had thought I had been very clever, outsmarting him by stopping him in the hotel corridor. He was obviously smarter than I was. And Marian was the absolute genius amongst us all, I thought bitterly. I still did not know what her game was, except that she had almost got me killed.

'Madam, I tried telling that day. This not safe for you, if you still hunting for girl. She gone; forget her.' Veeramma interrupted my chain of thoughts.

'How can you say that?' I struggled to sit up, while my neck and my head felt they would be dislocated any minute. My tongue was still swollen and I had developed a strange lisp.

'I must look for Liza. Someone saw her again yesterday. Her sister told me.'

'Sister, shister!' Veeramma spat out. 'Go see truth!'

'Where? I have been asking you since yesterday. Why don't you tell me what you know?'

Her eyes flashed with such venom that even I shrank back on the bed.

'Go ask her. She fool you. She no cry, no worry. Just pretend. Go see her at Arpora bazaar.'

The angry tone in her voice made me remember that tonight was the flea market, an occasion which gave stiff competition to vendors like Veeramma. That could be one reason she was so angry – with me, with Marian, with the whole world.

Every Saturday night the land adjoining the Anjuna beach at Arpora was converted into a giant bazaar, with hundreds of big and small stalls. It was a legacy from the hippie days, when foreigners who flooded into Goa needed money to buy their drugs, and they began to sell whatever they had with them. Slowly this became a weekly ritual, and while most of the original flower children had left, now all kinds of art and crafts were on sale. But the motivational factor had probably moved on from drugs to pure commerce. Music played in the background, and sometimes people danced and others performed. Temporary bars and long rows of restaurants selling exotic food sprang up overnight, ensuring the crowds which sometimes touched over a million would stay on till early morning. But while the sellers were both local and foreign vendors, the level of business was more organized than those of the wandering beach vendors. Many hundreds of thousands of rupees could be spent in a single evening. It was a 'flea market' only in name.

'Did you see Liza there as well?' I asked curiously.

Veeramma shrugged noncommittally. 'Seen many like her.'

Perhaps this was the time to show her Liza's photograph, to confirm we were talking about the same girl. The last time she had refused to look at it. I hunted for my mobile phone, buried at the bottom of my handbag.

Taking it out, I began scanning through for the message to which Amarjit had attached the photograph.

For a moment my breath almost stopped.

All the photographs and videos on my phone had disappeared. All my messages had been wiped clean. I went to my desk, and took out my laptop, quickly turning it on to check if, by chance, the videos and photographs were still in its memory.

Not only had everything been deleted, I couldn't even get into my email because my account had been hacked and my password had been changed. A lot had happened while I was sleeping off the effects of whatever drug had been slipped into my food or drink.

In a state of shock, I sat back.

So that was the reason I had been drugged. I wondered if Veeramma had managed, somehow, to get the messages deleted from my phone and computer. She was smart enough to do so. But she was still with me, and it was unlikely she would take such a huge risk.

Yet someone had realized that I had these damaging videos and decided that they needed to get rid of them.

I was beginning to feel hunted, and intruded upon. Violated and assaulted. Whoever was keeping a track of me was doing an extremely good job. Both the people who had sent me the videos and the others who had wiped them out were aware of what I was doing here. While one side was trying to keep me going, the others were obviously trying to intimidate me. I wondered where this would eventually lead. It could be more dangerous than I had thought. In fact, if I had actually fallen off the rocks and died, and everything had been wiped from my computer and mobile phone, no one would ever know what had happened to me.

And it was ironic that Marian who had warned me that everyone on the beach had colluded to cover up Liza's disappearance, because of their close associations with each other, might herself be part of that close-knit group. So what was her link with everyone here? It was pointless asking Veeramma, who seemed to have a pathological hatred for her.

Besides, Veeramma could be involved in the cover-up as well. Rather than looking after me right now, she was probably keeping an eye on me. Could her dislike for Marian just be a spoiler, so that I wouldn't know who to trust?

'Thanks for saving my life,' I said to her slowly, trying to sound genuine and to remember exactly what had happened yesterday.

How could I find out if she was involved? How could I be sure which side she was on?

I took out a handful of 500-rupee notes from my wallet and thrust them at her. I knew I was both thanking her and bribing her, but I needed to know more.

I knelt next to her, pushing the money into her hand, and said as earnestly as I could manage, despite the weakness I was beginning to feel, 'Tell me where you found me and how you brought me back here.'

She took the money and tucked it into her saree blouse. And to my surprise she shook her head.

'Not me, madam. Hotel call me. They say you calling my name. Then they call doctor.'

'But I was walking over the rocks to Fernando's. I slipped, and almost fell into the water. And then you came and helped me. You dragged me to safety.'

A slight smile crossed her face this time. 'What you say, madam? You lying in room when I came.'

Had it all been a nightmare, then, just another part of my drug haze? Had I imagined everything – the rocks, going towards Anjuna, Melvyn appearing there, Veeramma rescuing me?

She looked sympathetic, and waved one hand around my head. 'Madam, drug do this to you. You dream everything.'

I decided not to question her any more about my behaviour. I got up, and looked down at my jeans, which I had been wearing since yesterday, and found that though they were torn in a few places, I did not seem to be as badly hurt as I had imagined. I recollected the pain and then realized that Veeramma might be correct after all. I had been hallucinating.

'Did anyone touch my phone?'

She shook her head. 'I no see, madam. Your bag lying here. You check money, passport all there? Too many thieves on beach.'

I already knew that my wallet was where I had zipped it in. My passport and credit cards were fortunately in the hotel locker here in my room. So obviously only my phone and my computer had been tampered with.

She began to get up.

'I go now. Be careful, madam. I told you the other day that all this big trouble for you. Big big sharks. Go back to daughter.'

'Thanks. I'll see you on the beach.' I nodded to her feebly as she left the room.

When Veeramma mentioned Durga, I was jolted into remembering that I had promised to call her and my mother. Pushing aside my sickness, I rang home, resigned to a familiar harangue from my mother as she checked whether I was alright and, of course, if I had met anyone 'significant'. Over the years this had become her code for asking if I was finally going to bring home a partner for myself. But as time flew by, to her disappointment, though there were quite a few very special men, none of them had grabbed my hand permanently.

I knew she had given my number to Amarjit in the hope that perhaps now, as a fresh divorcee, he would show an interest in me. I could hear her sigh when I told her that I had no clue if he was going to be back in Goa anytime soon.

Calling home made me yearn for some normalcy in my life again. Compared to my Delhi life, my Goan experience seemed increasingly strange, and I longed for the few peaceful days I had enjoyed here before Amarjit had sent me that video.

My mother, unaware of my present plight, told me that Durga was out with her friends, while Sharda, her sister, was learning new recipes for making Italian food from my mother. So tomatoes were being whizzed in mixers, pasta being boiled and markets rapidly denuded of oregano and parmesan cheese. Or so I was told.

And then we discussed the Delhi gang rape survivor whose every breath the nation was praying for. Indeed, I too felt compelled to search for Liza because of this young girl's courage. Despite her terribly fragile state, she had identified and named each one of her rapists in a detailed statement to the district magistrate. One hoped that thanks to the media focus, the promised fast-track courts would come up and that her case, unlike that of Scarlett and so many others, would not languish for years.

Meanwhile, the news I conveyed to my mother, as can be imagined, was quite limited. I could hardly tell her that while I was hunting for a girl in Goa who had been raped and molested, I had apparently been drugged, and had hallucinated about walking on a beach calling out for a woman who sold sarongs and silver jewellery. It definitely did not sound reassuring.

Instead, after stating that I was still on the lookout for a potential husband, I said goodbye and gingerly tested my legs once more. Surprisingly, I was feeling better already, and I sat down again at the desk to make a forward plan, as well put down some notes.

I also needed to let Amarjit know what had happened so far. I ordered a couple of hardboiled eggs and some toast. I was suddenly feeling very hungry, as I realized that I hadn't eaten anything since breakfast yesterday; but I didn't want to risk anything more elaborate.

Just to be on the safe side I also decided that I would visit Fernando's tomorrow, but without telling Marian, as I wasn't sure if I could trust her. Today I would go out only in the evening, when I was completely recovered.

If I were to trust Veeramma's version of events, I had somehow come back to the hotel, or collapsed somewhere near it. The hotel staff had then brought me to my room, and because I was calling out for her, asked Veeramma to sit by my side till I woke up. But somehow I just couldn't believe it.

It was indisputable that I had passed out at some stage, and someone had brought me back, and perhaps it was that same person who had wiped the videos and photographs from my laptop and phone. Even if I asked the hotel management about who had brought me back, I had a feeling no one would give me any straight answers.

Nonetheless, I rang the inquisitive Maggie, who normally was never short of answers or questions, to find out if she knew anything.

There was a silence while she obviously thought about what to say.

Finally, very cautiously, she said the general manager had been out for lunch at the time, but she would inquire from the rest of the staff and call me back. She personally knew nothing about the incident. Her unusual reticence made me wonder how much she really knew. Of course she wouldn't call back, of that I was sure.

I put the phone down, wondering how I would ever learn what had really happened to me.

I took off my clothes and stood in front of the mirror on the wardrobe, twisting and turning, reading the evidence on my body. The scratches on my legs and bruises on my arms proved that I had slipped on the rocks but I could also have been dragged along or at least had been pulled and pushed a little. I ached all over, but thankfully there seemed no reason to suspect anything worse than a bit of rough manhandling.

Wondering who had seen me in that condition, and who had picked me up, made me feel further humiliated. Thankfully, Durga and her friends were not here any more.

Registering a fresh email account, I sent a long message to Amarjit, describing yesterday's curious events. I requested him to re-send me Liza's photograph and the two videos which had been deleted.

I also asked him, once again, if he had got anything further to share with me, especially any information on the men who were with Liza in the videos, and, if so, to send it to me as a matter of great urgency. In just two days my life seemed to have turned upside down and I seemed to be getting sucked deeper and deeper into this case. Now after what had happened to me, I felt outraged and more determined than ever to find Liza.

His reply was extremely guarded. He sent me Liza's photograph, as well as the videos, and told me that he would try to come down in the next few days. He also said I shouldn't take any unnecessary risks. He only wanted information, and not my blood on his hands.

His dramatic words did little to deter me. If someone was trying so hard to scare me, it might mean they had something to hide, and Liza was still alive. There was something they were trying to cover up. I simply had to find her now.

By the evening I had more or less recovered from the effects of whatever had been given to me. Putting on an innocuous plain white dress, I went down to the flea market, as Veeramma had suggested. But this time I hired a cab so that I would be certain to reach my destination and not be sabotaged once again.

I felt very unsure, though, what I should do next. The two people I had thought I could trust, Marian and Veeramma, had both turned out to be unreliable. Whoever had tried to destabilize me had quite clearly succeeded.

At any other time, the sight, sound and smell of the

Arpora bazaar would have delighted me. The sheer variety of craft, food and design on display was intriguing – and the entire landscape had been decked with a variety of lamps and tents. The music provided a steady beat to the ebb and flow of the crowd. But all I felt was a sense of betrayal.

I allowed a cold anger to brew within me. I wanted to nail whoever had wrecked Liza's life and made a fool of me. I was furious with Marian, and everyone else who at first seemed helpful but turned out to be uncaring and duplicitous.

Veeramma had suggested that something about Marian would be revealed to me here at the market. It was risky to follow her advice – it might be another set-up, after all – but in this fairly crowded place I thought I might safely pick up some clues.

But as the sunlight faded and the gas lamps were lit I still hadn't found any reason to be here. Christmas lights came on, and a few groups wandered about singing carols. Children ran about excitedly as parents bought gifts, but I was still aloof, uncertain and unhappy. It was far too crowded anyway to look for anyone here. I was irritated at my own gullibility.

Finally, as I stood at a slight distance from the bazaar, wondering whether I should weave my way through the narrow pathways of the market again, I saw the man who I believed had almost caused my death.

It was Curtis D'Silva talking to an Indian girl, barely 500 feet from where I stood. I quickly moved behind a clump of palms, and took out my phone to photograph them together. Even though it was dark and I would only get an indistinct image, I thought it might be helpful later.

It was difficult to say for sure, but the girl could have been Goan, as she stood there in a short black skirt and a red tank top.

They were having a fairly animated discussion, but I didn't dare go any closer. Luckily, after a while, with a kiss on her cheek, he walked away. Yesterday's experience had convinced me that behind the friendly mask lurked a very dangerous man. And to remain alive, I had to stay out of his way.

I kept to the shadows till he was out of sight, and then casually walked up to where the girl was now sitting at a bar inside the bazaar, smoking a cigarette, lost in thought.

I sat down at the chair next to her. Turning to her as casually as I could, using an icebreaker that has existed ever since the discovery of nicotine, I said, 'Excuse me, could I borrow a light from you?'

I looked straight at her. She was a very pretty girl with straight black hair and a pouting, red-painted mouth. I remembered her now, clearly. She had been talking to the two men at the bar at Bambino's, the night I had first met Marian. Interesting.

'Sure,' she said in a husky voice, and handed me her lighter.

'It's a nice evening, isn't it? At least we can still hear each other over the music.' I lit my cigarette.

'Do you live here?' she asked curiously, taking the lighter back from me and putting it in her handbag. 'I think I've seen you somewhere before.'

I tried to keep my tone as casual as possible. If she had seen me with Marian that night, I didn't want her to remember it.

'I'm just visiting. A friend told me to come down here because it's such a fantastic market . . . And what about you?'

'I've been in Goa for about two years,' she said, and then fell quiet, smiling at me, and then looking back at the sea.

'For work?'

'Yes,' she said. 'Actually I'm from Chandigarh. But I was offered a job and here I am.'

So she had left behind a fairly conventional lifestyle. And most likely moved from wearing salwar kameezes to miniskirts. It was a long way for a good Punjabi girl to travel, as I well knew.

'That's where I come from, too. So you're Punjabi?'

She gave me a smile but then nodded without saying anything. I couldn't help feeling that she didn't want me to know too much about her. I decided to change tack slightly.

'What sort of work do you do?'

She seemed to hesitate again.

'It's a pretty crazy job . . . I'm a manager on the *Tempest*. It's a floating casino.'

I felt as though a penny had finally dropped into the slot machine.

'That's interesting work,' I said encouragingly, hoping she would tell me more.

'Not really,' she shrugged. 'I'm really quite fed up. I wish I could leave it but, you know, sometimes it's tough to walk out of things. Complicated.'

'Are you working tonight?'

'I'll be going there later. My shift doesn't start till nine.'

It was close to eight already.

'And you stay there till . . .?'

'Almost three in the morning. Get home only at five or so. I work when the rest of the world sleeps!'

There was a sadness in her voice. I wondered if she could become a conduit to my getting to know something more about Curtis. Could the casino have a connection with Liza as well?

'Do you have any foreigners working there?' I asked casually.

'Just a few temporary workers. Sometimes they come to make some extra money, but they aren't regular like we are. They might do a performance of some kind. Or sing.'

That meant there was definitely a possibility of a link to Liza. If for some reason she had gone onto the ship, could it explain her disappearance? It was a long shot, but my excitement rose. There was some hope of cracking this case, after all.

'I would love to come and roll a few dice. Will you be there tomorrow?'

'Sure,' she said, stubbing out her cigarette and picking up her handbag. 'It's been nice talking to you. It's the first normal conversation I've had with anyone for a long time. Otherwise my life is all about hustling, and pushing and persuading and money and ...' She stopped and shrugged. 'All the usual shit.'

'And can't you just leave all this and go back home?' I asked.

She laughed, with nothing happy in the laughter.

'If only you knew what my life is like. I don't think I can ever go back again to Chandigarh. Even if I try to, these guys won't let me go. I'm ... I have a very tough contract, and I think my boss likes me a little too much.'

She grinned. I was taken aback by her frankness. But then she probably led a life as though in a goldfish bowl, chosen more for her good looks than her qualifications. And if her boss liked her, he would have made it obvious to everyone. In her placement, her promotions, her salary. The younger the better. And she looked barely eighteen years old.

Some of the similarities between her and Liza gave me pause.

A boss who liked young girls? I remembered the job offer, according to Marian, that was made to Liza by a man who was much older than her.

Why couldn't this girl just leave? Hadn't anyone told her these relationships can be very very dangerous?

'But if you take a flight home . . .'

'They'll still come after me. I've tried to leave a few times, but it simply isn't possible.'

She looked at me and said, 'I really don't know why I'm telling you all this. You remind me of my mother, I think.' She stopped and then blushed, thinking she might have offended me, adding quickly, 'I mean you could be her younger sister.'

There was something very vulnerable about her and I wondered if she realized how trapped she sounded.

'Listen, I'm going to definitely come to the casino tomorrow. I hope you'll be there,' I told her. We exchanged phone numbers, in case I needed to contact her.

She reached out to shake my hand. I could see she would be a good salesperson, as she flashed me a big, meaningless smile.

'Sure. Ask for Vicky, and I'll show you the ropes. It'll be very crowded, though, since it's Sunday.'

After an airy wave, she began to walk away. Overcome with foreboding, after the events of the day, I was tempted to stop her and say I would come with her today. But remembered that I couldn't leave without trying to find out more about Marian.

I got up and slowly started walking back into the flea market. Oddly enough, I felt much better after my meeting with Vicky. It had given me a glimpse into a world of which I knew little. But it could be one which connected all three: Curtis, Vicky and possibly Liza.

Of course, if I went to the floating casino I would have to take care to stay out of Curtis's way, which shouldn't be too tough. I knew he was a DJ on the ship, and I had already looked up the *Tempest* on the Internet. Gambling was organized on the first deck, while the music, dancing and dinner was on the second.

If I remained on the first deck chances were I could meet Vicky and go up only when I was sure Curtis wasn't performing. I would also have to find a way of looking around the ship. I also wondered about Vicky's mysterious boss. I remembered a few media reports alleging that the casino was owned by a powerful politician who was also a minister. Interesting. Could it be him?

I sighed and savoured a rare moment when a chance meeting seemed to actually lead me somewhere!

Meanwhile, the crowds at the flea market seemed to be increasing by the minute. Feeling a little claustrophobic – possibly a residual effect of yesterday's drugs – I was about to leave when I saw familiar long blonde hair, and a painfully thin figure, walking away from me towards some stalls at the other end of the bazaar.

Marian!

She had her back towards me, so I decided to follow her at a distance, curious to know where she was going. Unfortunately, as I reached closer, I got caught in a group engrossed in the music being played by a live band, flinging their limbs and heads rather energetically about. They tried to drag me into joining them, and ultimately completely blocked the narrow path between the stalls. This carnival atmosphere that occasionally erupted around the Goan beaches was usually welcome. But not today.

Helplessly I saw Marian walking further away. She stopped to chat with a few people, and looked at some jewellery, before disappearing from view behind a building. If she was feeling guilty about what had happened to me, or in a rush to escape somewhere, she showed no signs of it.

I kept pushing forward through the group of dancers, who finally parted reluctantly to let me through. By the time I reached the stalls where she had been a moment earlier, Marian was nowhere in sight.

Disappointed, I stood uncertainly looking around. I tried to call her mobile, but there was no response.

I sent her a message asking bluntly, '*Where are you? Wanted to meet.*' There was no need for any niceties as I felt she had deliberately and knowingly put my life at risk and was continuing to harm her sister's interests.

It was strange that she had neither called me today nor found out whether I had managed to reach Fernando's. She showed no concern if I was dead or alive. All of that was indicative of the fact that she knew what had happened yesterday. Yet Amarjit seemed to trust her and had sent me another message telling me how grateful he was that I was helping her, and that he hoped that soon my patient investigation would reveal the truth about Marian and her sister.

It now seemed that it might reveal a very unexpected truth.

Having lost track of Marian, I looked around and found that next to me was a woman selling deliciously fragrant homemade bread. Another had a stall of delicately embroidered Kashmiri shawls. At a distance I also spotted a makeshift tent advertising astrology, with stars and other motifs embossed on it. And just a little closer to me was an Australian man selling exquisite (and very highly priced) silver jewellery.

But there was no sign of Marian.

Pretending to look through the jewellery, I asked the Australian if he had met someone called Marian.

He looked at me blankly.

'She was here a moment ago; the girl with a scarf around her head,' I explained.

'Oh, that lady! Yes, she was interested in the jewellery. But then,' he shrugged, 'this is my first time here, so I don't know anyone. I have no idea where she went. She said she had an appointment, and she would be back later.'

I remembered Marian's interest in astrology and wondered if she had gone inside the tent for a consultation. I walked towards it, only to find three determined-looking women and a man waiting in a queue outside. But there was no sign of her.

Idly, I bought some tiny silver earrings for Durga and Sharda, while still looking out for Marian, and keeping an eye on the tent's entrance, which was covered with colourful sarongs and dupattas. I wondered if I should stop being so discreet and just peer inside. But I hesitated. I didn't want raised eyebrows from the waiting women, who would immediately think I was just another ill-mannered Indian hoping to jump the queue. After the terrible scenes I had created yesterday, the less attention I attracted the better.

So while I waited I bought a shawl for my mother, and mentally formulated a reason for an emergency session with the astrologer. *'Husband lost!'* I could say or *'Mother sick'*. But before I could try my guerrilla tactics and leap inside the tent, I received a message on my phone from Marian. She said she was sorry to have missed me, but she'd been looking for Liza since yesterday. Even now she was following a lead and she would meet me at my hotel at around 10 p.m.

So obviously I had made a mistake. Or had I?

Instinctively, after the way she had behaved in the past, I felt I couldn't trust her. Perhaps, I thought, I should stay here just in case it had been her I had seen, after all. She hadn't mentioned her location in the message.

There was still half an hour left before 10 o'clock and it would take me just fifteen minutes to get back to the hotel in a cab. I could wait a while longer and see if she emerged from the tent or if she walked by once more.

I sent her a holding reply that I would dine in my room and she should join me. I had bought some fresh bread and cheese, and if we were feeling up to it I would even open a bottle of red wine. She should call me once she reached the reception.

I also called the hotel to tell them to ask Marian to wait in case she turned up before me, and to call me the moment she arrived.

The past two days had taught me that there was something strange about Liza's sister, and I should be equally cryptic about my own whereabouts.

So, pretending to look through a few more shawls, I waited.

My instinct was to prove correct.

And in a short while, I would get a shock that would leave me reeling. I had thought I was close to discovering who Marian was, but obviously everyone here wore a great many masks, and it was my wretched task to peel them off.

Was this the reason why Veeramma wanted me to track down Marian? Or was there still more for me to find out?

Chapter 8

I don't expect people to be scrupulously honest, but it's always distressing to have been completely deceived. I already had my worries about Marian's real identity. Now it seemed I couldn't trust her at all, as my vigil outside the astrology tent had revealed.

As I followed Marian through the market and into the 'jungle' – the thick vegetation of shrubs and trees that bordered the neighbouring beaches – I felt devastated at my own naivety. How could I have continued to believe her, even when she had, over and over again, shown herself to be completely uninterested in finding her sister? And then yesterday it seemed she had wanted to lead me into danger and leave me there.

It was odd that I had missed all the clues, blindly believing whatever I had been told. Was it because Amarjit had, in a sense, introduced us, by sending her to me? I cursed myself for foolishly listening to Amarjit (yet again). But what if he had been misled too?

As I walked behind Marian – or should I call her 'Astrologer Anne'? – I kept a safe distance between us. Fortunately this part of the beach hardly had any light, so it was easy not to be seen. In any case, Marian was too absorbed in her thoughts to even notice I was behind her, and she seemed familiar with the winding path. A few people walked behind me; in the dark it was difficult to make out who they were, but from the little I overheard them say it seemed that there was a celebration ahead.

So much for Marian's claim she was looking for Liza, or even that she was worried about her!

Just to get a full sense of Marian's unreliability, I couldn't help sending another SMS to her, even as I tracked her, guided only by the occasional lanterns that hung from branches of trees, and a few enterprising tea vendors who had set up shop beneath the gaslights.

'*Am waiting, where r u?*' my message said.

She halted briefly to message back, not realizing that I was just behind her. '*Am still stuck. Meet tmrw.*'

I marvelled at the dexterity with which she could fool me, wondering why she felt the need to maintain such an elaborate facade.

I was still at a safe distance from the astrologer's tent when I had seen the last client finally leave. And then, to my surprise, Marian emerged, and I realized that the scarf she was wearing around her head, and her assorted beads and necklaces symbolized her status as a fortune teller. The long dangling earrings were just perfect, as were the harem pants.

When she had appeared, two local helpers had come up

to her to dismantle the tent, which was just an assortment of multi-coloured curtains, strung together from a central pole. She instructed them to take it home, handing them some cash. It was a well-established routine and she stood at a distance, sipping some water from a bottle, supervising them and chatting casually. I could see everything more clearly thanks to the gas lamp that she held up to conduct the folding operations. There was no doubt that it was her.

Mystified, I stood behind the jewellery stall in order to observe her without being noticed. So she had another identity – fair enough! But why hadn't she told me earlier, especially when I had seen the card fall from her hand-bag? I couldn't think of any good reason at all, unless something detrimental to her would be revealed if she confessed her real profession.

Mulling over her persona, I had kept far away enough not to be noticed, following her as she set off across the market. She made straight for the well-trodden path which led into the forest. Neither the distance nor the lack of light bothered her, as she seemed to know where she was going.

I knew this could be dangerous, but I thought I must resolve the mystery about Marian. Did Amarjit, usually a shrewd police officer, actually have any proof that she was Liza's sister? I resolved that I would call him as soon as I got back to my hotel room, but meanwhile I had to concentrate on where we were going.

Goa has an almost continuous range of small hills which runs through its length and breadth. It is the stuff of legends, with many mythological gods and goddesses associated with it. In fact, Goa itself is said to have been born when an arrow was shot into a churning sea.

Densely vegetated areas such as this looked beautiful during the day, as ancient trees with thick roots rose out of the ground. But it was fairly frightening to be walking at night among tall trees and along an undulating path spilling over with eager plants which thrived in the fertile land.

I had heard about the snakes and scorpions that resided here, but kept blanking out the possibility of an encounter with them and focused on trying to be as noiseless and unobtrusive as possible.

The group around Marian was quite large now, as a few more people mysteriously emerged from the jungle and joined her. She chatted comfortably with those by her side, stepping over broken twigs and what I imagined to be scurrying mice, stopping only when she reached a clearing with an enormous banyan tree in the centre. The unexpected sound of a soft guitar and singing voices had already reached us a while ago. Red Chinese lanterns hanging from the branches of the tree completed the surreal scene.

I felt as though I had entered a time warp, and had gone back into the sixties. On the cement platform under the banyan tree sat a man with a long red beard and flowing locks in the middle of a swaying group, strumming and singing a Bob Dylan song. I had seen enough documentaries to know that I was probably in the presence of some of the early flower children who had stayed behind and made Goa their home. And from the marigolds scattered around and the smell of marijuana it was obvious we had reached the celebration.

I was taken aback. Geared up to expect that Marian was leading us into a drug den, or something equally dangerous, this was the last thing I expected.

An almost meditative environment prevailed, while the people who sat cross-legged on the platform around the tree and on the ground below clapped and swayed with the music. It was obviously a peaceful gathering, and I could see no sign of the drug mafia in the soft light of the lanterns.

I had been told that there were at least a thousand of these hippies (or 'Goa Freaks', as they were once called), all past their prime, still living in Goa in the way they had dreamt of. They had arrived as young men and women in the sixties and seventies, and found themselves unable to return to their old lives. Staying on, they formed a bond with each other and the golden beaches of Goa.

And the odd thing was that once again their lifestyle was attracting people from today's high-flying generation, disillusioned by the vagaries of the financial world.

Not in any significant numbers, but still enough to merit an article or two in a magazine, or a film on YouTube.

These ageing hippies were almost like gurus now, speaking from an iconic status about a unified world of 'love and peace'. It was a universal message that resonated with each new generation, as they repeated oft-heard platitudes about leading a simple life, and seeking nirvana.

I slipped into the back of the crowd, which was not visible from the platform because of the darkness, and found a space next to a tall, curly-haired man. As I joined in the singing and clapping, he turned his head to give me a grin, which I returned while making sure that Marian could not see me. I was reassured as there were no lamps near us.

The crowd, a mixed one of Indians and foreigners, all seemed to be absorbed by the medley of hippie anthems that the red-bearded man was performing. He sang in a slightly nasal voice and for a moment I really calmed down, forgetting my silent rage.

Like the others, I drifted back in time to what must have been a period of idealism and hope, till it got mired in the haze of hallucinogens. And, sadly, no one realized that this invasion of foreigners onto the beaches of Goa in the sixties would not only give Goa the look of a contemporary haven, but eventually also contribute towards many of the problems that the state faces today. Because it was these nonconformist flower children who had brought with them Goa's never-ending fascination with drugs. I looked around, wondering if the police knew about today's event? I could smell marijuana even more strongly now – did that mean that this party was likely to get busted?

Or, as seemed increasingly clear to me, this was probably happening with the blessings of the local powers that be, and only if the required sums were not doled out, or someone's ego not massaged, would the plug be pulled.

In that case, was dumping her sister's investigation the price Marian paid in order to continue having this kind of freedom? The fact that she had something to do with the organization of this 'celebration' definitely meant that she knew how the system worked. So why did she need me, and why had Amarjit insisted I help her? It all seemed more and more absurd.

As I was thinking, I noticed Marian climb onto the stage; her thin, usually nervous face was looking relaxed and animated, prettier than ever before. She was obviously a familiar figure and well known to the singer. He stopped strumming briefly to give her a kiss, as she swung by him, unselfconsciously, and then half sat and half sprawled near him. Someone handed her a cigarette. Was it loaded with more hashish? Was it safe for her to smoke it openly, I wondered.

I looked nervously at the man next to me, who wasn't smoking anything and didn't look like he was tripping, and raised my eyebrows. I didn't want to be busted in a police raid. He smiled and shrugged, obviously getting the implication. 'Don't worry,' he said. 'It's all cool here. They have all the permissions – everyone has been paid off.'

The celebratory atmosphere puzzled me, too. There were congratulatory cards 'To Stanley' hanging from some of the branches, and posters of the man who was singing in a younger avatar, without his beard and dreadlocks.

He wasn't so thin back then. Was all this fuss because he was someone famous? A forgotten lost member of the Beatles when they had come to Goa more than five decades ago?

Intrigued, I asked the man sitting next to me if he knew who Stanley was.

He looked amused and astonished at my ignorance and replied, 'You don't know about the legendary Stanley? He's a real icon. They say that about a thousand years ago Stanley used to work in the City of London. I believe he was a millionaire, but he gave it all up to come to Goa and live on the beach.'

I had not encountered a single myth about the hippies in Goa which did not refer to the fact that they had once been fabulously rich and had renounced it all, or else that they had made a lot of money in Goa through drugs, so this did not surprise me much. Though why they would abjure a decent lifestyle with private aircraft and Gucci shoes to live in penury under a banyan tree was a mystery to me. And equally, why would they want to give up a peaceful existence that promised nirvana, for a life on the run once they began making money from drugs? I just didn't get it.

'Thanks,' I told the man as appreciatively as I could. He had a very pleasant smile and I decided to let my guard drop a little. Why not?

'My name's Simran Singh. You might not believe it, but I'm actually a social worker who seems to have gone a bit astray in Goa, as you can see. Not many of us around here, I think. And what brings you here?'

'Good to meet you, Simran. My name's Dennis Pinto. I'm in between jobs, really. Start work in about ten days, so thought I'd take a break. I'm a scriptwriter for TV serials in Mumbai. All that masala stuff you can't bear to watch.'

'So how come you know so much about Stanley?' I asked. 'And who's that sitting next to him? That girl?'

'To answer the first question, because I wanted to meet some of the older hippies. I was intrigued by their stories; might make a film on them one day, I guess.' He peered to see who I was pointing to. 'And the girl? Anne? Oh she's his daughter.'

His daughter?

Marian never failed to surprise me.

How many lies had she – or rather 'Anne' – told me? I tried to remember if she had ever mentioned her father in our very brief meetings. And I was pretty sure that she had not. It was my fault – I had been working to a written script, as Dennis was only too well-qualified to point out.

I had not asked Marian any questions except about Liza, I realized, and nor had Amarjit given me much information. I had been so deeply affected by the videos of a young girl in trouble, that I had allowed myself to be manipulated throughout, trying to be sensitive about a difficult subject. It was possible that everyone knew much more than I did, because I had blindly accepted the fact that all I was looking for was a girl who had been raped on the beach, and that her sister, though unreliable, was too distraught to be cross-examined. I secretly believed she would eventually tell me everything. And I rather single-mindedly and foolishly stuck to that narrative.

'That's right. She's an astrologer. You must try her. Her predictions are always spot on. She told me last year that I would leave my TV company to work for a new one, and I did. And that it would be a great move. And all indications are that it should be. She's got an instinct for it.'

Last year.

So what Curtis had told me was correct. It was possible that Liza had been here a year ago – and Marian had been here for equally long, if not longer.

None of this surprised me any more. As I watched, a few people waved their hands in front of her and she pushed them away laughing. Astrologer Anne was not going to prophesy anything right now. No wonder

Veeramma had tried to warn me time and again, and why she had been so upset. She probably realized I knew very little about Marian or the story behind Liza's disappearance, which probably bore little resemblance to the one I had begun to build up in my head.

Where did Liza fit into all this? I looked around, wondering if she too would suddenly appear. But though there were a number of curly blonde heads in sight, I didn't think any of the faces matched the photograph.

The music stopped temporarily as another long-haired, equally wrinkled man came onto the stage and spoke about 'My friend Stanley' and how much he was a local treasure, a part of Goa.

And then everyone began singing and swaying once again, enjoying themselves hugely, including Dennis.

Had I been less tense and worried, in another time and space, and despite the sweaty bodies around me, I would have been charmed by the atmosphere, too. But right now there was too much on my mind.

Why had Marian (as I continued to think of her) kept all this information from me? And, more dangerously, had she kept it from Amarjit as well? I remembered her telling me about the Oxford degree she intended to take, and about not doing drugs. Obviously she had hidden a lot from us. Why? Simply to give herself a more respectable appearance? Or could she be involved in her sister's disappearance?

Then the thought struck me:

That is, if she has a sister at all!

My face flushed with renewed resentment and mortification, as I suspected I might have been sent on a completely wild-goose chase. Why had my daughter and her friends been made to leave? Why the hell had my holiday been stalled?

Just to trail a lying, dishonest woman, who probably had some very grim secrets to hide? Or who was simply a complete fantasist? I knew that when people were addicted to drugs their sense of the real and unreal got increasingly blurred. And if she took drugs it would also explain her scrawny appearance.

On the stage, the speeches weren't over yet. Now it was Stanley's turn. He slowly got to his feet. I wondered if he would devote a few words to the fact that his younger daughter was missing. Wouldn't this be a good place, with so many people present, to talk about her and how much he had loved her?

Instead, he gave a completely predictable speech.

'This is the place of my rebirth,' he said looking around nostalgically, obviously enjoying the moment. He could say whatever he wanted, because most of his audience wasn't even born when he had first come to Goa. As he rambled on, I listened to every second word, distracted by what I had learnt of Marian's duplicity.

'I was working with money,' he said. 'Making tons of it,

and was totally depressed. Strange, isn't it? Money can't buy you love, it's true. I was looking, just as many of you are today, for the meaning of life. But exactly forty years today I came to Goa and found the sea, the sand, a great life and a few other things. But most importantly I found myself! And today, I'm a lucky man because you – all my friends and my daughter – are all here with me to celebrate the moment.'

He laughed and I could see his nicotine-stained teeth, some of which were missing. And like Marian (or rather 'Astrologer Anne') his bones jutted out. It seemed that the years of drinking, drugs and living on the edge had taken their toll. Yet none of that mattered because Stanley seemed a happy man. Life had not defeated him – as long as he had his peace amulets and his shocking-pink sarong tied way below his emaciated waist.

He pulled Anne/Marian into the circle of his arms. Father and daughter, they looked good together, even though between them they must weigh less than 90 kilos.

It was far from what I had imagined.

Watching them sing and dance, without a single mention of Liza, made me uneasy. I wanted to rush out and talk to Amarjit, but instead I took some pictures to mail back to him, and decided to stay a while longer so I could gather as much information as possible.

Thinking back, I remembered that Marian had

specifically said that she sent photographs of Liza back to her parents to keep them from worrying. But I realized she had only mentioned her mother, who worked in a bank in London. Was it another 'embellished' truth? I felt a tight band of tension spread from my head down to my shoulders.

It was inexplicable that she had been pretending to be isolated and overwrought at having lost her sister, when actually she had a large circle of friends and knew so many people. And so did her father. How long had she hoped to go on fooling me, and of course, Amarjit? Could she have invented this story about the plight of her missing sister just to get sympathy from the police force? Why?

The other thing that bothered me was that she obviously wasn't a tourist at all. I now suspected that she actually spent a large part of her time living in Goa. I didn't know her present address, nor had she given it to me, but I was certain she would have a well-maintained apartment.

She appeared very comfortable in the way she moved around and greeted the people who had come for the celebration. In many ways she was better equipped than I was to find out the truth behind Liza's disappearance. If indeed any disappearance had taken place. In fact she could probably teach me a thing or two about how the system worked in India.

As these thoughts ran through my mind, a tall man,

who looked Goan, climbed onto the platform and put his arms around 'Anne'. They retreated to the far side and she kissed him. He said something to her which obviously changed her mood. Looking sombre, she whispered something to her father, before setting off with the man. Then, over the music, I heard the distant roar of a motor-cycle, and it seemed she had left.

When she did not reappear, I decided it was time to go back to the hotel. This whole case was becoming a giant puzzle. I felt as though there was a conspiracy to fool those who were interested in finding Liza, and I didn't know why. Why would anyone want to create such an elaborate hoax, anyway? What a waste of time.

I got up to leave and then sat down again, realizing that I didn't have the faintest idea how I would get back to the hotel.

Luckily, as I asked for directions, my newly found friend, Dennis, said he was also leaving, and that we could walk together through the 'jungle'. Reassuringly, he mentioned that he even had a hired scooter parked near the beach. It was the normal mode of transport in Goa, and because he looked so dependable, I accepted his offer to drop me off at the hotel.

Exhausted by the events of a tumultuous day, I decided not to worry as he led the way out. He didn't look like he was about to assault me. But then I couldn't claim to be a great judge of character any more.

'You must have heard the story about the stash of drugs that Stanley put away somewhere forty years ago, that everyone has been hunting for ages, haven't you?' he asked me as we chatted on our way back through the dense vegetation.

'Really?' My response was guarded. 'Isn't that just part of the usual hippie mythology?'

'Anne told me how hundreds of people have been looking for it. Whenever Stanley mentions that he might have buried it at a particular house or in a particular location, everyone rushes off there and starts digging. It can be quite funny. There have been quite a few of these false alarms. Supposed to be real Afghan opium, worth a million dollars at today's prices.' Dennis's tone was light-hearted and gossipy.

But for me suddenly the evening had turned grim again.

'She's an astrologer so she should know where it is,' I said nastily.

'It's not exactly like water divining, you know, and Stanley can't remember where he left it. He said he put it in a plastic bag and buried it somewhere. But it was a big consignment and even the cops have got to know about it, I believe.'

'So are they interested?' There was still no sympathy in my voice.

'Everyone's interested. It will be amazing if that stash is ever found!'

'Why?'

Dennis looked serious. 'Well, for one it might take the heat off Stanley and Marian, you know. Right now people are circling them like vultures, because someone started a rumour about it again. The whole beach knows what's going on, but no one will talk.'

'Does this mythology mention his second daughter?'

'Does he have one?' Dennis looked surprised. 'No idea!'

We had now somehow reached the small pathway which led to a makeshift scooter stand. I was starting to realize that, since there were no directions written anywhere, Goa divided people into two categories: those who knew the way, and those who didn't.

I most definitely fell into the second category, and it was pure luck that had brought Dennis into my life. As I told him, delightedly.

He drove me to my hotel, and with surprise I realized that it was already past one in the morning. I gave him my phone number, and hoped he would be in touch.

Back in my hotel room, I collapsed onto the bed, and stared blankly at the ceiling. What was going on?

I wasn't too concerned about the tale of the drug treasure trove because, as I said, I had already heard too many similar stories. But I still didn't know whether Liza's disappearance was real. I knew she existed, because everyone had seen her on the beach. And I had seen her photograph and her videos.

But how was she linked to Marian and Stanley?

I wrote an angry email to Amarjit, accusing him of hiding things from me.

Sending off the email did not reduce my anxiety, however. Now I was even more worried about why Liza had been written out of the script, and why her own father hadn't mentioned her tonight – if indeed he was her father. Getting into bed, I tossed and turned, going over the various possibilities.

Early in the morning my phone buzzed, and I sat up in bed with a jolt.

When I saw the words 'number withheld', I broke into a sweat, unable to bring myself to open the accompanying photograph.

Chapter 9

Perhaps it was the sheer dread about what the message would contain which led to this unreasonable reaction.

After the events I had witnessed last evening, it was obvious that neither her 'sister' nor her 'father' were concerned about Liza. If people had not told me that they had actually met her I would have begun to think she was an imaginary figure. How could her family celebrate when – supposedly – a child was missing, perhaps raped and murdered? Their casual attitude was shocking.

Because they seemed so unconcerned, I wondered if she were already dead, and they knew about it. Or if the father and daughter had other information that they did not care to share with me. So why had Marian (that was still the name I associated with her) made such a fuss about her missing sister? After all, Liza had been seen so rarely around these beaches – especially recently – that even people like Dennis, who was closely following Stanley's story, knew nothing about her. And others, like Curtis, claimed she had forgotten those she had once known well.

I wondered at Marian's relatively early departure from the event yesterday with the man I presumed to be her boyfriend. Why had she left so suddenly, when even I could see that the celebration was going to carry on for a while?

Right now all bets were off.

I couldn't help thinking that the message, which had just arrived on my phone, would almost certainly be about Liza's death. The final blow because, barring some miracle, she wouldn't have been able to survive the last assault.

So it took me almost a whole hour before I screwed up all my courage and with a sense of foreboding, checked it.

The picture which opened up with excruciating slowness made me forget that this was still early in the morning and I was in a hotel room with very thin walls, as I shouted out, 'The bastards!'

In many ways the image was worse than what I had expected. It was far too close to home. In tears I hugged myself for comfort.

It was 4 a.m. by now. When the phone rang, my nerves were so jangled that I sat there shivering and finally had to force myself to pick it up when it would not stop.

'Is everything alright?' It was Maggie, the girl at the front desk. She sounded concerned. 'I was passing by your room and heard you call out . . . Are you okay?'

Hearing me shout in the middle of the night would have whetted her curiosity even more. How could I tell her what I had seen? The photograph had looked so innocent but it had opened up a cornucopia of worries.

'All fine,' I said, trying to sound as nonchalant as possible.

Someone was definitely trying to scare me. Otherwise why would they have sent me a picture of a chain of broken hearts on a bare arm. The pattern that had been painted on Durga just a few days before. And it was I who had photographed it. I began to worry if this was some kind of coded message which meant she was in danger.

After the recent shocking gang rape on a bus no girl could be considered safe in Delhi where she was right now, and this made me fear that something terrible might have happened to her, too. I wondered if someone had got hold of her?

Again I felt under personal attack, as the psychological pressure built up on me. After the stress of those earlier videos now I had to deal with this innocuous-looking image that had far too many implications for me. How much did whoever was sending these files know about Durga? Or me?

Perhaps much more than I had realized?

After all, they had hacked my phone and probably stolen my numbers and checked every message. And so they were aware that sending me this image could push me to breaking point. I sensed a palpable threat in that silent photograph.

Curtis D'Silva had been the prime suspect for some time, but now I realized that there could be many others, people like Marian and even Veeramma who knew about the tattoo, who could be involved. Not everyone, though, had the same agenda. It was puzzling.

In fact I had only seen Curtis twice since I started working on this case. But perhaps the reverse wasn't true and I was under some kind of full-time surveillance, either from him or from the 'others'. I wasn't sure if, with this latest image, the unknown sender had wanted to scare me off or keep me here. But had he (or she) really known me and wanted me to leave, this was the last thing to have tried. It only made my resolve to find the culprits stronger.

Yet, though I was reluctant to quit, and fairly certain Durga was alright in Delhi, I wondered if my investigation would create a problem for her. I paced up and down the room, drinking whisky and chain smoking till 6 a.m.

Then, at last, I finally called home, as I knew my mother, who was an early riser, would be awake. I would not be able to speak to Durga at this hour, though, since it was the Christmas holidays and she would sleep late.

Once I had reassured myself that she was fine, I asked my mother to keep an eye on Durga. I told her I had called her early in the morning only because I hadn't slept very well last night, but there was nothing really to worry about. The case was going well and I was sure I would soon reach a conclusion. But I didn't tell her anything more than that, and I had also requested Amarjit to be equally discreet, in case he spoke to her.

All I had told her was that I was looking for a missing British girl. And I was fairly optimistic of finding her soon.

There were some advantages to being a (sometimes cantankerous) spinster in your mid forties. Even your mother didn't dare cross-examine you too much.

I sent yet another message to Amarjit with photographs of last night's event, and asked him to call me as I needed to speak to him urgently.

His call came through at 9 a.m. and I told him all my suspicions about Marian and how I was now convinced that Liza was just a very small pawn in a larger, more dangerous game, though I wasn't sure what it could be. Perhaps drug running? Did that account for the recent interest in the story of Stanley's fabulous drug stash? My other hunch was that Liza could be on that casino ship, because of the connection with Curtis. I asked Amarjit to check up on the owner.

He was quiet for a moment and then said he would inquire. But his earlier marked silence made me uneasy. Was this another area where I was not supposed to ask any questions?

And then I told him my real anxiety, after last night. That we were wasting our time, and Liza might actually be beyond our help. From the attitudes of Marian and her father, either Liza was very, very safe or very, very dead. Further, it seemed we would learn little from Marian whose behaviour raised more suspicions than it allayed. I told him bluntly that she was unreliable and so he was my only hope of more information. He should tell me anything he might have kept to himself thus far, not wanting to prejudice me in my investigation. I was still trying to be polite.

I also told him about the latest photograph of the tattoo, expecting him to offer some kind of protection for Durga. After all, I was doing him a favour by staying on here and following this case.

To my surprise, instead of being supportive and appreciative of the progress I had made, and impressed at my uncovering of Marian's double identity, Amarjit abruptly said he would call me back. He needed to find out about something. He definitely seemed a bit off-colour.

When he rang back, fifteen minutes later, he sounded even more subdued. He said my concern was proven correct and that he had been mistaken to be so worried about Liza. According to fresh information he had just received, she was probably alright. The government was no longer concerned about bad publicity, as it was thought Liza would turn up on her own. It was very likely, he said, that Marian had concocted a story to deflect attention from her own family history of drug abuse. After what I had told him, he would ask the Goa police to run a check on her credentials.

Liza, he told me, in all likelihood had simply run away, and would soon be back. The videos were probably staged and had no relevance to the case. It was just the resemblance to Liza of the girl in the videos which had sent everyone into a panic. There was no reason to believe it was her.

It was a long explanation and while Amarjit kept all emotion out of his voice, I could sense that he, too, had been severely embarrassed by my findings.

It appeared, he said, the urgency was over and that there was no need to pursue her any more. It was a false alarm. He had been wrong to involve me and he would feel happier if I were to return to Delhi. The sooner the better. He apologized profusely for any inconvenience, and promised to make it up to me.

What struck me, though, was that apart from being a lengthy speech, it sounded like he had written it all out. Listening to him, I became increasingly bewildered at the complete contrast between what he was saying today and what he had told me previously. This was not going to be a full-scale war or even a skirmish. The troops were being withdrawn before the enemy had been sighted or a single shot was fired.

In his voice I heard all the resignation that I myself had experienced and then rejected. The more he tried to persuade me to come back, the more I knew I had to stay where I was.

Except that now I wouldn't even have him on my side.

Yet I did not really care, because I did not believe a word he had just told me. Something was amiss.

To fob him off, I told him that I would probably return in a day or two. I wanted to relax on the beach after the frightening events of the past few days.

'I'll spread the word I'm no longer interested in Liza,' I said nonchalantly. 'I'm sure everyone will leave me alone.'

My plan, of course, was completely different. I was going to find out which bastard had sent me this last picture. Now all my protective instincts as a mother had been aroused. Towards both Durga and Liza. But I still had a couple of questions for Amarjit.

'You're right. It's obvious that these people know more about me and my family than I would like. I really should withdraw from this case, but I'm curious about two things. Liza may have vanished recently, but she was here last year as well. And just for my information, didn't Marian name even a single suspect when she spoke to you about her disappearance?'

Amarjit sighed. 'I knew you wouldn't give up so easily, and I feel guilty because I'm the one who got you into this. I thought you might find some more information about her, but frankly I had no idea about Marian's double life. I was asked to move on her complaint and I got in touch with you.' He sounded defensive. 'Yes, as far as I know, Liza did arrive sometime late last year.' He paused and then asked someone for a file. 'Let me check. I didn't tell you all this because I thought you would hear it from Marian. She gave very little information to us anyway, and there were large gaps in her version of what happened when her sister vanished. Because I couldn't involve the police in Goa I left it to you to find out the rest. You've always managed to do that.'

Yes, I wanted to say, I normally do manage that. But it is a different matter when one is dealing with a woman who is apparently hysterical about her missing sister but shows no outward sign of grief, nor of trying to help anyone find her.

There was some rustling of paper as Amarjit turned the pages. Then he said, 'Right, here it is. Marian had told us that Liza had gone back to London a few times. She returned more than a year back, and there was an incident at the time, involving some sort of molestation. In fact, Marian complained about it, a case was registered with the police and an arrest was made. But Liza disappeared a few months *after* that. These videos actually appeared very mysteriously *after* a year, just a few weeks back. And then the girl was sighted, once again, very recently, according to her sister. But no one else has any information about her return. So we began to wonder where she was and what had happened to her. Had she been raped? Was she still alive? Or had she been killed and these sightings were just a case of mistaken identity? As I told you, there was a fear that the sister would go to the media, and besides, we didn't know who else had seen that first video. That's when we started thinking about getting someone like you to look into it. You happened to be in Goa and so it was perfect timing.'

I said nothing, maintaining a stony silence. Obviously I had been useful at that time and I no longer was. And so it was best that I left. Quietly. It no longer suited the government to follow Liza's trail. Could Amarjit have been told to stay away by someone? Was my presence here causing them more problems?

I had a strong feeling that he was still not telling me everything.

There was some more rustling of paper as Amarjit went through the file once more.

'And here is some more information about that first molestation case. About a year ago there was a boy who knew Liza quite well, who was later suspected of raping her. But, honestly, Simran, take my advice. People here seem to have lost interest in the case, so there's very little point in your staying on.'

'And what happened to the boy, the suspect?' I ignored his last few sentences. He might be willing to believe that the videos were part of some pornographic film but then they would have been of better quality, wouldn't they? With bright lights, steady tripods and with much of the anatomy revealed. These films looked real because they were so gritty and raw, and the audio and video quality of the second video was hardly professional even though it was clearer than the first.

Amarjit paused, as though going through the file, and then replied, 'He was an odd-job boy who used to hang around Fernando's shack. He was supposed to be terribly fond of Liza and couldn't let go of her. Followed her around all the time, and Liza had complained about it, that's how Marian got to know. She thought he had misbehaved with Liza in revenge, and there was a bit of a bust-up about it last year and the police were called in.'

'What was his name?'

'Vishnu Braganza. Twenty-three years old.'

It no longer surprised me that Marian hadn't even mentioned this incident, or the possibility that Braganza could be involved in the present case too, to me. It was the same reason why she had requested the current investigation and then, as I discovered to my regret, not shown much interest when she probably realized it might make her life on the beach far too uncomfortable. To enjoy the golden Goan sands, you had to maintain the equilibrium. Pretend not to notice if anything bad happened.

Unless she was blackmailing someone, after all. Instances of women falsely implying rape, though rare, were not unheard of. The modus operandi might have been to insist on an investigation, and then withdrawing when the right amount of cash, or whatever it was she was looking for, was offered. Could that be the reason behind Amarjit's odd reaction? Was that why, as I suspected, someone important had decided the case was closed?

So Marian had seemingly 'helped' me with a pro forma investigation. It would suit her only too well if I left the matter now and returned to Delhi. If anything had happened to Liza we would find out in due course anyway. The frequent 'sightings' she had referred to, if true, were common in cases of runaways and missing children and over the years would soon be forgotten.

But it was also possible, as Amarjit claimed, that Liza could soon be found, or would return, and that she was playing a game with all of us. Perhaps she had run away because she wanted to put a distance between herself and her sister's odd lifestyle? Remembering the hippie gathering under the tree, I wouldn't blame her. It was alright as a Unique Experience, but it might have got a bit tiresome on a daily basis. From the little Marian had told me (assuming she could be trusted), Liza struck me as a headstrong but ambitious girl, hardly the sort who would want to spend her nights under a banyan tree with a bunch of fading flower children.

So if both Marian and Liza had been deceitful, why had the last photograph, of Durga's tattoo, been sent to me? Was it just to jolt me into leaving? Or to steel my nerves? Or to remind me that I too was the mother of a young, vulnerable girl?

Multiple questions pressed upon me and I was

disappointed that Amarjit had succumbed to pressure and decided to close the investigation.

Whoever had sent me that last image might have wanted to discourage me from becoming complacent, to remind me that he or she was still around, and that I should be careful. But it had had the opposite effect. I had decided to head for Fernando's and dig out some more facts.

Even though it was a short ride, I caught a taxi to Anjuna and walked only the last bit over the cool pale sand (since it was still early in the morning) to Fernando's. It turned out to be a nicely structured rectangular shack with a slightly more upmarket ambience and clientele than the others.

It was laid out on two floors. On the ground floor were the normal plastic chairs and wooden tables, while on the first floor were more upmarket silk-covered couches and divans, a deliberate private setting. From here, through the large windows, the sea, a deep blue today, was clearly visible. I was told that, at this time of the year, most Indians had to pay an entry fee. Foreigners were welcomed free of charge, as the shrewd owners wanted to attract those who spent in dollars (or at least at a dollar rate) rather than rupees. What the foreigners did not realize was that they would be also charged higher-than-normal prices for food and drinks, more than making up for the entrance fee they had forgone.

But possibly because I was a woman alone (despite the

colour of my skin) I was given special treatment today. I had been allowed up to the first floor. Free of charge.

I looked around, imagining the scene that night when Marian and Liza had come to meet the travel agency owner. As well as someone who could have been 'a minister'. Who could it have been? I wished Marian had taken a little more interest in her sister's life, and wondered if the detachment could be due to the eight-year gap between them.

Slowly, as it was barely 9 a.m., a few more people straggled upstairs, mostly because they could smoke here in privacy. I noticed that there were lots of hookahs or sheeshas, as they were also known, scattered about, promising different flavours of smoke.

At night the scene would be quite different: dim lights, trance music playing, people smoking, eating, drinking and glancing out of the windows at the dark sea. For young people to be unfettered, with this amount of freedom, was probably impossible anywhere else in India.

But so much could go wrong as well. I remembered the terrifying video of Liza walking on the beach, and then the attack on her by the two men.

The other girl who had died here, Scarlett Keeling, had also spent a lot of time around Anjuna. If I looked out of the window, I could probably see the spot where her body had been discovered.

Looking around, I wondered if any of the boys working

inside the shack had been a witness to anything that had happened on that night, when Liza had come with Marian.

Probably nothing they would admit to.

As Marian had already pointed out, the shack owners and the locals they hired – the *panchayat* heads, the police, the politicians, and even the media – were all closely associated with each other. Through their youth and schooling, and through marriage, these villagers had known each other for far too long to betray each other over the rape or death of an 'outsider'. And the other reason was that these shacks had mostly migrants working in them. Their jobs were at stake if they were to confess to what they had seen or heard. They would never be able to return the next season, as they would be blacklisted. The same applied for the beach vendors – they too had to follow the rules laid down by the close-knit community of local leaders.

The waiter who served me was in his early twenties, dressed in shorts and a t-shirt – exactly the sort of person these shack owners hired. Usually the workers came very cheaply, for less than 20,000 rupees for five months, plus free food and drink. And, as I had found out earlier, even drugs could be supplied as part of their pay. Though, according to the newspapers today, the beaches had finally become drug-free zones.

This particular boy was probably from one of the northeastern states, like many of the others. Thanks to the lack of jobs in that part of the country, a sizeable number of migrants had come to work in Goa, as restaurant helpers, cooks, guards and so on. The booming tourist trade had provided fairly regular employment and, being young, they no doubt enjoyed the cosmopolitan character and the informality of the beach.

'Hey – do you know someone called Vishnu here?' I asked as pleasantly as I could. I wanted to encourage him to speak.

'No, madam. I come recently. I know no one.' He looked at me, startled, as though I was asking him something which would get him into trouble. I had a feeling he had been instructed not to speak too much.

I couldn't mention either Marian or Liza as that might alert others. But after my last experience I had a ready-made reason to meet Vishnu. I now knew what would work.

'Don't worry. Vishnu is a friend. I'm looking for him because I have to give him some money. Someone sent it for him.' Among the many lessons I had learnt, especially after my interaction with Veeramma, was that on the beach the only way to get even the slightest bit of information, or anything done, was to pay cash. Otherwise no one knew anyone or anything. Or remembered anything. It was too much hard work to do anything for free.

'I just find out, madam.' He scurried away, looking a little more thoughtful than he had earlier.

After a while another man strolled up. From his more leisurely gait, well-massaged, shiny body, oily hair and the jogging trousers I assumed he was slightly higher in the hierarchy. He even pulled out the earpiece connected to his mobile phone in order to hear me.

I was honoured!

'You looking for someone?' He came straight to the point. But at least he was smiling a little.

'Someone called Vishnu. He used to be here a lot.'

'What for?'

'I have a message for him and some money.'

'He left. The police came and took him. I think he go to jail.'

'Why?'

'He trouble some girl.'

'Is he still in jail?'

'I don't think so. That long back.'

'Do you have an address for him?'

He hesitated.

I took out a 500-rupee note and handed it to him.

'Thanks. He also friend of mine.'

Giving a big grin, he put the money away quickly and then looking over his shoulder to ensure no one was looking, scribbled on a piece of paper and handed it to me. I looked at the address, which was of a shop, 'Rummy Electronix', at Anjuna village itself.

'But, madam, be careful. He sometimes get very angry.'

I briefly wondered if I should ask this man about the incident with Liza, then thought better of it. Nor did I want to meet Fernando. I didn't want anyone to know why I was actually here or else I might not even get a chance to meet Vishnu.

On my way to the village, I kept a lookout for both Marian and Veeramma, wondering if I could try to get some more information from either of them. But to my pleasant surprise I bumped into Dennis, my 'Sir Galahad and Sir Lancelot rolled into one', as I told him.

'You've added meaning to my dull life,' I said, gently flirting with him. It seemed a long time since I had done that.

He obviously decided to humour me, and that felt nice, too.

'It's always great to help out lovely damsels in distress,' he said, sounding old fashioned and gallant, living up to the reputation of the legendary figures I had compared him to.

Hopefully I wasn't looking so distressed this morning, after all, in my white-and-red dress. For the past few days I had been too involved in other things to pay any attention to my appearance, but now I was pleased I had (quite accidentally) chosen flattering clothes.

'Do you want to meet later, for a drink in the evening?' he asked.

That seemed like a good idea, in more ways than one. I had planned to go to the floating casino, the *Tempest*, this evening, as I had promised Vicky. Apart from the fact that I liked his affable manner, it would be better if I had an escort with me. I didn't quite know what I would find in the casino, and it would be good to be accompanied by someone whom I could rely on.

To my quite visible delight, he barely hesitated, his genial features spreading into a smile.

'Why not? It should be very enjoyable, and perhaps give me material for my next script!'

If only I could tell him the story behind my casino visit, he would have more material than he could handle for several TV serials. But as yet I wasn't confident enough about sharing my information with anyone. Not even with men I found interesting and attractive.

We fixed to meet at around 8.30 at Panjim, where the ferry motorboats picked up customers. Dennis said he would be at the beach for the rest of the day, so I left him and trudged into the village, where I hoped to find Vishnu. After a little meandering through various paths which led through crowded streets, I found the 'electronix' shop.

It seemed deserted but for an elderly woman who was half-heartedly dusting the shelves, on which were piled all kinds of electronic gadgets, wires, lights and plugs. I noticed that there was a whole section of both basic and expensive mobile phones and their parts, as well as an array of SIM cards. A few desktop computers and keyboards had been dismembered and lay clustered at one end of the narrow room.

I watched, amused: she was shaking the duster in the direction of the goods, while her attention was fixed on the tiny television screen jammed between cardboard boxes full of plugs and extension boards. An evangelist was on screen urging sinners to repent.

I waited till he had completed one round of exhortations and then quickly said, 'Hi – I'm looking for Vishnu?'

Her attention barely shifted. 'Gone out,' she said.

'Shall I wait for him? How long gone? I mean,' I corrected myself, still resisting the urge to speak in incomplete sentences, though it was very infectious and somewhat good fun, 'when is he likely to return?'

'Soon back,' she said, giving me a quick grin, showing off a surprising set of sturdy, white teeth that belied her age. 'Sit, sit.'

I had barely sat down on a plastic stool near the counter, when a large young man appeared in the shop. The left side of his face was covered with scars, as though he had been recently injured. The skin was red and an eyebrow was missing. One arm hung loose at a strange angle. It would be difficult to forget him. And I hadn't.

He had 'repaired' the Internet in my room on the day that Durga left. The receptionist, Maggie, had been in my room with him, I now remembered. I think she had mentioned that he was an expert with the Internet. As well as with computers and mobile phones, I could see.

I couldn't be sure, but I thought she had said his name was Vishnu. Small world, getting smaller all the time.

I hadn't made the connection and had frankly forgotten about him till this moment. But at least this coincidence gave me a pretext for starting a conversation with him. Perhaps things were finally moving in the right direction.

The woman smiled again. 'She waiting for you, Vishnu.'

'Yes?' He looked at me and there was (or so I thought) a flicker of recognition in his eyes.

'Didn't you come to Hotel Delite? To my room with Maggie? You repaired the Internet?'

'That's right.' He looked a little concerned. 'Internet gone down again? I come? You should tell Maggie, no? Why you come all the way?'

Even though the manager at Fernando's had warned me that Vishnu could be problematic, he spoke in a very gentle fashion, belying those accusations of molestation and a quick temper.

In fact he appeared quite amiable, his soft mouth twisted in a semblance of a smile. He didn't seem like a street fighter, unless something had provoked him beyond tolerance. So what had gone wrong?

'Not Internet today, Vishnu. I needed to talk about a common friend – Liza.'

On hearing the name he became wary and started backing away from me.

'Too much work today. Talk tomorrow.'

Perhaps his stint in jail had frightened him, and he was worried about any mention of Liza. She was the girl who had put him behind bars, after all. Had there been any truth in the molestation charge?

I looked around and found to my relief that the woman in the shop was now unabashedly watching TV, and didn't seem to be listening to us.

I took out my mobile phone and scanned down to Liza's photograph, the one that Amarjit had re-sent to me.

I could sense that Vishnu was becoming increasingly tense. His breath was whistling through his teeth and I knew he wanted to leave. Beads of sweat broke out on his forehead.

He wasn't just stressed, he was scared.

'Madam I got work. I late.'

He picked up a bag of equipment and started to leave the shop without even looking at my proffered phone or the photograph. Exactly as Veeramma had done at first. Things hadn't changed here on the beach, despite what Amarjit may have said. No one still wanted to talk about Liza. Which could only mean that the message had still not gone out that she was safe.

I reached out to stop him but he shook my hand off.

'I go now.' Ignoring Liza's smiling photograph on my

phone, half running, half limping out of the shop, he got onto his ramshackle scooter and quickly left.

'Poor fellow. After the police arrested him, something gone wrong with his brain. He very scared of his own shadow. Cries at night like baby. They beat him badly.'

It was the woman in the shop. Obviously she had been listening to our exchange, after all, and not to the evangelist on the screen.

'What was he arrested for?'

'That Liza you talk about. Some man molest her, you know. And then this foolish boy stop him. The police come at night and take Vishnu away. They say *he* wanted to rape her. They say Liza sister say like that. Nonsense. This boy impotent, you know. Very weak. Born like that. Thrown in jail for full one year. No case against him, only beatings. Just come back. Now he too scared to speak even. Only work all the time. Police still catch him now and then. Any trouble they come for him. *You did, you did* – like that, they say. Poor boy.'

'You are his—'

'His auntie Elizabeth. His parents died long back. His father Christian and mother Hindu. I his father's sister.'

'And Liza, did you meet her?'

'She came to thank him that first time he looked up. Because he help save her from that fellow who try to rape her. But Vishnu already in jail. No one listen to her. Brought him flowers, gave this book. Say sorry, sorry. But no point. Now he come from jail, but she gone.'

Reaching under the counter she took out a book; it was a collection of well-known quotations. It didn't look like it had ever been opened. Somehow I doubted if Vishnu – despite his undoubted Internet skills – was interested in reading.

On the first page, scrawled in a large, uneven childlike handwriting, was the inscription: '*For My Superhero Vishnu, Be Who You Want To Be, Many Thanks, Liza xx PS sorry for the trouble. See you when you come back*.' She had drawn a curly-headed smiling face under her name. It sounded like she was wishing him well for a holiday with little idea of what would happen to him within the confines of a jail. She did not know that by protecting her, Vishnu had annoyed someone who would never forgive him.

It gave me an odd pang to see Liza's name like that, at the bottom of the page. It made her more real, somehow. Up to this point I had been uncertain of her existence outside the videos that I had almost believed to be faked, especially after Amarjit had said they may have been staged. Her signature and the innocent, idealistic message made it even more imperative that I try to find her. She sounded just like any other young girl.

Like Durga.

'His face . . . is it because of the police beating?' I asked Elizabeth.

The woman looked away. 'Who knows who did? Police

also have big boss, you know. Only Jesus Christ knows who did it and why.'

Perhaps if I persisted Elizabeth would tell me a little more.

'What happened to Liza?'

'Madam, we live here fifty years. Girls come and go. She wasn't first and she won't be last. White white legs, golden golden hair. English passport. French passport. German passport. Jew passport. Tcha! I seen same story from hippie days. My husband had shack down there. Now we old, so out, out. Young people's business, they say. Foreigner business, they say. They buy land, property. But need money for land, for drugging. Spoil our boys, our family.'

She didn't sound bitter at all, as she became more and more animated telling the story of how the beaches of Goa had changed. If you saw life through her eyes, the fault lay with some of the foreigners who came here, not, as others said, the beach boys who had learnt to exploit them.

'These white girls carry drugs, smile at customs, spread legs for police. Carry drugs everywhere – you know, push in there, push in there.' She simulated putting something between her legs and up her backside. I watched, fascinated, as this very traditional, God-fearing woman now gave me a quick lesson in drug smuggling.

'And they get big big money. Also shack-fellows get

money, because they get drugs at night, from sea. Minister get money, police get money. One night even some minister from Delhi come for Vishnu in car with red light. He own shack on beach. Fernando's. He come with siren blaring. He ask Vishnu about that girl. But he don't know nothing. Still they beat him.'

I nodded. This might not be evidence I could produce in court, but it corroborated what I suspected. Liza had been molested by someone – possibly Curtis – who then chose to make Vishnu the scapegoat. Perhaps Liza had consumed too many drugs that night to remember who had assaulted her. So Vishnu took the rap. But why would a minister come down specially to check what Vishnu knew? Because he was worried that Vishnu had seen something at Fernando's? Even a cursory look at Vishnu would tell anyone that the man was barely capable of violence. But it was still not clear to me how these events were linked to Liza's final disappearance.

The story was not as simple as Amarjit would like me to believe. Clearly the minister must have been the reason why Amarjit had pushed me into this case. And it could also be the reason why he got orders to stop me from going further. If I could discover the trigger for both his original request and his subsequent command that I halt my investigation, I would be able to solve this puzzle.

What surprised me, listening to Elizabeth's frank and

lucid description, was how openly this supposedly illicit smuggling was conducted. Obviously the people involved were confident that nothing of this would ever be reported to the police. Or that, even if it were, no one would ever take any action, because the police were possibly involved in it as well.

'Do you remember the minister? Who he was?'

'No, madam. I only remember he had big moustache.' She twirled both hands around her lips graphically and laughed, and from her dismissive tone I gathered that she wasn't going to say anything more. She had turned away, and to make her point even clearer she made the TV a little louder and the evangelist began denouncing the weak ways of the flesh once more.

From her perspective it was really a straightforward story. Though parts of the narrative were shocking to me, it had become a way of life for her. A perfect example of Hobson's choice: you either got involved or you stayed away from the beach entirely. But either way you ran a risk of being attacked by the sharks in the water, and mauled by the wolves on land. Just as Vishnu had been.

That was life. Nothing had changed in the last fifty years.

Auntie Elizabeth continued to flick the duster in the air over the shelves as though she were conducting an unseen orchestra. I thanked her and left the shop, after taking

Vishnu's phone number. In case, I told her, the Internet needed repairing.

Thinking over what I had just heard, and feeling desperately sorry for Vishnu, I decided to take a slow walk back to the hotel.

Having spent a large part of the morning being puzzled over Marian, I now knew enough to ask her frankly why she had concluded – or had allowed Amarjit to decide for her – that there was no point hunting for her sister any more?

Because, in either case, where was Liza?

I also wanted to know why Marian had framed Vishnu over something he obviously hadn't done. One year! It was a long time to be locked up for someone else's crime. And, of course, why she had hidden the truth about her father from me. The questions went on and on.

To my surprise (it must have been my lucky day), when I rang her, she answered almost instantly and even agreed to join me for lunch back at my hotel.

It was a strange coincidence that on the day I had been asked to give up my hunt for Liza I was finally making some degree of progress on the case.

It was important to be honest, and so as soon as Marian and I sat down for lunch, I let her know that I had attended Stanley's anniversary party the night before. And I told her I had seen her there, too, playing the perfect daughter.

I tried to keep the irritation out of my voice as much as possible. But today I needed her to stop telling lies, allow some of my anger to simmer through.

She looked at me and then looked away. I could see that this wasn't easy for her to hear.

'Marian, you and I both know that there are two sides to life on this beach. One side is very visible and very loud. This is the world where you can be a simple tourist, have fun, indulge in water sports, eat, drink and go home. The other side is where you and I seem be trapped. I could have had a lovely holiday here with my daughter, without a care in the world. But because of you, that night, I was forced to abandon my holiday, send my daughter away, and got sucked into this case. And I still don't know why you haven't been honest – either with me or with Amarjit.

'It may involve just a few people, but I know there is something very dangerous going on. I don't quite know how Liza got caught up in it and why you decided to pretend you were just two simple girls who were misled one evening.'

I enjoyed watching her flush with discomfort, as she lit a cigarette with shaking hands.

'I now know that you've been here for a while,' I continued, 'and that things are not quite so straightforward as you told me and Amarjit. So when, exactly, were you planning to tell me the truth? After those guys who messed with your sister had done the same with me? After they had given me those drugs so that I almost killed myself? What's going on here? Whose side are you on? And why didn't you tell me about being an astrologer? It makes no sense. You've hidden a lot of facts from us. I seriously don't even know if Liza is really your sister. I don't know what to believe.'

It was a long list of accusations, and I could not help the harsh tone of recrimination in my voice.

Marian looked at me, white faced, as tears rolled down her cheeks. I ignored her distress and ordered some wine – I needed to calm down and keep the anger out of my voice.

'Yes, yes, she is my sister,' she said finally in a choked voice. I hoped desperately that this time her anguish was genuine and that she was telling me the truth at last. 'And I am sorry I couldn't share everything with you when we met. I know you probably thought I didn't care about Liza but I was caught in . . . in a trap. I had to get justice for Liza and I had to survive. Sometimes it seemed only one of the two was possible. Not both.'

She smoked nervously for a few moments before she spoke again.

'I was wondering when you'd find out. About my dad and me. Quite honestly I wanted to tell you on the first day, but I thought you might get the wrong impression. Most people, especially Indians, have a definite view about hippies and I was scared that you would have concluded that Liza was also some kind of tramp, and not helped to find her.'

I bit my tongue. She was right. The lifestyle choices of others could prejudice us towards judging them, often erroneously. What she didn't know was that usually I was on the receiving end of those judgements, and was unlikely to criticize anyone else for unconventional behaviour.

'So what exactly is going on?'

'Well, you've already seen Stanley, my father, who is very easy-going. But Liza and I grew up with my mother in London, and she's very different from my dad. They had come to Goa together in the late seventies and stayed on for a long time, running through the money my father had made. Finally Mum got fed up of the lifestyle. She had a job in finance before she came here, and she went back to London to work for the same bank she'd left. Both Liza and I were born in London, and my dad came for short visits, but he never liked it there. He had got too used to this carefree life. So he left us and came back to Goa. Liza and I arrived here for the first time around two years ago to meet the father we hadn't seen for nearly fifteen years.

'I discovered I'm a lot like my father. I could empathize with his need to stay here, though I wanted to stay for different reasons. I have an eastern sensibility, and I'm into yoga and astrology. I love the whole spirituality bit.

But Liza wanted something else. She was more physical, so she got caught in a different crowd, because she wanted to make money and have an adventurous life. I guess she was attracted by the beach glamour. The fun, the aimless drifting from one party to another.'

She paused as though recollecting her life before and after.

'Yesterday, while I was at Stanley's celebration, my boyfriend got a message from his brother, who is in the police, that I shouldn't worry about Liza. That's why I left the party. So I wanted to tell you: it's okay if you want to stop looking. We don't know where she is, but the police seem to think that she will show up. In fact they even gave my passport back to me finally, so I can go home at last.'

I noted how her conversation still kept slipping in and out of the present and past tense, when speaking about Liza.

I decided not to tell her that Amarjit had more or less told me the same thing, that there was no need to bother about Liza any more, and I should leave. But her last comment surprised me. Was it she who had made the deal with the police? Her passport in return for calling off the search for Liza? It sounded like a very strange bargain. And, as far as I remembered, this was the first time I heard about her missing passport.

'Why did they take your passport away? Surely they didn't suspect that you had been involved in your sister's disappearance?'

She looked embarrassed and said, 'It's a long story and I wish I could tell you everything. But it's my story and isn't related to what happened to Liza. Seriously, I know my behaviour has been odd and erratic, but there is little connection between the two. Simran, please, please believe me, there is no point investigating this any more. There are many reasons. One compelling factor is that there are some rather awful people involved. You saw how they drugged you the other day, they are capable of anything. *You must leave at once.'*

Marian looked around, just as Amarjit had when he had met me here. She seemed as nervous as he had been. I wondered if she realized that she had contradicted herself. On the one hand, she had told me Liza was fine. On the other hand, she just said that I could still be in danger. Surely that meant that Liza was not safe either?

Over her shoulder I got a glimpse once again of those two almost identical men, whom I had begun to think of as Tweedledum and Tweedledee, standing behind the glass door.

These were the two men who been arguing with the manager at that very spot on the day Durga and her friends decided to leave. It was strange that they always seemed to be here when I was meeting with anyone related to the case.

Were they here once again to keep an eye on me? Or Marian?

I didn't want to mention their presence to her till I had got a bit more information, so I pretended to acquiesce.

'Fine. I'll leave. But only on the condition that you answer my questions. To begin with, what made you decide to stay on here for almost two years, and did Liza go back to London in between?'

Fortunately Marian had her back to the door and did not notice the two men – unless, of course, she had come with them; I pushed away the thought so that I could concentrate on her.

'Well, initially Liza did go back to London a couple of times. Then someone floated a story about my dad's mysterious stash of opium or cocaine or whatever. Every now and then there will be rumours about it and it comes back to haunt him, and us. I don't know if it was ever true, because he says he has checked every place he can think of and he can't even remember if he ever had it. But now everyone believes it. And they think he knows exactly where the stash is. The cops harass him, the junkies harass him, and he survives by playing his guitar and pretending to be the last of the great white hippies. It's all about peace and love. But actually it's all fucking ridiculous.'

Now the mask had completely slipped. Finally in front of me was a desperate woman, worried about her father, uncertain about her sister.

'So why didn't you leave and just force him to come

with you? I mean, obviously he's living in some fantasy world.'

'I couldn't. As I just told you, they'd taken my passport away. Look, I can tell you how wonderful Goa can be when things are going well, and how one bad experience can make everything turn to ashes. But I don't think you'll believe me.'

I sipped my wine slowly and counted to ten. I kept my voice as soft as I could. If she was going to take me on another long ride it would be very difficult. But if she had something genuine to tell me I was certainly interested.

'I've wasted a lot of time over all this,' I said, keeping my voice even, with enormous effort. 'I need to know why your passport was taken away. And you keep saying that "they" took it. Who *are* these people who seem to be persecuting you?'

'Your beach friend is involved in this. Are you sure you want to know?'

My beach friend? For a bizarre moment I thought she meant Dennis.

'Which beach friend?'

'Veeramma. I wanted to warn you about it the other day. But I kept quiet because you were so sure you'd get some information from her. She can be very dangerous.'

So the dislike was mutual, though Marian had been better at hiding it.

'What happened?'

'She planted drugs on me.' Her thin face seemed to become even more gaunt.

I nodded patiently, though still slightly unbelieving. Wasn't it Marian's scheming that had led to my being surreptitiously slipped drugs at Cozee Home?

It had been Veeramma who rescued me. I tried not to be judgemental as I listened to her.

'Have you ever wondered why someone has taken the trouble to teach that group such perfect English, German, French? It's a lot of effort, you know. They only do it because it is profitable. Haven't you realized that yet? Only a few of the beach vendors are involved – but definitely Veeramma and her gang are part of it.'

I admitted I hadn't thought about it. I had imagined that these girls had picked up the languages, despite all their disadvantages, simply by interacting with foreigners on the beach. Slowly I began to understand her meaning.

'I was very impressed, too. These lovely traditional-looking women, so fluent in so many languages. Well, it's very useful for them, because they chat up the tourists and find out who is worth how much. The richer ones are then sold the more expensive drugs. And some of the poorer ones, like me, are caught in a web, from where it's difficult for them to ever get out.'

I was shocked at her words. Marian, the calm, cool, detached woman, who was barely ruffled by her sister's disappearance, had her own very troubled history.

'So what happened?'

'It was sometime last year, just before Liza vanished. I used to see Veeramma around and she was very friendly. Then she offered me some hashish, very cheaply. I refused. Honestly, I don't do drugs. Only once in a while, very, very rarely, I might smoke a joint with Dad. Or take a drag from someone, like I did last night. Also, at the time this happened, I was quite happy getting to know my father, learning yoga and practising astrology. I seemed to have an instinct for all of this and I never needed an artificial high. I enjoyed myself anyway.

'But for some reason Veeramma had targeted me. She just wouldn't let go. And her bosses at the time had told her to look out for potential victims who looked young, who were mostly alone, were vulnerable and not very rich. They usually tell these women the profile of the person they are looking for. And they also wanted a woman with a foreign passport, because they are easier to manipulate. Veeramma kept hitting on me every day, telling me how beautiful I was and bargaining with me till the price of that marijuana was brought down to a few hundred rupees. It was so ridiculously cheap that I bought it, thinking that I could give it to my dad, or the groupies who hang around him.

'So I took it back to my room. Liza and I were staying at Cozee Home at the time. I didn't have my own place. And as I said, this was just the day before Liza disappeared. I hadn't realized that it was a trap. Three anti-narcotic guys came in the middle of the night a few days later and raided my room. They arrested me for that small packet of marijuana that had been practically pushed on me. So I had to be "nice" to them.'

She paused. Tears poured down her cheeks again.

'I was desperate not to go to jail. Can you imagine what the story would have been like? Father a former hippie, sister who had vanished, and now I was caught with drugs. I had just got admission into Oxford, I didn't want to screw that up. So I did whatever they asked me to do.

'I had sex with all of them. Gave them whatever pounds I had. They still impounded my passport before letting me go. But they agreed they wouldn't make it into a police case.'

'So did you tell these anti-narcotic guys about Veeramma?'

She looked at me pityingly.

'You are obviously even more innocent than I was. Don't you get it? She gets a cut from them, whatever money they make. The cops, the beach boys, the women, they are all aware.'

I was now completely shocked. The prism shifted once more as I realized that it could have been Veeramma after all who had tipped off Curtis at Cozee Home to slip the drugs onto me. In all likelihood she had seen me walk towards the guest house with Marian.

'But I didn't give up. As soon as I got involved with my present boyfriend – his brother is in the police – I complained to him about Veeramma, a regular police complaint that she was a drug peddler. She was banned from the beach for a while, but now she's back. And I am sure she would like to destroy me in any way she can.'

Even though I hated to believe any of this, it seemed too far-fetched for her to make up. But I also wanted Marian to understand that Veeramma was as much a victim as she herself had been. She had to succumb to the demands of the drug mafia and the police if her group was to continue working on the beach. In some ways, being poorer than Marian made her more of a pawn.

Now I could also understand Veeramma's reluctance to give me any information about Liza. And why she wanted me to leave without helping Marian. She might have had an underlying worry that I would find out the truth about her. Because after all, Marian was right. I did regard her as a friend.

Was there anyone on this beach, I wondered, who hadn't been corrupted somehow, seduced by the idea of a good life?

I remembered the blonde girl running on the beach, and Veeramma's remark about the tattoo.

'Did Veeramma also do a tattoo for Liza?'

Marian looked surprised.

'How . . . how do you know?'

'And was it lower down, near her pubic area?'

'That's right. It was a little daisy chain of broken hearts.'

Even though I had expected it, I felt the answer like a body blow. Did the design hold a deeper, darker symbolism?

I felt a huge sense of relief that Durga and her friends had left Goa when they did.

'Why did you accuse Vishnu of molesting Liza?' I asked her, looking for the other missing parts of the jigsaw.

A puzzled look crossed her face.

'I never registered any complaint. I know someone put my name on the form, but at the time I didn't even know who he was. He's been to jail twice because of her. The first time he went Liza felt terrible about it because he had actually saved her from rape. She insisted on thanking him, but it was too late. I think you might have met one of the persons already who assaulted Liza.'

I hoped she wasn't acting once again.

'Do you mean Curtis D'Silva?'

She gave a tiny nod, and quickly added. 'But please don't say anything to anyone. And I have to apologize for that day, when you were given those drugs, I really had no idea what they would do to you. I can only say I had nothing to do with it.'

Grudgingly I nodded and then said, 'Is there any evidence at all on Curtis?'

She shook her head.

'And do you think he raped her? With some other men?'

For a minute I thought she might say something further, but instead she said quickly, 'It's such a long time back, and it will be difficult to prove anyway. Look, I must thank you for everything, and I'm really sorry we couldn't take this to a logical conclusion. But let's meet in a day or so, if you're still here.'

As she got up to leave, I thought I'd better warn her about the men hanging around at the door. 'Did you come here alone?'

'Yes.'

I passed her my compact mirror, which I used solely for situations like this.

'Just pretend to settle your makeup and aim it towards the door behind you. Do you know those two men? They keep turning up.'

Marian glanced in the mirror, and frowned as she quickly shut the compact.

After a pause she said, 'They've been stalking me for a few days. Ever since I met you that day in the shack. That's the main reason I've been rushing away from our meetings and not turning up and so on. I don't like the way they look at me. Something worrying about it. If it wasn't for Liza I think I would have left this beach long ago. Who wants to lead a life like this? This is really becoming crazy.'

She stopped abruptly. I noticed she had said she had stayed on for *Liza*. So there was probably something more that she couldn't tell me. And that probably involved Curtis D'Silva, Vishnu, and the cover-up. And these two men as well. A larger story, which she still hadn't shared. Nor did she seem likely to do so.

So I decided not to persist any more; I didn't want to completely alienate her. She had given me a few hints that might make it easier for me to find things out. Besides, I thought she should leave soon as those two men outside looked decidedly untrustworthy.

The French windows next to us, when opened, led directly to the beach. Putting down enough cash to pay the bill, I quickly picked up my handbag and asked her to follow me out from behind the tall plants in the restaurant, which effectively hid us from view. No one would see us from the door of the restaurant if we moved fast enough.

Once Marian had run down to the beach and was safely on her way home, I strolled past the two men who were still lounging at the entrance to the cafeteria, no doubt waiting for us to emerge.

As I went by, they actually had some expression on their faces, for a change.

They looked completely baffled, seeing me appear from a different direction.

After many days, I felt like laughing.

Chapter 10

No matter what I had said to reassure Marian and Amarjit, I had no intention of giving up on my search for Liza. I thought it was both ridiculous and frightening that a young girl could vanish and a year later we still had no idea where she could be, or what had happened to her.

And so, for many reasons, despite the fact that I'd had a really difficult day, I had decided to go to the 'floating' casino.

Not that I am a gambler. It's one of the few addictions that I've avoided – I even stay away from lotteries. Perhaps because I hate losing!

In fact, I avoided card games of all kinds if I could help it, because of a well-known family fixation. My grandfather had been so besotted with playing bridge that he often did not come home for days on end, staying on at the club with his cronies, playing rubber after rubber. That convinced me that I should never go near a pack of cards.

Luckily other pursuits – drinking, smoking and flirtatious relationships – have added quality to my life. I would hate to exchange them for nights in cold card rooms or overheated casinos.

So, some of my present excitement had to do with the fact that I was going to the casino with Dennis. It had been a while since I had seriously thought about interesting men, or men that I wanted to take an interest in. Till a few months ago my attention had been taken up by Edward, a wonderful British man I had met in London last year. We had shared 'memorable moments' (as mentioned in the last postcard I had sent him), first in London, and later in Delhi. But I knew I would never shift to London and he could not abandon his lucrative career and come here.

And frankly, both of us were just a little bit relieved that these hurdles existed. If there had been none, possibly we would have invented them. We had both been on our own for far too long now to fall into any kind of permanent arrangement.

Thus on our last evening together, over a candlelight dinner in a suburban Delhi restaurant, we had mutually concluded that long-distance relationships simply did not work.

My mother was disappointed because she had (with difficulty) adjusted herself to the idea of a British son-in-law, and Edward was very helpful in so many ways. He loved staying at home, cooking, lending a hand with the household chores and chatting with her about all her ailments.

But once Edward left, she had begun pushing the idea of the newly divorced Amarjit in my direction, though I knew we probably had too much baggage between us. Too much love and too many fights. It was a volatile relationship and strangely it only worked when we had a third person in it to provide a certain piquancy.

I sometimes wondered if I sought out flawed relationships because I hated to commit 100 per cent. So I looked for men who would not demand it. It is always so much nicer to search for love than actually find it. Because then you'll discover that love is fleeting, anyway.

Right now Dennis seemed an interesting option. We were only on our third meeting and could choose to engage or disengage as we wanted. There was definitely an attraction, but I didn't know which way it would develop. We knew very little about each other, aside from the fact that we were both on our own, and, for my part, that he had an interesting life. He certainly wasn't as good-looking as Edward, but I liked his sense of humour. In a world full of pompous, self-important men (which, at times, certainly included Amarjit), this was a huge relief.

I knew I had a very serious investigation on my hands, but there was little harm in taking Dennis with me.

Just for a little while I even pretended that I was going out for a normal date. When I got back to my room, I took some time to decide what I would wear, settling finally for a mid-length black dress. It was well-fitting but not too obtrusive or low-cut, as I didn't want to attract attention on the ship. The only person whom I hoped would notice me was Dennis.

After many days I decided to put on some mascara and lipstick as well, just to get into the mood for doing something other than getting sand between my toes.

Finally, clasping a string of pearls around my neck, I reminded myself of all the things I had to look out for tonight.

Once we got onto the casino ship, I needed to know where Curtis D'Silva fitted into Liza's story. And of course I should try to find out if Liza had any connection with the casino. It might be impossible to explore the ship, but I could certainly try to find out if she had ever been on board, or indeed, though it was unlikely, if she was still there somewhere.

It was also important to look out for the mysterious owner of the casino who was supposed to be quite influential. Despite my best efforts I still had no idea about his identity, as he was deliberately kept nameless in the press, possibly because it would be difficult to prove any links between him and the casino. If he had a share, or owned the ship, it had to be through a third-party transaction, and his involvement would never surface. Perhaps Vicky would have an answer to some of these questions. I decided that, no matter how tough it was, I would definitely ask her more about Liza.

Reaching the jetty at Panjim, where the casino

speedboats departed, I almost didn't recognize Dennis, even though I had thought about him all day. Because we had only met in our shabby beachwear, I overlooked the dashing curly-haired man in his dark trousers, crisp blue cotton shirt, and shiny black shoes, sitting and reading a magazine. It wasn't till he looked up and walked towards me that I realized who it was. It was infinitely more invigorating to smell Pierre Cardin perfume than seawater and fish.

'You're looking lovely,' he said, as chivalrous as ever, his eyes creased at the corners.

'And so are you. Are you always this nice or are you making a special effort?' I asked a little dreamily, basking in the compliments, as we joined the queue for the speedboats.

The reflected lights on the dark water lent a romantic hue to the moment, and I couldn't help a slight skip of my heartbeat, which was just as swiftly followed by regret. What was the point of a romantic evening when my mind would be engaged with the story of Liza?

'No need to make any effort with you, Simran. You and I met under a holy banyan tree, and you know the real me! We've already been blessed by marijuana smoke. We've seen the light, and the rest is all *maya*, a mirage.'

He pointed at his clothes and around. I could see why he would make a good scriptwriter. The self-deprecatory style was nice, too.

Interesting, but not presumptuous.

Laughing, and feeling a bit like characters from a James Bond movie, we got into the speedboat and headed for the *Tempest*, which was lit up with dazzling neon lights. A largescreen commercial ran in a loop on the ship's side, depicting beautiful women endlessly dealing out counters and collecting money.

The commercial turned out to be much more exciting than the reality.

Uniformed attendants guided us into the ship, though they could have done with a little more sprucing up, and I was surprised at how unremarkable everything looked. I expected alluring music and ethereal beings throwing flowers at us, enticing us to the gaming tables, festooned with gold and purple.

Instead, almost as soon as we arrived and got our tickets, we walked up a dull black staircase and found ourselves finally inside the heart of the crowded casino floor. Disappointingly, instead of wild excitement, there was a nondescript ambience, more like a downmarket version of an airline lounge. Later, I was to find out that the owner had once owned an airline, which he had shut down, transferring most of his staff to the casino. Perhaps that way he saved money on the uniforms – and the staff had already been trained to seat and feed people. And if they could make their customers believe it was a long-haul flight to the US, they could trap them into gambling for fourteen hours. The only difference being that they didn't have to announce the emergency exits, and probably had been retrained to block them in case people tried to get away with undeserved cash.

'Shall we walk around, and see what you'd like to play?'

Dennis put a friendly hand on my arm to steer me around the tables, as I continued to be a little distracted. I couldn't tell him the real reason I was here, so I replied in the affirmative – but my eyes were searching for Vicky. Where was she?

We picked up our counters from the cash desk, and then slowly did a tour of the room. Unsurprisingly the tables were rather crowded, mostly with Indians; there were fewer foreigners than I had anticipated. Perhaps international tourists had no need to come all the way to Goa to gamble. For them the beaches would always be the greater lure.

Many of the players, in any case, looked rather the worse for wear, as though they had been there for days and would have to be prised away from their table with a crowbar. Few bothered to look up as we approached, or even noticed each other. They were absorbed with the gods of fortune, spread out in front of them in red and black discs.

In fact the seriousness with which they were staring at their roulette wheels, card decks and dice made one feel as though this was really the last-chance casino. Dennis and I seemed to be the only people who were relaxed as we strolled around, drinking and joking about the general gloom which hung like a pall over the place. If anyone had found a magical world where money dropped from the chandeliers onto their laps, they were keeping very quiet about it.

Finally, to my relief, I spotted Vicky guiding a client to a roulette table. She was looking prettier than ever, in her full regalia of short skirt and black jacket.

'Hey, Vicky,' I called out.

She turned her large startled eyes towards me.

'Oh, hi,' she said, bursting into laughter. 'Oh lovely, lovely, lovely. You look gorgeous. You made it. Fantastic!' She rushed towards me, dripping charm.

It was as though she had met a very old friend, instead of someone she had bumped into accidentally on the beach just yesterday. But of course, I knew her affection would increase as the evening progressed and we donated more and more of our hard-earned cash towards the well-being of the *Tempest* and its owners.

Yet it was impossible not to warm to her. She was like an affectionate puppy, sitting us down and beckoning a waiter to bring food and drink for her guests. She was obviously a senior and favoured member of the staff. Cocktails and snacks appeared, while she kept up a steady flow of chatter about how popular the casino was and how many people came here.

The sad girl I had seen on the beach yesterday was completely hidden behind the veneer of sophistication and good cheer.

I found myself wanting to tell her to relax, but of course I couldn't. This bright unnatural banter was part of the uniform she had donned.

Taking out his phone, Dennis aimed it towards us for a photograph. Suddenly one of the bouncers, a tall young man standing to one side, lunged out at him as though he had pulled a gun.

'No photography, sir. Too many VIPs around. Not permitted.'

Looking a little surprised, Dennis shrugged and put his phone away.

Vicky touched his arm, saying apologetically, 'My boss is here tonight and so they get extra strict.'

Dennis was intrigued. 'And why would he want anonymity? After all, he should be like Richard Branson, and want to be the face of the business!'

Glancing around, Vicky leant forward confidentially. 'Actually he's a minister in the union government and that's why he likes to keep it low key. Very few people know he owns this place. If you look to my left you'll see a bunch of people around a table playing blackjack behind the screen. Vinay Gupta. That's the man in the blue safari suit, and all those with him are members of parliament.'

'But what if something happens and we all have to be evacuated? Or if someone from the media comes on board? Then he won't be able to hide!' Dennis pointed out.

I couldn't help smiling as I remembered how, just the other day there had been headlines in the newspapers when some Goan police officers had been spotted on board a casino. They quickly locked themselves in with the manager, claiming that they were present only to 'familiarize' themselves with the way a casino works, as a media mob descended on them. Named and shamed, they had to face a severe reprimand from the state Home Minister. But it was natural that these casinos, which had been legalized only recently, should carry the fascination of the illicit. Lawmakers would be as attracted to them as anyone else. And once they got addicted, why would they not want to do some 'revenue sharing', as some preferred to call it?

I looked towards the group, as casually as I could. The screen gave them privacy from the rest of the ship, but from where we were sitting, close to the VIP area, they were clearly visible.

There was the familiar-looking face of the Panchayati Raj minister, Vinay Gupta, with his trademark ferocious moustache. I almost laughed out loud.

'Vicky, you said he's very fond of you. Does he ever come down to the beach? It would be lovely to meet him there sometime . . .'

I paused, wondering if that sounded a bit desperate. But finding myself so close to the man who had probably been present on the night Liza disappeared, and who might have had Vishnu unlawfully jailed, I didn't want to let him go so easily. Surely there would be a way for us to meet him.

'But if that's not possible,' I added, 'I have so many friends in Chandigarh. I am sure both of you would know them. And he must know my friends in the government. So we can also fix to meet either in Delhi or in Chandigarh.'

I tried to escalate the comfort level, deliberably dropping a few names of people in the central government who now held important portfolios. Some of them had been with me in either school or college.

'Sure, I'll ask him. In fact he has a share in some beach shacks, so perhaps he might want to host you. It should be fun.'

'Is Fernando's one of them?' I couldn't help asking, sipping my vodka, and remembering Auntie Elizabeth's reference to a man with a moustache.

Vicky looked at me and then said quickly, 'How did you guess? And also some at Baga beach.'

'I read about him in the papers,' I said. 'I think he came for a Christmas celebration. Choir-singing or something.'

Dennis raised his eyebrows. 'Really?' He looked a little puzzled, but I hoped he had the good sense not to say anything. I shook my head at him slightly, and he smiled and casually put a finger on his lips, taking it away before Vicky could catch the covert signal.

Pushing a chicken tikka towards him, I asked Vicky casually, 'And how long have you known him?'

'Nearly two years. I met him in Chandigarh when he was interviewing us to become air hostesses in his airline. I had just finished school at the time.'

'What happened to that airline?'

'It's been shut down,' she said cheerfully. 'I think we sent more passengers by road than air, because there was too much competition from the established airlines. We only had two aircraft. Both were quite rundown and Vinayji was far too busy all the time with his government responsibilities to expand the company. But he made sure no one lost their jobs. Even though he can barely come here twice a month, he decided to consolidate this business at least. He already had this casino and he transferred all three hundred of us here.'

'You obviously have an important post for someone so young!'

'I look after the operations,' she said. 'Vinayji trusts only a handful of people. I'm one of them.'

None of this was said with any hint of pride or modesty. It was a matter-of-fact statement. It reminded me of what she had said yesterday – and how difficult it would be for her to leave her job.

'You don't mind staying here all night?'

'I have to look after everyone. And especially when Vinayji is here, just in case he needs me.'

As though reminded of her duty, she began to get up. 'It was so nice to see you, Simran and Dennis. Enjoy your evening and let me know if you need anything. I must see if Vinayji and his guests are alright.'

Vinay Gupta, who seemed old enough to be her father, had managed to create a very loyal employee. Paradoxically, while she had indicated her discomfort over her boss on the beach when we had met, it was obvious that there was something more between them. What surprised me once again was that Vicky didn't even try to hide it. She must have seen photographs of Gupta with his wife and children. And why would she, such a young and lovely girl, throw away her life like this?

I knew I might not get this chance again, so I asked, 'And Curtis? You know him, don't you, the DJ and singer here? Supposed to be very good.'

A nervous look crossed her face, and the cordial smile faltered a bit.

Could she and Curtis have a relationship as well? I had seen them exchanging a fairly chaste kiss at the market, but that might not tell the whole story. They had looked like they were discussing something confidential. Something that Vinayji might not be aware of? That was an interesting twist.

'Of course, everyone knows Curtis. He's very popular around here and does a wonderful imitation of Elvis Presley, too. You must hear him. But if you'll excuse me . . .'

Perhaps mentioning Curtis had been a mistake. She turned to walk away rapidly, as I sprang to my feet. There was little time to waste, as I could see that when we next met she might not be as friendly as she had been today. No doubt when she next spoke to him, Curtis would tell her about my visit to Cozee Home, looking for Liza. And possibly also what he or his accomplices had done to me subsequently.

'I must meet Mr Gupta. Why don't you introduce us?' I began to gather my handbag to follow her.

Dennis got up as well, looking a bit confused as he tried to figure out what was going on.

'I . . . I think I'll introduce him to you a little later. Let me just catch up with some other guests? I promise I'll come back.' There was less warmth now in Vicky's voice.

Not sure if I would see her again, I took out my phone and scanned down to Liza's photograph, where she was smiling into the camera. I decided to take a chance, and bluff my way through.

'Just one last thing. I was also looking for this girl. I believe she's been on this ship recently and might even work here. I have a message for her from her mother.'

I added the last sentence so that I could pretend that I

226

was only a messenger for Liza's family and not investigating the case in any way. It might help not to set alarm bells ringing, especially since we were confined on a ship and more or less at the mercy of the *Tempest* team.

I already knew how ruthless Vinayji could be.

Vicky turned pale when she saw Liza's photograph. But she still shook her head.

'I have no idea who she is,' she whispered. 'Please, Simranji. Let me go. I would request you to just try your luck at some of these tables and then leave. Perhaps we can meet on the beach tomorrow and we'll talk.'

She was no longer smiling, and in fact her expression was a bit steely. The friendliness on her face had been replaced by a distinct frostiness. Behind the cold look, I glimpsed a touch of very real fear.

'What are you scared of?' I asked gently. 'Why don't you tell me?'

I could have sworn that her eyes glinted with unshed tears.

'Go away. Please. You don't know anything about my life or this world. I'm not scared of anything.' But her voice quivered, giving her away, and she glanced around. No doubt we were being watched closely. I wondered if our conversation was being listened to – I knew that some casinos even hid microphones strategically in various places, as well as hidden cameras to track customers. That could partly explain her nervousness.

I still had to force her to tell me something. She was my one solid lead.

'But just tell me, have you ever seen this girl? Does Curtis know where she is?'

I put my hand out to stop her from leaving.

As I spoke she pushed my hand away roughly, and suddenly her expression changed to something quite nasty.

'Please don't ask me any more questions, and it would be best if you left immediately,' she hissed, signalling to one of the managers.

'Perhaps I should ask Mr Gupta for some information then,' I said, and started moving towards the screen before she could react. I had barely taken a few steps when I found the way blocked by the same bouncers who had almost snatched Dennis's phone away. I stepped back, wondering what to do, as Dennis quickly stood between me and them, and put his arm around me protectively.

'I don't quite know what this is about,' he whispered into my ear, 'but I think these people don't like us very much.'

I looked around, and for a minute, everything around us seemed to have come to a halt. I hadn't realized that other people had noticed the altercation. A few of the less-involved gamblers had actually abandoned their careful calculations about winning and losing, and were staring at us curiously.

Vicky, far from being the friendly person she had been before, was now at Vinay Gupta's side, saying something into his ear, something that annoyed him, and I could see his expression change as he looked towards us.

Perhaps, as Vicky had suggested, it was time to leave. But I was relieved that at least I had found out that Liza was almost certainly connected to this Vinay Gupta. And that Vicky had known her. There could be no other reason for her rather severe reaction.

So Liza was the common factor. Something had definitely happened to her, and even mentioning her name had made Vicky change from a friendly hostess to an ice maiden. Something so terrible perhaps that none of these people wanted to admit that they knew her well at all.

And the one person who had the most to lose from any revelation was probably Vinay Gupta himself.

I was beginning to understand why I had been drugged on that first day and my mobile phone wiped clean. This was a very powerful man. No one could afford to mess with him.

What, then, could be Vicky's stake in this, I wondered, as I whispered to Dennis, 'Sorry. I'll explain when we get thrown out of here.'

Fortunately he still managed to look amused.

'I thought we were going to have a quiet evening gambling away our family fortunes. And perhaps our families as well, like the Pandavas. I don't have a wife to give away – but I do have a former brother-in-law whom I was hoping someone might want . . .' Dennis said softly, trying to make me laugh. I could see that he didn't want our first evening together to be entirely ruined, even though he was unable to fathom the dynamics between Vicky and me.

We still stood where Vicky had left us. I was undecided if I should at least try to go upstairs. With Dennis by my side I felt a little more brave than I would have otherwise. The only problem was we seemed to have attracted far too much attention.

'I suggest we try to make a quiet exit before we're made to walk the plank,' said Dennis, keeping his arm around me.

'I wouldn't have minded a guided tour of the ship, but something tells me that these guys have other ideas,' I said ruefully, as one of the bouncers approached. I wondered why it was so essential that we be thrown off the ship. Was Liza still here, possibly in one of the rooms?

I was quite sure that there would be a few areas where only Vinay Gupta and his cronies would be allowed. There were several doors around the casino area which were marked 'Private' and 'No Entry'. It was a large ship and it didn't make sense to use only two areas. Perhaps some of the staff lived on board.

Mr Moustache and Vicky were now herding the other

MPs out of our view, no doubt so they wouldn't see us being led away. I thought it might be best to act as though there had been a genuine misunderstanding and that, once we spoke to Vicky or Vinayji, all would be sorted out.

I picked up my handbag and waved to Vicky cheerily. But she pointedly turned her back towards us and strode off after Vinay Gupta. Despite her tears yesterday, and the fear in her eyes today, she obviously knew who her future lay with. It was certainly not with me.

We were asked politely to leave by the four bouncers, who now stood in front of us. It was difficult to persuade them to change their minds. I insisted that we had paid the full amount for dinner and the entertainment upstairs, neither of which we'd had the opportunity to enjoy. But my argument fell on deaf ears. It had been a foolish move to reveal my cards so early, in front of Vicky. I wished I had waited before I showed her the photograph. It was highly unlikely that I would ever see Vinay Gupta or Vicky ever again. Nor would I be allowed on board the *Tempest*.

I felt angry at myself for having wasted a wonderful opportunity.

It was in dismal silence that we walked out onto the platform below to await the speedboat back to shore. The four bouncers stood on guard.

Dennis tried to look nonchalant, but I was aware I had put him in a dangerous and embarrassing situation.

Not a good start to what I had hoped would be a life-long relationship!

I apologized to him once again, when we had been unceremoniously put back on the speedboat and sent back to shore. Trying to sound as remorseful as possible, I buried my own anger and irritation over my mishandling of the situation.

'It wasn't fair. I really should have warned you about my search for Liza. And the possible implications when I started talking to Vicky about it. Sorry. Evenings with me can get out of control.'

'Out of control can be fantastic,' Dennis laughed, apparently unperturbed by the disruption to what should have been an elegant evening in a casino.

'Perhaps, as you said, you can use this in your next script.'

'Tell me, do you do this very often? Get into scrapes, find yourself surrounded by bouncers? Man, those guys looked like they could really crush us with just two fingers.'

'With me, life will never be boring, though you might have a few broken bones,' I told him, attempting to match his light-hearted tone. Obviously he wasn't going to allow anything to wreck our evening, or what was left of it.

By now we had been hustled off the ferrying speed-boat, rushed through the waiting area, and deposited rather rudely onto the streets of Panjim. I wondered what anyone observing me would have thought: I had been walking around, stoned out of my mind, the other day, and now I had been thrown out of a casino. Vinay Gupta probably looked like a saint compared to me.

It was close to 10 o'clock, and the streets of Goa's capital city were already deserted. Most of the action would be taking place, as we knew, along the beachside restaurants. But I didn't want to return there so quickly.

'Now, ma'am,' said Dennis, 'why don't you tell me why we had to lose out on our ticket money? I didn't even get to play a single game! All I got was one mojito and a couple of chicken tikkas! And I still don't even know who Liza is.'

'Why don't we find a quiet bar?' I said, thinking that it might be good to confide in someone so unflappable. 'And I'll tell you the whole story.'

Chapter 11

Waking up next to Dennis was surprisingly nice. It felt even better than I had imagined. He was still sleeping, lost in a happy dream, perhaps, as I saw the sides of his mouth quiver in a smile. So, wrapping a bed-sheet around me, I slipped away and tiptoed to the bathroom. Fortunately we were at his hotel, so I would be spared more curious looks from Maggie the receptionist at Hotel Delite. She already had a dubious impression of me. If I had arrived with a strange man in tow last night, I would have been surely damned for life.

I didn't quite remember our journey back to his hotel as I had dozed off in the cab. But the rest of the night (or early morning, to be more precise) had passed by in a sensuous embrace, and deserved an encore. It had been a long time since I had felt so relaxed and euphoric.

As I looked around for my clothes, and picked up my handbag, I saw the familiar flashing red light on my phone. We had been so busy that I wouldn't have noticed it earlier. That part of me which was still floating on air hoped that it would be a friend greeting me, because the next day was Christmas Eve.

I was suddenly filled with dread. I picked up the phone and sat down on a chair next to the bed again, suddenly unable to move.

What if . . .?

I didn't want to complete the sentence. The experience at the casino had made me realize once again that Vinay Gupta was a very dangerous man. Whatever Liza had done to annoy him might have been considered intolerable. Was that why Vicky had become so nervous when she had looked at Liza's photograph? Or was she jealous because Curtis had also been involved with Liza, albeit in a crass and brutal manner?

I stared down at the phone again, and finally, saying a silent prayer, opened the message. As I feared, it said 'number withheld'. A chill went through me.

I clicked on the accompanying video, dreading what I would find.

It was again a video of Liza. She was with a group of around eight people. It was a rather raucous cocktail party from the sound and look of it.

On closer examination I realized that one of the men was Vinay Gupta. Could this have been shot on the ship, or at the beach shack? It was difficult to tell.

Vinay had an arm around Liza. They weren't really talking very much to each other, but both had drinks in their hands and were sharing a cigarette. He pulled her towards him and made her sit on his lap and began kissing her, pressing her close to him. A 60-year-old man feeling up a 16-year-old girl. It was not a pretty sight.

They were the only two people I could immediately recognize in the video, as the lens was focused on them. I would have to play it again on a computer, at a larger size, to see the others clearly.

It was a shaky, short clip, only about two minutes long.

But looking at it, all the pleasure I had felt after waking up next to Dennis emptied out of my mind. Who had sent this to me?

Could it have been Vicky? I had spoken to her about Liza last night and then this video of her boss molesting Liza, in full public view, arrives on my phone. It was certainly an odd coincidence.

I lit a cigarette and watched the video once more. This tiny film changed everything. What I had suspected for a while was now clear: I had located the master puppeteer. The shadowy figure I had been searching for. The link between Liza, Curtis, Vicky, Vishnu, Veeramma, Fernando, and countless others on the beach. Even the police.

This man owned the beach, and decided the punishments, doling out his own form of justice, when, for instance, Vishnu had made the mistake of protecting Liza.

This man, who had the power to run the government, now demonstrated enough hubris to molest a young girl, knowing he would get away with it. If anyone had to pay the price, it would be Liza, unless she showed unswerving loyalty towards him, like Vicky did. Had Liza fallen out of favour somehow and had to 'disappear'? Vicky's nervousness had alerted me finally to the possibility that Liza might not be alive at all.

She wouldn't have looked so anxious if Liza was safe and well, and had simply run away. Did Marian know about this? Was this something else about which she had made a bargain to keep from me?

'What's happened?'

I snapped out of my thoughts and found that Dennis was looking at me perplexed. 'Has Mr Moustache been in touch with you?' he asked, stretching out on the bed, and leaning towards me. I was startled at how close he was to guessing the truth.

'Not really. In fact, I have no idea who it's from. I told you about these mysterious messages and videos I keep getting. This is not the kind of thing you want to see before breakfast, but if you want to take a look . . .'

Dennis reached out to take the phone from me. 'Sure. Now that you've told me so much, I'm intrigued. I didn't know things like this happened here – though it depends on the company you keep, I guess.'

Perhaps I could find some consolation in his statement. Maybe I was even relieved that this kind of occurrence was not routine in Goa.

Dennis knew Goa much better than I did, having spent the first few decades of his life here, before leaving to study and work in Mumbai. But whenever he returned home he enjoyed mingling with the international crowd on the beaches in North Goa, before he caught up with his parents, who lived in the south of the tiny state. The area around Anjuna reminded him of his own slightly wild youth, he said, before he became a card-carrying member of the hard-working middle classes.

He particularly liked being where I had first encountered him, with the ageing flower children and the hippies, but he equally enjoyed the quieter, more culturally rich, family-friendly atmosphere of Benaulim, another small Goan village. His father was an artist and his mother a well-known fashion designer who had brought out a very successful range of Indo–Portuguese fusion clothes. Yes, through him I was definitely learning about another side to Goa, while alas, I was introducing him to a much darker aspect than he had imagined.

'Oh, Jesus!' he exclaimed, horrified, looking at the video clip. 'Is this . . . is this the girl you're looking for? Liza? That's Vinay Gupta with her, isn't it? The bastard. Poor girl. I mean, she's only around fifteen or sixteen, isn't she? What's she doing at this party?'

'She seems to have done a lot of things perhaps she shouldn't have done. Or, excuse me, shouldn't *be doing*. It's difficult to say why she's there at all. But she seems fine, which surprises me, because in the last video sent to me, as I told you, two men were literally attacking her, so I'm still trying to figure out the sequence of events.' I got up and then stumbled, remembering that I was still wrapped in the bed-sheet.

Unbothered about how I looked, I distractedly picked up my clothes, which were scattered all over the room.

'Unless this video was actually shot before the one in which she was attacked,' he said. 'The person sending them to you might not be sticking to any sequence. These might simply be the most important parts of the story. Whoever sent this might have found out about your visit to the casino last night and thought you would want to know the link between Vinay Gupta and Liza, since you had asked about it.' Spoken like a clever scriptwriter.

'Which means that whoever it is either knows I went to the casino, or saw me there. Could someone be following me?' I thought about my suspicions about the two men. But why would they send me this video? I had thought they would be more keen on preventing any information from reaching me.

'Anyone at the hotel? Did you talk to anyone about your wanting to go to the casino last night? Ask for directions, perhaps?'

I could see that even Dennis was getting involved in this now, and with a familiar twinge of sorrow I realized that we had almost forgotten our romantic night. It already felt like it was in the very distant past.

I considered his words. 'You might be right. I asked the manager when I was booking the cab. Maggie – the receptionist at the hotel – thinks I am weird anyway, and was definitely listening. But they would only be interested in me if they have something to do with Liza. And why would they be involved as well? That would mean that almost every person that I have met so far on the beach has been involved in Liza's disappearance. That's practically impossible, isn't it?'

Dennis shrugged. 'Not everyone, but I think a lot of people know what happened. After all, the girl has been missing for a year. Her sister and father are still around. I didn't hear about it because it's all been hushed up, but people who live here, as you said, know each other very well. These frequent messages and the videos make me think that someone wants you to carry on the investigation. They are sending you clues, keeping track of you, but obviously can't come out in the open because of the problem you've stated over and over again – that everyone here is very closely linked with each other. And if, as you suspect, Liza has been murdered, then they have to keep quiet, otherwise someone like Vinay Gupta will make sure they are food for fish very soon.

'So someone, perhaps even that inquisitive Maggie from the hotel, is passing on information about you to someone else, that's all. You are working on your own and no one seems to be supporting you in this, or giving you any information apart from those videos. But data about you might be going through to others, from different sources.'

That made sense. So far, I had tried to be discreet in my interest in Liza, but as I had already found out, time and again, it was entirely possible that many knew what I was doing. Those two men turning up again when I was meeting Marian could not have been a coincidence, surely. Besides, lately I was no longer behaving like a relaxed tourist. Had that attracted attention as well?

'Do you think it's really impossible to trace this number?' I tried to remain positive, looking down at that wretched 'number withheld' message.

'We need someone who knows something about mobile phones, who can tell us what kind of phone this video would have been shot on,' Dennis pointed out. 'But getting hold of a private number would be very tough, and you'd need help from the police. They could get in touch with phone companies and so on. But in your case, even though Amarjit could do it easily, you said he doesn't want you involved any more. Besides, can you really trust him?'

And that's when I thought of Vishnu. I remembered the pile of phones lying in his shop, some for sale, others obviously left for repairs. And the computers lying half dissected, with keyboards and the motherboards all over the place. Although he wouldn't be able to crack the phone number behind this anonymous message, he might be able to tell us what sort of phone had been used to make the video – and he might even know people on the beach who carried phones of the same brand or specifications. It was a long shot – but we had to try everything.

The last time we had met I had made him quite nervous, as I was an obvious outsider. But perhaps he would be less worried if he saw Dennis with me. After all, Dennis was a Goan, a local person, and if he spoke to him directly, Vishnu might be a little more forthcoming.

We decided that we would have a quick breakfast and then ask Vishnu to come over to Dennis's hotel. Dennis would speak to him initially, explaining that he needed him to fix his computer. He would first talk to him downstairs, and then bring him up to the room, where I would be waiting. Together we would try to convince him that he should share all he knew about Liza, especially if he had any suspicions or knowledge about who had assaulted her.

Perhaps there was a sliver of a chance that he would tell us that she was still alive. So far, he was the only one who seemed to have cared for her; he had even gone to jail on her behalf. Twice.

Troubled by this latest video implicating Vinay Gupta, I considered getting in touch with Marian, to update her. But her connection with the police, and the deal she had made already, stopped me. Besides, thus far I had not shared any information about the videos with her. She might get upset if she heard about them, and do something reckless.

Or, as was more likely, she might not do anything at all. Right now she was far too concerned about her own security to be of any use. Now that she had received her passport back, I had a hunch she would want to leave the country before she was stalled once again. Indeed, whoever wanted to wrap up this case probably wanted to get her to leave as fast as possible.

Dennis agreed that it would be best if I completed my investigation before we spoke either to Amarjit or to Marian.

But my fear was that they might not even want to know anything further. The case, according to them, was closed. Or if it wasn't, then it soon would be, whether or not anyone discovered the truth about Liza's disappearance.

Over breakfast I loaded the video onto Dennis's computer to check if there were any other familiar faces in it. The grainy quality of the video was actually worse than in the others I had been sent, and I wondered why. This seemed much more of a surreptitious recording than the others.

While going through the video frame by frame I realized that one of the figures in the background resembled Vicky. She was standing next to a man who had his back to the camera. His hair was tied in a ponytail, and when he turned around I was sure it was Curtis. He and Vicky stared towards the very animated and possibly drunk Vinay Gupta, who now had Liza on his lap and was kissing her.

Their expressions were not clear, but Dennis and I tried to work out what was happening. Vicky wouldn't have been very happy with the turn of events. Perhaps she was jealous that her boss had seemingly switched allegiance?

What would she have done next? She was just a few years older than Liza, but was she ambitious enough, and upset enough, to get Liza kidnapped and raped? And even killed?

Was that why she had looked so scared yesterday? Because she feared exposure?

Or was someone else responsible?

Just as I was staring at the last few frames, I noticed that another two men stood in the corner. They looked familiar. I enlarged the still image, clicking on it over and over again, thinking about the men who had attacked Liza – could this be them?

But in fact I was now sure they were Tweedledum and Tweedledee. The same two men whom Marian feared had been following her around. And had surfaced twice at my hotel too. In this video, they were as usual trying to look unobtrusive, surveying the place as though they were noting everything. It was odd that they were the only ones not having a drink. But even at the shack party when I had seen them, they had been lounging at the bar, toying with a couple of glasses. I hadn't actually seen them take a sip of anything. Each time, they had seemed slightly more formally dressed than others, in trousers and shirts.

The only possible explanations were that they were part of the minister's security, or put there by someone to keep an eye on him. In either case, looking at his behaviour, pawing a young girl openly at a party, they would be concerned.

And that's why they would also be very interested in what had eventually happened to Liza when she disappeared – and, no doubt, in my efforts to find her.

It would also explain their interest in Marian.

When Vishnu arrived, Dennis went downstairs to meet him, and after about ten minutes, while I paced restlessly in the room, I heard Dennis knock on the door.

Despite all the effort Dennis put in, Vishnu almost left when he saw me. Perhaps he had spotted me with Marian and was worried because, despite Marian's denial, it was her complaint – according to the police files, at least – that had got him locked up.

The slightest mistake by him might see him behind bars once more. I could sense his fear.

'Please, Vishnu. Do sit down. We are both on the same side.' Dennis put a friendly arm around him.

'I'm only interested in finding out more about Liza, and nothing else. Believe me. I'm not from the police. I don't want to report anything about you to anyone,' I added.

I tried to calm him down as much as possible, but he backed away from us and looked accusingly at Dennis.

'You told me repair laptop. I go now.'

He started walking purposefully towards the door.

Dennis spoke to him again, very gently, in Konkani – which I understood a little – and told him not to feel so worried. There was nothing to fear. We were on his side. We only wanted to find out if he knew anything about Liza. We cared about her. We were not connected with the police. The anxiety did not leave his face, but at least he was, reluctantly, persuaded to sit down.

In the morning light his wounds looked even more fresh. I remembered Auntie Elizabeth mentioning that every time there was a problem, the police nabbed him for an interrogation. Perhaps they had been around recently as well. Did that mean that there was news of Liza? Or did it mean that he knew something about her that the police were nervous about? I thought I had better clarify that with him before we went any further.

I decided not to mention the anonymous messages just yet.

'We just need to discuss Liza with you. We are very worried about her,' Dennis reiterated gently.

'Please tell us about when and how you first met her,' I added, with a grateful glance at Dennis.

'On beach,' Vishnu said truculently, sitting down on the edge of the chair next to the bed. We sat across from him, while he gazed at our faces with nervous blinks, his eyes still searching the room for hidden traps.

'You found her pretty?'

He nodded.

'You fell in love with her?'

He literally jerked his head back.

'No love,' he said quietly, looking down at the ground. 'But give protection. They no like.'

'Who's they?'

'The same who come for me.' There was a desperate note in his voice, and he looked around as though he expected someone to jump out from behind the sofa or the curtains. He was trembling like a nervous horse faced with extreme danger. It was heartbreaking to think of how 'they' might have tortured him. It was true that in many ways vulnerable, poor and thus marginalized young men in this country were as much at the mercy of the police as women were.

Dennis patted him on his hand.

I looked straight into his eyes. 'You know I am here to help Liza and no one else. In fact, everyone wants me to leave, but I have stayed on only because I feel I must try to find her. They tried to hurt me too. Gave me drugs. I almost died, on those rocks, you know. If I had slipped and fallen no one would have ever known that it was murder. I am sure you heard about it. Everyone knows everything on the beach. But I survived, and I haven't given up, though I still haven't been able to find her. I know we have to rescue her, somehow. I'm praying she is still alive.'

I hoped my words were getting through to him.

He appeared to be listening, at last, and I saw him nod his head, though a shadow crossed his face. Perhaps the fact that I was clearly as vulnerable as him made the situation a little less frightening. He wasn't alone in this.

'You were with her all the time when she was here, hanging around Fernando's. Did you see what happened to her that night?'

He vigorously shook his head.

'Vishnu,' I said gently, 'you don't even know which night I'm talking about! Let me rephrase that. I am talking about the night she disappeared. I believe something did happen and you probably saw it, which is why you are denying it.'

Dennis spoke to him again, convincing him to answer my questions. I was impressed. For a man who had just been thrown into the deep end of a case in which he had no obligation to be involved, he was very persistent.

Finally, with great reluctance, Vishnu turned to him and said, 'Don't tell police or they beat me. But Liza always at Fernando's. She get free drugs there, free drinks, food. They want her to carry drugs for them, because she young, needs money, has foreign passport.'

He stopped and looked down at his hands, clenching and unclenching them. Perhaps he didn't quite know if he should tell us everything – not knowing that Auntie Elizabeth had already told me quite a lot.

Making up his mind, he took a deep breath and said, 'Then . . . then Gupta come to Fernando's, two, three times and he like her very much too. I tell her go home, she no listen. I shout at her. That when she complain to Marian and Marian tell police. They lock me up.'

There was something terribly gut-wrenching about his innocence. His was a story I was familiar with, but the constant victimization of helpless men and women like him was depressing. What was also frustrating was that Marian denied ever having registered his name with the police. And yet someone had deliberately made him believe she had trapped him. Perhaps because it would give them a good reason to make him a suspect when Liza disappeared for good, as it gave him a motive to take revenge. It was a classic sting.

I looked at the welts and scars covering his face, and probably most of his body as well. That one arm which hung almost uselessly by his side. Tears came to my eyes, and I didn't try to hide them. I let them fall.

He looked at me with something close to childlike surprise. Perhaps he didn't think his pain could ever be understood.

I found it difficult to speak but Dennis stepped in, carefully framing the next question. We had to be very sensitive with our words, as whatever we asked chipped away at his fragile dignity.

'Was there any incident, any time, that made you worried about Liza's safety?'

For a while he said nothing. I feared he might retreat into his shell again, but then he took a deep breath and said, 'You won't mention to anyone? One day I see two men. And she.'

I knew how dangerous this admission could be. I remembered Liza falling on the sand while she begged to be left alone. Later, her golden hair falling over her face, as she was forced to lie down and spread her legs. Her screams echoed in my mind, so that even if I plugged my ears I still heard them, louder and louder.

'Do you know which men?'

'No. Too far.'

He closed his eyes as though it were a painful memory.

'What were they doing?'

'Too far, no see.'

His eyes were still shut. He was a tall, well-built man, but he seemed so guileless that I understood very well now why his aunt felt he was incapable of any kind of sexual assault; and yet I had been warned about his anger by the manager at Fernando's. He refused to speak, but his silence was eloquent.

I tried another tack. 'Why do you think Liza went to Fernando's the night she was raped?'

He didn't realize that it was a trick question, and didn't deny she had been raped.

'Because she got too used to drug. She only sixteen, but they give her too much. She keep going back because they keep cocaine for special customers. They want to hook her.'

I remembered Veeramma's quip about the fishermen, and the young girl who was running on the beach.

'And the drugs were all for free?'

'That's right. They no charge her for anything.'

'And was Curtis D'Silva part of this as well?'

Vishnu remained quiet. For him to implicate Curtis was far too dangerous. Anyone mentioning that Liza might have been groomed by Curtis as a drug mule risked the most severe punishment.

Most people are jailed and tortured so that they reveal the truth about criminals. Vishnu was jailed and tortured to silence him forever. He could now only give very slight and oblique references to what he knew.

I looked at Dennis helplessly, who gave me an encouraging nod, as if to say that I was doing quite well. So I ploughed on. But this time instead of the rape, I decided to focus on the drug trade.

'Does Curtis have a stake in Fernando's or the drug business – or both?'

Vishnu kept silent, but it felt like an affirmation. I was making progress, and many of my suspicions were not unfounded.

But Vishnu was an unreliable ally, as it was likely that, in public, he would deny everything he had told us, not only because of the risk of repercussions from the police, but because he, too, was dependent on Curtis and his father. They all had to live together in the same village. And everyone knew the consequences of talking too much and too frankly, even about a girl who had vanished and whom no one really wished to bring back.

'And what happened to her afterwards?'

'Don't know.'

He seemed to have decided that he had given us enough information. I couldn't press too hard; I didn't want to scare him away.

'Do you know where she could be?' I asked gently.

He shook his head.

'How well do you know Marian?'

He frowned and then shrugged.

'Do you really hold her responsible for getting you locked up? You know she says she did not go to the police.'

He looked away. But surprisingly, at this moment he didn't seem as angry with her as I had imagined he would be. He might have learnt, after coming out from jail, that she had been trapped into a fake drug charge and used for a variety of purposes.

She had been cheated and lied to, just as he had been. They were both victims, weren't they?

'Do you think she has also carried drugs for Fernando? Or Vinay Gupta?'

He said nothing. His aunt had alluded to the possibility of their involvement in the smuggling, but whether it actually happened would be difficult to prove.

'Did you want to save Liza from that life?'

He nodded, and a strange expression crossed his face. It was like a flash of sudden anger, and I was taken aback.

'I try but she no listen.'

The anger that I had been warned about strengthened his voice suddenly. The softness had been replaced by a furious and unsettling tone.

I felt Dennis look at me with concern. For a moment I was confused.

Was his oppressed demeanour a facade? Had he hurt Liza because she had betrayed him by allowing Vinay Gupta to seduce her? By taking too many drugs?

Had the police been right after all and Vishnu was involved in her disappearance?

I pushed these thoughts away, and tried to sound as conciliatory as possible.

'But she thanked you. Gave you that book.'

He shrugged. 'She change. Not good.'

He stood up and slung the rucksack he had come with over his shoulder. 'I go now.'

'Vishnu, Liza was . . . no, *is*,' I corrected myself quickly, '*is* your friend. Friends stick with each other in difficult times. Please don't abandon her. Don't give up on her. I want to find her and I think you can help me. Do stay for just a few more minutes.'

He shrugged, and when Dennis held out his hand, Vishnu reluctantly shook it, and sat down as though a compact had been made. I noticed he sat back with a little more ease. We were finally getting through to him, though I still didn't dare to ask him about the first video I had received from Amarjit with Curtis in it.

I carried on, feeling slightly less worried about my ruthless interrogation.

'Have you ever been on the *Tempest*?'

He remained silent, without looking at either of us.

'And Vinay Gupta, the minister? What do you think of him? He owns the place, doesn't he? And lots of shacks on the beach, too.'

He seemed to want to say something, but then changed his mind.

'What did you think of Vinay Gupta anyway? Was he too friendly with Liza?' I repeated the question again, though with a different emphasis.

'Don't know him well,' he said finally.

'But you've been on the *Tempest*?'

Again he wouldn't speak. I wondered about his reticence. Thus far he had tried to cooperate. Now he simply wouldn't say anything.

'Your aunt said you had met Vinay Gupta. That he came looking for you.'

Giving up, I decided that shock value might be better. 'Alright,' I said, 'I want to show you this video, and please don't run away this time.' I deliberately put a lighter note in my voice. I played just the opening sequences of Liza dancing along with the other boys.

He shifted uncomfortably, but Dennis patted his arm to reassure him. It seemed to help, because he sighed, and though he barely seemed to look at it – possibly it was one of the 'bad' things that he did not want to remember about Liza – or did he already know what it contained?

'Do you recognize the people in the video? Who are these other boys with Liza?'

He jumped up. Again without admitting anything.

'Do you know what happened here?'

'I go now.'

'Were you at this party?' I asked persistently.

Shaking his head, he went for the door.

Dennis leapt to his feet as well.

'At least tell us if you know what kind of phone this would have been shot on?' Dennis asked, trying to block his exit. But in a fiercely determined fashion Vishnu stood at the door with his back to us.

'Open the door. I go,' he said.

'Wait, Vishnu – when do we meet again?' I pleaded.

He left without saying a word.

Dennis looked at me, and I could feel the empathy flowing between us. Strange. I hadn't known him till two days ago and now I felt he understood only too well this terrible situation I found myself in.

'That was a gruelling session. We didn't learn anything about the phone, but I think you managed to get some information out of him. The problem is that he has to still live among the same people who ruined his life. He was obviously very fond of Liza. Can't even bear to look at her picture now.'

'All of us keep on using the past tense for Liza, you know. I'm worried about that. I don't know where this girl could possibly be.'

We decided to walk back to my hotel, so I could grab a change of clothes, and then I suggested that we call Marian one last time and find out if there were any further developments. Or if she would tell us about Vinay Gupta's ruthless seduction of her sister. I still hoped she might drop a hint.

As we passed the spot where Scarlett Keeling's body had been found one morning five years ago, I realized that it was a forlorn hope.

Chapter 12

Reaching my hotel, I immediately called Marian, but unlike her prompt response last time she didn't pick up her phone. I wondered if, ironically, she was in an astrology session. Though, of course, one might argue that it was very strange the stars hadn't revealed the truth to her about her sister.

By now it was nearly afternoon and while Dennis went for a swim, I remained in my room to make notes about what we had found out so far. A hazy picture of what could have happened was emerging, and I needed to clinch the final details.

My mind wandered to Liza's mother, and I was intrigued by how both she and Stanley had been written out of the story. I hadn't even thought of meeting Stanley, as I had assumed, from what Marian had told me, that he was completely detached from his younger daughter's life. Liza's mother was still in London, and apparently hadn't been told about her daughter's disappearance. A young girl had been missing for a whole year, without anyone, even her parents, being aware of where she could be. It all seemed to have been very meticulously planned.

And it had been Marian who had made sure no one found out about it, till she decided to go to the police. More and more curious.

I remembered that Marian had said that she had been advised by Amarjit to not tell her parents about it, and that she sent an occasional email to her mother so that she would not worry.

But now that there was no need to take Amarjit's wishes into account – he had withdrawn from the case – had Marian informed her mother? And had her father been told anything at all? After all, he lived in Goa and even if he didn't care, someone would have mentioned the case of his missing daughter to him by now, surely?

This silence was strange. Possibly she hadn't even told the High Commission.

Once the police had assured her Liza was safe, was this silence necessary at all, or was it also part of the bargain she had made? Or could there be still more to this case, something I still didn't know? Surely it was silly, after all that had happened, to just accept the police version that Liza was safe and would return in the near future.

I knew that if Durga disappeared like this I would be on a rampage, despite the fact that I'm not a very interfering or possessive mother. Or so I hoped.

Perhaps it was time I had another serious conversation with Marian, and asked her some more tough questions. Obviously I had let her off too easily the last time, distracted by the two men who had been following her, worrying for her safety.

At the very least I would try to persuade her that she must keep the pressure on the police and ask them to produce some hard evidence of Liza's safety.

I sent a message to Dennis telling him that I was going to walk around this beach and the next one, to try to find Marian, because she had again failed to respond to my calls or messages. Failing which, I would go down to the 'jungle' and try to talk to Stanley and get Marian's home address. She had promised to text it to me but she still hadn't done it and Amarjit hadn't replied to my email asking for it.

No doubt Dennis was still swimming and so he wouldn't see my message till later. Which was okay, as we had already agreed to meet for a late lunch at Yankee Doodle (the name never failed to make me smile). It was such an aberration on a beach on which the shacks mostly had Goan names.

I walked onto the beach, still preoccupied with Marian's contradictory behaviour and the impact it had had on Liza's life. Apart from the indifference she had faced from Marian and Stanley in Goa, she'd had other things to worry about: she was a young pretty girl, left more or less to her own devices, on a beach that was far from safe.

I thought of her being sexually assaulted by the boys, and then the rape, and her molestation by Vinay Gupta. It was strange that Marian seemed to have little idea about any of the incidents, and denied having even registered the case against Vishnu. According to Marian, her involvement only began after she and Liza had their drinks spiked at Fernando's.

I didn't know why I found it so difficult to be sympathetic towards her, but I wished she had shown some more spirit or interest in finding Liza, instead of telling me to back off (albeit politely). She claimed a connection with the police, which was how she got the latest information about Liza, but that too was a contradiction. She had been conned by one set of policemen, only to become romantically involved with the brother of another cop. It made no sense.

Even if I were being very kind towards her, she seemed dishonest and indifferent towards everything except her own survival and getting her passport back. I could not suppress my antipathy.

My questions for her had still not decreased, despite our fairly cordial lunch the other day. I wondered if she had any of the answers. Was the minister she had mentioned as being present the night Liza disappeared, Vinay Gupta? And was this latest clip taken at the party she had attended with Liza at Fernando's? And if this was the case, had she herself done the recording? After all, she wasn't in the video. While appearing to share information, was Marian actually concealing a lot from me?

With rising excitement I realized that I might have found the answer at last. Could Marian have been spying on her sister throughout. Did she want to get rid of her? Was that why she appeared so indifferent to Liza's fate? I called Marian again but she still did not pick up her phone, so I sent her another urgent message. She was back to her old ways.

I wondered if Marian or Stanley could give me Liza's email address and password. If we found some emails they might shed some light on her job offer and possibly her relationship with Vinay Gupta. I remembered that Marian had mentioned that Liza was intending to meet her future boss that evening at Fernando's, and perhaps get a job in a travel agency. Could that mysterious boss have been Vinay Gupta, who had multiple interests and businesses? The pieces were definitely falling into place.

While walking around the beach, I thought of other unsolved cases of young girls who had died in Goa, and hoped we would be able to find Liza alive, though the possibility looked more and more remote. But at least we would know what happened to her and perhaps ensure some penalty for those who had made her life hell, and exploited her so mercilessly.

At least in Delhi, thanks to the street protests by women's groups and relentless media pressure, the six men who had raped the 23-year-old woman in the bus had been arrested. Perhaps things were beginning to change.

But I also knew that the record of the Goa police in nabbing criminals was not exactly glowing.

I was reminded of the murder of a Russian girl who had been found on a train track leading to Mumbai a few years ago, with her throat cut and her arm hacked off. Strangely the police concluded that she had abandoned her friends on a whim on the night of her death, and boarded a train to Mumbai. And then she had fallen off while leaning out of the train to smoke a cigarette. When that theory was trashed in the media, it was suggested that she had actually committed suicide, and her throat was slit and arm cut off when she leapt from the train and somehow got under the wheels. Regardless of the fact that it would have required extreme and improbable gymnastic skills to have achieved that.

Like Liza, this girl was strong, healthy, robust. Making plans for the future. Not the kind of girl who wanted to come to Goa to die. But in Liza's case the mystery deepened further, because nothing had been found to prove whether she was alive or dead.

Despondent and increasingly pessimistic, I had walked the whole length of the beach; but Marian was nowhere to be seen. I stopped and asked a few people who might have known her as Astrologer Anne, but they said she hadn't been around all morning. Nor could they give me her address.

From a distance I saw Veeramma and her group with a couple of tourists.

I waved at her but gave them a wide berth. It was pointless asking someone who hated Marian with such ferocity. Even if Marian's story about Veeramma's involvement in trapping unsuspecting tourists was untrue, the animosity between them was obvious. I could do without any further complications in this case.

I called Marian again but now her phone was switched off. It was coming up to 1 o'clock and I was getting more and more irritated with her, thinking it was typical of her to behave so selfishly, and not answer or call back. Surely she would understand that there was something urgent I needed to discuss with her if I had called so many times.

Sighing with frustration, I walked down to the banyan tree where I had witnessed the hippie reunion, and where Stanley still 'hung out' after forty years. I wished Dennis was with me, because even though the 'jungle' looked harmless in the morning, I was still preoccupied with thoughts of so many young women being raped every day. Those who died were quickly forgotten, while their murderers roamed free – and those who lived were often ostracized by society.

Fortunately, I found the path through the jungle much more easily this morning, and it definitely was well trodden, large enough to accommodate scooters and motorcycles. However there were far fewer people around today, and just a couple of individuals emerged from the direction of the banyan tree. They waved at me as they passed, and I raised both hands with 'V' signs to radiate peace and love on earth, feeling a bit silly, trying to look like I belonged.

Around me the greenery seemed soft and friendly. And yet, from my research, I knew this particular stretch could be terribly dangerous. The 'accidental death' of another young couple had taken place somewhere around here, too. Media reports did reveal later that the boy had probably been killed by a lethal blow to his head, while the girl was sexually assaulted and then murdered. But the matter was quickly disposed of by the police, with the rather imaginative explanation that the couple had simply been 'struck by lightning'.

By now I had reached the banyan tree, but there was no sign of either Stanley or Marian. In fact, there was no one around at all. Not even a single groupie. The place was completely deserted and a morgue-like silence surrounded it.

The banyan tree, with its lovely long smooth pale-brown roots descending into the earth from ancient branches, looked like a dramatic sculpture against the morning sky, a strange architectural grid from which grew flags and posters bearing antinuclear and greening-the-earth slogans. Chinks of the sky shone through the thick foliage above, and even though it had been a hot afternoon, I could feel the damp cool of the undergrowth, thick and messy as it crept around my feet.

The circular cement platform around the tree was bare today, barring a little steel box and a hookah. No one seemed to have touched these for a while. The guitar was not to be seen, either – perhaps it was kept somewhere else. I had a feeling Stanley only came here for effect, and he probably lived in a proper flat somewhere. Stupidly, I remembered that Marian had mentioned that she had a home in this area. She had also said she would text me the address and call me over, while we had chatted in the coffee shop, but she never did. Foolish of me to have believed her.

The silence around me grew more dense.

It was no longer friendly or serene, and a shiver of fear ran through me. I wondered if it had been sensible to come here alone. The sound of the crickets and the birds seemed to get louder and louder.

I told myself to stop imagining things. After all, I knew that if I shouted out, somebody would wake up from a drug haze and stumble out of the jungle wondering at the noise. But even that thought didn't make me laugh.

I got onto the platform to see if there was anything which could give a clue to Stanley or Marian's whereabouts. But there were only the steel box, the hookah and the love-and-peace posters.

The breeze blew and the leaves rustled loudly, sounding like the swish of an expensive silk saree, and it reinforced my sense of loneliness. My footsteps were unnaturally loud, and as I walked around the tree and to a nearby little stream which ran through the jungle, each crunch of the fallen twigs under my feet reminded me of the words 'accidental death'. The boulders here would easily crush anyone's head. As a burial place it was perfect. This was one of the best spots in the area to get rid of an overenthusiastic and nosy social worker.

'Are you looking for someone?' The sudden question made me stop in my tracks.

I swung around quickly. For a moment the dark figure standing on the platform with the sun behind him looked like a madman, wearing loose pyjamas, his hands raised over his head. It looked like he had a knife in one hand. I almost screamed.

As I took a few steps backwards and stumbled into the stream behind me, the figure leapt down, and grabbed me. I gasped, ready to push him away, and found that it was Stanley, swaying and grinning.

He didn't seem murderous at all.

Even though I was still shaking with fright, he gave me an encouraging and friendly smile.

He was a bit the worse for wear, with his straggly red

beard and his thinning hair, tied in the ubiquitous pony-tail. The 'knife' in his hand turned out to be a bong used in these parts for smoking marijuana.

'Oh, thank God it's you,' I said, once I was steady on my feet, and my heart resumed its normal pace.

'Who did you expect, my darlin'?' he said in a familiar lilt. 'It's my patch. I grew this tree from a sapling. Been here as long as it has.'

I wondered if he was stoned already, and then, as he gave me a smile through nicotine-stained teeth, I realized that he was just joking. I tried to laugh, but it came out as a choked cough.

'I . . . was looking for you. And Marian.'

'I don't know where she is today. She's normally here quite early. Sometimes I go over to her place, but last night a friend called me over for some music. Man, what a night, what a blast.'

Looking at him I was, frankly, envious. Despite his time-worn appearance, he had managed to both simplify his life and remain an adolescent forever. While the rest of us were moving irrevocably towards certain death, he seemed to have discovered the secret of rebirth.

'I loved the music you played here,' I couldn't resist telling him. 'Made me feel so nostalgic. I was here for your anniversary celebration.'

'Oh man – wasn't that rocking, rocking? I hope you don't mind, I got to bathe, man.' He got up onto the platform and without the slightest embarrassment stripped in front of me and walked to the stream.

I was amused by his casual nudity. I had seen enough of the early nudists on the Goan beaches not to be surprised. Stanley had obviously stuck to his natural life-style through the years. His stubborn desire not to change was admirable.

'Tell me,' I asked gently, facing the other way so I wouldn't have to watch his ablutions, 'do you know where I could find Liza?'

'Wild child, wild child,' he said, while splashing water on himself. 'Haven't heard from her for a long, long time. Unlikely. Unlikely.'

I turned and looked at him, startled. He had rubbed himself clean with some sort of soap and now was vigorously towelling himself down with a well-used piece of cloth. He reminded me of the sanyasis who often trekked around the Himalayas, looking for spiritual succour, with little else than a loin cloth and a lota. Though, of course, in Stanley's case he was not exactly looking for a spiritual higher power, having already found his salvation at the end of a reefer, no doubt.

'So, where is she? Aren't you worried? She's your daughter.'

He shook water from his dreadlocks, hopped back onto the platform and slipped on his pyjamas again. Then, bending over the small steel box, he took out a sleeveless red t-shirt, mumbling to himself while pulling it on. It seemed he hadn't heard me.

'Good as new, good as new.' He had a disconcerting habit of repeating phrases every now and then. 'Looking good, good looking?'

'Oh, you're looking wonderful. The colour suits you,' I said, for lack of anything else to say. He shared an annoying habit with Marian of not quite being there.

Like father, like daughter, I thought.

'I'm *looking* for *Liza*,' I said abruptly and emphatically, barely controlling my irritation, realizing that if I didn't come to the point quickly the conversation could go on for ages.

'So am I,' he said surprisingly. 'I've been looking for her for a long time. She came and left, left and came. If you find her, do tell me. But don't tell anyone else. Because too many people are looking for her.'

'Which people?' I asked.

'Raman and Joseph, for instance. Or Joseph and Raman.'

'Who's that? I don't know them.'

'Oh, if you go onto the beach, you'll get to know everyone. Everyone . . .'

He only seemed to have heard the second half of my query.

'*Who* . . . are . . . *Raman* . . . and . . . *Joseph*?' I asked slowly.

'Hang around Fernando's. Ex-policemen. They work

for Gupta, you know, he owns the damn place – that fellow who's in parliament. I don't know why you guys have these fellows there. Bullshit parliament here. As bad as the British. Why did you choose such a bad system? Bloody capitalists, bloody bloodsuckers. Look at the UK, what's the point of living there?

'And look what this Indian government has done to Goa. It used to be so beautiful. Turned into a shithole. You know, man, when we came here it was so clean and beautiful. The sky was blue, the sea was blue and the beaches were white. Now the sea is grey, the sky is grey and the beach is grey. Man, sometimes you can't even see the fucking beach, it's so covered with plastic. And people. Lots and lots of people you don't need. You call this development? I call it bullshit.'

I sighed. I knew this outburst only too well, having heard it a million times from all kinds of people, including Indians.

He would now launch into a faux-Marxian tirade against the industrialists, and then about the class struggle, against war, nuclear power, and so on.

'Alright,' I cut in before he went any further, 'can you describe Raman and Joseph? Are they sort of tall and well-built? Always in trousers and shirts? Shoes? Slightly formally dressed?'

'That's them alright. Fucking wear that shit to the beach, you know. Haven't bought me a drink in their life.'

That was them. No drinks in their own hands either.

I wondered if I could risk showing him the party video, but hesitated, as he might get upset, seeing Vinay Gupta with Liza. What father, even one who was totally on his own trip, would remain calm and unemotional watching his daughter being manhandled by a central government minister?

On second thoughts, I decided to show him just the last frame, with the two men who I thought were Raman and Joseph. I didn't know why it was so important that I knew if these were the same men, but so far my instinct had been working well for me today.

I handed my phone to him with the frozen frame of the two men.

'Are these the two guys?' I almost said 'fucking guys'. His language was catching.

'Rotten photograph but it looks like them. You got to fucking change your photographer, man. He's terrible. Can barely see them. Hopefully he doesn't charge a lot of money,' he said chuckling, rolling a cigarette. 'You want a drag?'

It really was like being in the last century. I hadn't heard this style of speaking since I was in college. I shook my head firmly and took out my own cigarette; memories of the drug nightmare still stuck in my head. I had no idea what he was smoking, and even if it was just tobacco, I wasn't taking any chances.

Meanwhile, I located the photograph of Liza on my phone and handed it back to him.

'Great. And here I have Liza.'

He immediately looked up at me. A shrewd look crossed his face.

Then he blew out smoke, and his lips straightened into a grim line as he looked down at the phone in his hand.

'That's her alright. Where did you get this photograph?'

The chubby-faced Liza smiled into the camera, and at him.

I didn't know what to say, so I bluffed again.

'She sent it to me.'

'So how come she only sent you half?'

I looked at him, puzzled by his sudden observational skills. Was this laid-back and 'cool' attitude only a cover?

'How do you know it's only half?'

'Look at it closely. Don't you see that man's hand on her shoulder?'

I tried to zoom in as much as I could. And then I realized that with her tangled hair flowing down, I hadn't seen the hand at all. But now looking closely I could make out the shape of the dark fingers with a gold ring on one of them.

'Have you seen the whole photograph somewhere else?' I asked him.

He nodded.

'Who is he?'

'Someone you should know if you've met the other bastards you just showed me.' For just a moment I thought his voice was far too brittle for someone who claimed that he did not care.

'Vinay Gupta?' I asked.

'Shhhhh. These trees have may not have any bark, but they bite,' he smiled.

'Why didn't you stop her?' I said. 'He's old enough to be her father, but you're her real father.'

'Ever tried to argue with a 16-year-old? Man, I left that life long ago. I didn't even fucking remember she was my daughter till she turned up one day. Don't lecture me, ma'am.'

I could sympathize with his inability to force an adolescent into behaving in a socially acceptable fashion. I had lost too many debates with Durga over the years.

'Please don't call me "ma'am". My name is Simran.'

His eyes crinkled a little, and I found myself warming to him. Alright, he was a bit strange, but he seemed like an honest man.

We smoked silently for a while, and it was obvious that he was getting more and more relaxed, as he spread his legs out and leant against the tree trunk. I sat on the edge of the platform, not too far away from him. I waited for him to tell me the rest.

'She thought he was going to give her a job. He had an

Airline. A Travel Agency. A Casino. All in capital letters. So she thought she was going to go straight from Goa to Las Vegas. I told her I've seen this too often. It's not so simple.'

'So then why did she leave?'

'No idea. You ask her. If you can ask her. She gave you that photograph. Or ask the other half of the photograph. That may be better.'

He laughed again. His eyes twinkled. There was no remorse, no guilt. If he had deliberately forgotten his daughter, there was no way I could force him to remember her, or to even want her back.

'What about your stash? Did Liza know about it?' I don't why I asked – perhaps it all seemed connected to her disappearance.

Suddenly he started laughing so much that his eyes watered, and tears rolled down his cheeks.

'Stash, oh God, the stash. Fucking yes. She took it. She took it. You want some too? Everyone wants that stash. But it's g-o-n-e. Gone.'

He had become uncontrollable, speaking faster and louder.

'And where did she go?'

'She went back to London, of course.'

'When was that?'

'Oh – about a year ago.'

'And when did she come back?'

He shrugged.

'Did she come back?' I persisted.

'Maybe, maybe not.'

He seemed to have suddenly sobered up. The hysteria had gone.

'Would you like some lunch? I've got some friends waiting for me.'

Possibly feeling sorry for me and my unenviable quest for answers about Liza, he paused and added, 'The short answer is, no. I've been looking for her because everyone is looking for her. Then I heard that she hadn't gone to London, and she's still around. But she never came back. Shit happens.'

'You saw her last a year ago?' I was still grappling with that information.

'That's right.' He nodded peaceably, as though we were not discussing his daughter's life, but the weather.

'So then why is everyone looking for her now?'

'Ask those goons, Joseph and Raman. They're the big gremlins. They know everything. And I mean everything. They say she's back. She sent someone an email. Then Marian says someone saw her around. Something like that. Marian has been looking for her as well.'

'Not gremlins,' I said. 'I call them Tweedledum and Tweedledee.'

He laughed. 'Yes, that's so apt for them. Apt.'

'Do you have Liza's email?' I asked hopefully.

'Not much use for Internet here, is it?' he said grinning

275

and pointing to the banyan tree. 'Though I do get the occasional postcard. Snail-mail will do for me.'

'And Marian's address?' I asked. 'I've got a few questions to ask her.'

'Sure.' He took out a piece of paper from his pocket, scribbled on it and gave it to me.

As I took it, he held on to my hand. 'You know, I really like you. You seem so pure, so intense.'

He gave me what could be considered a very deep look. Perhaps a thousand years ago, when he had just arrived in Goa, I might have been taken in. When he still had all his hair and all his teeth.

I nodded. 'You're so pure too. As pure as Afghan opium.'

Stanley laughed. 'If you ever want to have fun, come to me, come to me.'

'I will.'

'Shall I escort you out of here?' he said, standing up a little unsteadily. The loose pyjamas barely clung on to his hips, and the t-shirt, which left his belly button bare, seemed to be a child's size. If he was any thinner nothing would have fitted him.

'I must share a secret with you,' he whispered, but there was no happy note in his voice. 'Perhaps there is magic in this place, because once you are here, you can never leave. The gremlins can trap you, you know.'

Pushing forward, battling the air, he walked ahead of

me. Carefully putting one foot ahead of the other, he appeared to be negotiating a path he had walked for forty years, as though he was doing it for the first time.

'Look out for the gremlins,' he said every now and then.

I followed closely behind, but my fear had disappeared.

Saying goodbye to Stanley, I realized it was almost 2 o'clock, and began to walk back to meet Dennis, so we could have our long-awaited lunch. I couldn't wait to discuss my encounter with Stanley him, and then rush off to Marian's home.

But halfway there, I checked my phone and found that I had a new message. Rushing along the beach, thinking it was from Marian, I opened it.

It was certainly Marian. But not the way I thought I would see her. Or the way I wanted to see her.

Chapter 13

I stood on the beach unable to move. Then I sat down on the sand and called Dennis, asking him to meet me at the rocks which divided the two beaches.

Because on my mobile phone was a shot of Marian falling onto those very rocks. It must have been late yesterday evening when it happened. After we had met for lunch.

And after I thought I had saved her from Raman and Joseph.

She was just a tiny figure in her trademark loose trousers, her long golden hair splayed against the evening sky as she tumbled down. It was too dark to tell if anyone had pushed her, but I knew it was her because the next shot showed her lying awkwardly, wedged amongst the rocks, dangerously near the water. She lay face down, her hair spread out, as the torchlight, possibly held by her assassin, flashed down on her. Blood streaked along the rocks and bloomed at the back of her head. She had probably been brutally hit and then thrown down. The scarf which she so often tied around her head drifted from the hand she had stretched out to break her fall.

Poor, confused, vague Marian. Another statistic to be added to the growing numbers of 'accidental deaths'.

I put my head in my hands, trying to get over the shock.

Then I realized that I must do something about this. I must get up and find her. If her body had not been discovered, she might be still lying there, pulled underwater, perhaps, by the waves that crashed roughly against the rocks.

It was odd that no one had found her so far.

Certainly Stanley had no idea about her accident.

Around me, no one seemed perturbed or spoke about any unusual happening. Everything seemed so weirdly normal. Was it really possible for someone to have been murdered close by, and for the world to simply carry on, uncaring?

There had been nothing in the national news this morning, or in the local Goan newspapers.

'Madam, you okay?' I looked up and saw Veeramma standing in front of me, looking curious. 'You want massage for headache?'

'No, no,' I said and pushed myself to my feet.

'You drugged?' She looked at me with a strange half-smile.

But I was so numb I couldn't even smile back.

'No, I'm okay.'

As she continued to gaze upon me solicitously, I decided to abandon my earlier resolve about not mentioning Marian to her. After all, there was little that these wandering vendors did not know, as they moved from beach to beach, gathering gossip. And this was someone Veeramma took an avid interest in.

'Have you seen Marian anywhere today?'

Other vendors like her were peacefully going about their work. Tourists were crowding the shacks for lunch, while others were being browned in the sun. The edges of the sea were dotted with adults and children splashing into the water, and making sandcastles. And deeper into the ocean I could spot jet-skies skimming along the surface, while speedboats lifted parasailers high into the sky. There was colour and energy everywhere. But there was little sense of a life extinguished.

Normally a death would have meant a higher police presence, cordons, questioning of the beach boys, shack owners, tourists and vendors. But there was no excitement of any kind anywhere. No visible fear or tension.

As soon as I asked the question, I thought I saw a look of triumph flash across Veeramma's face. It was gone so quickly I wondered if I had imagined it. My mind was already ravaged by hundreds of conspiracy theories, but I questioned whether this was why Veeramma was hovering around me? She wanted to enjoy the moment when I discovered that Marian was dead.

'No, madam. You meet her today?' she replied with a slight smile. It might have been her way of being nice to me, since I was obviously unwell, but even the smile appeared fake to me right now.

Something held me back from allowing her any sense of victory. Nothing would please her more than to know that the person whom she held responsible for her harassment was gone.

In this battle, Marian was the loser. Forever.

I struggled to keep my voice casual.

'Nothing urgent. We were to have lunch together. If you see her let me know.' It felt strange to say that, since I knew Marian was dead. Was I the only person on the beach who had learnt about this tragedy?

It was difficult to pretend that everything was fine, but I had to do it, till I reached those rocks and found out more about what had happened there.

This felt almost as bad as when I had been 'drugged', as Veeramma had put it. There was a surreal quality to everything, as I walked faster and faster to the other end of the beach.

Nearing the rocks, I found Dennis sitting outside a shack and drinking a beer, waiting for me. He waved and got up to give me a hug and a quick kiss when he saw me.

'What's happened? Thought you'd forgotten about our lunch!'

Then he saw my face and asked, 'Bad news?'

'I'm afraid so.'

I put my arms around him and hugged him tight. Silently he held me close, rubbing my back for comfort. I allowed myself just a moment or two to pretend everything was fine.

Then I forced myself to pull back and showed him the message.

He took a deep breath, blowing it out with full force. 'Jeeesus. Is this . . .'

He'd never met Marian. And now he never would.

I was overcome with remorse at being so irritated with her, when she was probably on the run and had been threatened – not just by the gremlins but by the police as well. I had thought she had got her passport and would escape – but Curtis or even Vinay Gupta might have decided that she was becoming a nuisance and it was best to dispatch her.

Who could have executed the actual order? Had Raman and Joseph got to her? It seemed the most obvious explanation. I remembered their confusion when they discovered that she had escaped from the hotel. Had they tracked her down after our meeting and bludgeoned her to death?

She had even told me how she had to stay on the run from those two men. Perhaps I should have at least warned her to take care. But because she said nothing, I had kept quiet too.

Could she have predicted her own fate? Did she have a premonition of what was going to happen to her? Was that why she had met me and told me her side of the story that day? And she had also explained about the bargain she had made.

Lost in thought I suddenly realized Dennis was still waiting for an answer.

I found myself shivering as I said,'Yes, it's Marian. Liza's sister. This probably happened just yesterday.' I gestured towards the rocks.

'Right here? That's odd, because no one has mentioned anything. Surely someone would have found her body.'

'Perhaps the water sucked her in, she might be still stuck somewhere. Let's go down and check.'

I knew I was hyperventilating and sounding high-pitched and hysterical, but I didn't care. Nor could I help it. I was overcome with grief that I hadn't tried to help Marian a little more. Though I didn't quite know what I could have done differently.

Dennis quickly paid the bill and we scrambled towards the rocks. Waves lashed across them and I remembered my own wasted attempt to cross here. The memory of almost falling into the sea swam back to me, and hanging on to Dennis, I peered into the water for any sign of Marian. I checked my phone again and again. The picture showed the same overhanging hill, the same type of vege-tation. The placement of the rocks seemed identical as well. But there was no body trapped anywhere. There was no blood, no sign of struggle. Nothing.

Marian's body had completely vanished. Had it been taken away swiftly by the police, early in the morning? Or by someone else? Or had it been dragged out by the tide? I knew the current could be very strong in this area. In which case, either she'd already have become fodder for fish – the fate Dennis had predicted for whoever challenged Gupta – or her body would be washed up a few days later.

Over the sound of the sea, I shouted out at some of the beach boys, who were idly fishing, to ask if they had seen anyone come this way yesterday.

'Lot of people come here,' one of them yelled back. 'Who you want?'

'A woman. Long blonde hair.'

He shook his head and carried on fishing.

Dennis suggested that we go to Marian's home. It was good that he was there to negotiate the way there, because I was still feeling like a criminal, castigating myself for doubting her.

After some hunting we found ourselves in front of a slightly rundown four-storey building. Most of the bright green paint was peeling off, revealing a shocking-pink undercoat. Like many house owners in Goa, this landlord had an interesting taste in colours.

Marian lived in the 'penthouse', as someone on the ground floor described it. It was a euphemism for a studio apartment right on the top floor. There were no immediate neighbours and she probably had a private terrace from which she had a fine sea view.

When we reached her flat it looked as though someone else had already entered unannounced. The door was slightly chipped and broken around the latch, and still ajar. Either the lock had been tampered with or it had always been like that, and she had left in too much of a hurry to lock it. Nervous about what we would find, we entered the flat cautiously.

There seemed nothing overtly suspicious or disturbed in the sitting room and open-plan kitchen at all. Everything was neatly and rather interestingly arranged. In fact we were confronted by a colourful mélange of textiles draped from the ceiling and around the windows. The sofas were in bright colours and the walls had hand-painted murals on them. The whole ambience was very Indian, just right for a fortune teller. No doubt she took appointments at home as well.

On the kitchen table I noticed that there were two glasses and a water bottle. It seemed someone had been visiting her. An empty sandwich-box with two plates lay in the sink.

In the bedroom, too, nothing looked disturbed, except that the computer chair was at some distance from the computer, as though someone had got up very fast, or been pulled up by force, and it had skidded away. The computer light was still blinking. When Marian left, or was taken away, there had been no time to shut it down. Or maybe it had been left on deliberately.

The cover of the bed had been pulled down and folded at the bottom of the bed. She obviously hadn't been able to spend the night in her own bed. Again, there was no sign of a struggle.

But there were two coffee cups on the computer table. One cup had spilt, and the coffee was still dripping slowly onto the floor.

Careful not to disturb anything, wrapping a handkerchief around my hand, I used the mouse to open the computer screen. To my relief and excitement, Marian's inbox opened up. I clicked on a few unopened messages, which turned out to be innocuous requests for astrology sessions and invitations for beach parties. They had all arrived in the last hour or so.

Curiously, all the emails prior to that had been opened, which meant someone had been here after Marian's death, and was here until one hour ago. It was one opened message in particular which astonished me, especially the attachment.

It was the same video that had been sent to me on my phone. And it had reached this inbox at just about the same time it had been sent to me. It was of Marian's body on those rocks.

Why had a picture of her body been sent to her computer? It seemed like a cruel joke, and it made no sense at all.

I noted down the sender, victoryatlast@gmail.com. It sounded like someone had wanted to see her dead.

While Dennis looked around the cupboards and the bathroom, checking to see if Marian had left any clue of her seemingly hasty departure, I decided to find out if I could track down Liza's email.

Thankfully, I didn't have to spend too long on it, as I found it was registered to this computer: lizakay@gmail. com. The password had been saved as well. Perhaps when Liza was here, she had also used this PC.

But to my shock, as it opened up, I found it was still an active account; the last email had been sent only yesterday.

Did that mean Liza really was somewhere around? That all the sightings of her had been real? That she had been coming to this flat and using the account? In that case, why had Marian pretended to us that she was missing? She would have known about her sister's visits, surely?

I called out to Dennis to help me go through the emails. I also needed a witness to note down what was on the computer. Fortunately, he had a memory stick with him, and we quickly downloaded whatever we could find that could be useful. We didn't know how long we had before someone came in. The best would be to copy whatever we could and study it later.

The last opened email said simply, '*Look out. We'll meet*

soon.' It too had been sent by 'victoryatlast'. It sounded as though Liza and this unknown person knew each other quite well.

Each of the emails sent from Liza's address was accompanied by the photograph of Liza smiling into the camera.

In the sent items I found the three videos of Liza that I had received so far, though my name did not feature in the list of people to whom the videos had been sent. Was it possible that they had been sent to me by someone else? Also, mine had arrived on my mobile phone, and the number had been withheld. Anyone who had received the emails could have been responsible for forwarding the videos to me.

I went through the list of others who had received the videos but found I knew only one of them personally, Amarjit. Apart from the Inspector General of Police in Goa, they had also been sent to Vinay Gupta and a few ministers in the government. As I opened them one by one I found that, unlike me, the others had also received written messages. All the videos had been sent to the same people.

Liza was not making an effort to hide the fact that she was back, and wanted to create a stir.

The first message, sent out just a few days before Amarjit had met me, was accompanied by the video of Liza dancing with Curtis and the other boys, after which we had feared she had been raped. The message said, *'Hello everyone. It's nice to be back.'*

The one where Liza was brutally raped on the beach simply said, '*Remember this?*'

And the video in which Liza was sitting on Vinay's lap said, '*Miss you, baby.*'

The close-up of Durga's tattooed arm was not in this list. So, obviously whoever had my number was solely responsible for sending that. Perhaps it was a private message, meant to scare me off, as it had been copied from my phone.

All of this appeared to point to the involvement of more than one person, and I couldn't discount the possibility that Liza and Marian had been working together. Though I still didn't know the identity of the person who had sent *me* the videos, I finally felt we were reaching the endgame. A pattern was emerging, and unless there was yet another twist to the story, I was sure we would soon be able to learn who had sent the videos and why.

As we quickly went through the list of sent items, we found that Liza's account had been dormant for about a year; it was only around two weeks ago that it had been activated again. The password had been changed at the same time.

One possibility was that someone was misusing this account. Perhaps Marian was playing a dangerous double game to get revenge for her sister's death? But then why would she wait a whole year before she started to do so?

Wouldn't it have been better to start the sting operation last year, when the evidence was fresh?

The timing made me wonder once again if perhaps – bizarre as it seemed – Liza was actually back. After all, there was no evidence to prove that she was dead.

Possibly she was in hiding till she had succeeded in exposing, or at least frightening, those who had assaulted her, and Marian had decided to protect her. Maybe she had hidden her in this very room? That could explain Marian's secrecy and her hurried exits; her confusion and her reluctance to give me her address or tell me the whole story; her desire to shake off Vinay Gupta's men.

Could it also mean that Liza had run away after the assaults on her, and then, with Marian's help, come back to nail the culprits?

I remembered that Curtis had said he hadn't seen her for at least a year. He had been very surprised when I had told him that Liza was back. My information would have alerted everyone concerned to keep a close watch on Marian. And on me.

But where had she got the videos from? She obviously couldn't have shot them herself. And they seemed very authentic.

Perplexed, we walked around the room, hunting for any further clues.

I unlocked the terrace door and had barely opened it when something hissed and leapt out at me. I screamed and ducked, only to find it was a fluffy white cat. No doubt she was more terrified than I was, having been left outside in the heat, without food or water. There was no sign of any feeding bowl. How long had she been locked out? She wasn't a stray and she ran swiftly towards the kitchen, obviously sure about knowing where she would find food and water.

Watching her pad imperiously through the apartment, I doubted that Marian would have deliberately locked her out so callously. It had to be whoever else had been here, and from what we had seen so far, that person had broken in, shut the cat out and then explored the 'penthouse'. There were no signs of a fight or a struggle anywhere, so possibly Marian was not here at that time. Was she already dead? Had the killers come here after they had got rid of the body?

Perhaps it was they who had hacked into her computer, drunk coffee and been startled to find that video of her murder on the computer. Assuming they did not film it themselves, they might have suspected that someone had seen them kill her.

Crucial parts of all the videos sent to me so far had been edited out. This one, I realized, was no different. The first part of the video, in which there would be information of how she had fallen onto the rocks, was missing. One thing which I rejected outright was that somehow Marian had tripped and died.

Whoever entered this room and left just one hour ago were either the assailants themselves or they now had an idea who her assailant was. Something in the video had startled them, spilling coffee as they rushed out.

Or it was someone unconnected with the killing, who had found the video on the computer and then gone to check, as we had, whether her body was still stuck on the rocks.

Either way, the person or persons had left in a hurry. And it was likely they would be back quite soon.

Which meant that we had better leave. But there were still a few things we needed to do.

Hearing my shout, Dennis had rushed out to the terrace to put an arm around me (as he was beginning to do quite frequently) and I must say at that point it felt good to have someone with me. Now both of us stood in the kitchen, discussing all these possibilities.

After taking some milk out of the fridge and pouring it into a saucer for the cat, I thought hard about Marian. She was becoming a bigger mystery to me than Liza. Was she really Liza's sister?

'Let's see if we can find that passport of hers. She said the police had just returned it,' I said, determined to check everything. This was no time to break down or become emotional. But it was very difficult for me, as I kept thinking of how mistaken I had been about Marian and whether I was misjudging her again.

'Let's also see if we can find anything connected with Liza, in case she actually came back and hid out here for a while. But we must be quick, because I have a feeling that whoever was here earlier will soon be back,' I added.

We did a quick search through the cupboards, under the bed, inside the set of drawers. For the passport, photographs, for anything connected to her past or her identity. But Marian – or her killers – or Liza, had left no documents behind. Not a single photograph or piece of paper. So perhaps we would never know the truth about the two girls and how and why they had disappeared. This was worse than I had imagined.

The thought had barely crossed my mind, and Dennis had just slipped the memory stick into his pocket, when there was a sound at the door.

Both Dennis and I became rigid with tension. We quickly went into the sitting room, just as the front door creaked open. For once in my life I wished I had a gun. My instinct was to run, as the people who had been here previously, especially if they had eliminated Marian, were not going to be kind or understanding towards us.

Helplessly, we watched the door creak open.

And I sighed, giddy with relief.

It was Stanley. It was the second time in a single day that his appearance had startled me.

Seeing me in the room with Dennis, his sleepy eyes

opened wide with surprise. But then he grinned with his now-familiar insouciance.

'Hi – it's you again,' he said cheerfully. 'Come to meet Marian?'

I didn't know what to say to him, as he stood there smiling, swaying on his feet in his tiny red t-shirt and loose pyjamas. I couldn't even remember the morning clearly, so much had happened since then. It seemed like I had met him many years ago.

It was obvious he still knew nothing about his older daughter's murder.

I felt a surge of sorrow for him, because I knew that he and Marian had, in many ways, considered each other kindred spirits. I doubted if he would be able to accept Marian's death with the same ease as he had accepted Liza's disappearance. I remembered Marian under that giant banyan tree with him, barely a few days back, kissing him, obviously proud of the father who had decided to follow his own path in life, however unconventional it might be.

This was the most tragic anniversary celebration he could have imagined.

On the other hand, I did not know if it was safe to ask him if he knew that Liza's email address was still being used. It, however, was not clinching evidence; it might only mean that someone wanted to give the impression that she was alive.

Even as I puzzled over what to say, while Dennis stood silently by my side, I heard footsteps on the staircase outside, and the door swung open again. All three of us turned to look at the door, and once again my throat constricted with fear.

And that fear, this time, was completely justified.

Walking in now was the duo who had probably stalked Marian to her death. The two tall mystery men who had a habit of appearing at awkward moments. The gremlins. Tweedledum and Tweedledee.

Raman and Joseph.

Their look of annoyance was probably matched only by my look of utter contempt. Theirs could not be a friendly visit, as now I was quite sure it was they who had been here before and left in such a rush. While I wasn't completely sure if they were the killers, I realized that, even if they were willing to let us go, Dennis and I could not leave them alone with Stanley. Having arranged the vanishing of his daughters, they might now want to attack this harmless man.

How would he react when he found out what they had done? Would there be an altercation? I was sure the two men must be carrying guns, as they had the annoying swagger of self-righteousness. What gave them the authority to break into a woman's home, possibly murder her, and still look smug?

But I decided to keep my tone as light-hearted as that of Stanley.

We had to pretend that we knew nothing, that ours was an innocent visit – and then we had to exit fast, hopefully along with Stanley.

'We dropped in to see her, actually,' I told Stanley. 'But the bad news is that she's not here.' I injected a carefree tone into my voice, and waved a hand towards the two men, who, after being taken aback by our presence, had dismissed us with a glance and were now rather rapidly looking around the room.

'I don't think we've met,' I said to them. I couldn't help adding, 'But I think I saw you at the hotel yesterday.' Then I glanced hopefully at Stanley, who understood the cue.

'This young lady says she doesn't know who you are. Simran, please meet Mr Raman and Mr Joseph, Mr Vinay Gupta's right-hand men. And left-hand men,' Stanley said smoothly, as though he were having a laugh. I shot him a quick look, wondering if he were quite as naive as he appeared to be. I also noticed that he no longer looked like he was flying without wings.

'Great to meet you.' I shook their hands, trying to appear enthusiastic. I hoped they did not remember my triumphant expression as I had passed them by in the hotel lobby after Marian had escaped to the beach. Again, it could have all happened a century ago, and I regretted feeling so exultant. It was always a mistake to taunt men who closely resembled the bouncers in the casino.

Their faces were expressionless once more. Perhaps they could even kill someone while maintaining that aloof demeanour. I thought of Liza's cold-blooded rape on the beach by two men whose faces were obscured. Was it them?

It could certainly be part of their job description.

I now had to give them a reason for our presence here. But I knew I couldn't mention Liza. That would be like showing a red rag to a pair of bulls.

'Have you seen Marian?' I asked them, as innocently as I could, thinking rapidly of an important enough reason for our wanting to meet her. 'Dennis and I plan to get married, so I thought we could get an auspicious date from her.'

I hoped it sounded plausible, and I tried not to look at Dennis as I said it.

I could feel him shooting me a very quizzical look, but he fell into line with the practised ease of a seasoned actor.

'And also,' he added, 'to find out whether we should do both – a Hindu wedding and a Christian one. She told us to come today. We must know if the stars agree with us, since we have fallen madly in love.'

He sounded crazy about me alright, as he gave me a besotted look and reached out to press my hand.

If I hadn't been so tense, and upset both about Marian and Liza, I would have burst out laughing.

Stanley shrugged. 'I already told Simran this morning that I haven't seen her since last night.'

Raman and Joseph shook their heads.

'The boss received a message which was a little worrying; he wants to meet her, too, so we came here,' said Raman, looking anything but worried.

Did the message Vinay Gupta received include the last video? Were they trying to cover their tracks, hinting that someone else had killed Marian?

Stanley put up his hands. 'I wish I could help you, but without Internet or a phone, you know I have no idea about messages or anything like that. Usually we meet every morning. I wanted to know why she didn't show up today—'

But he wasn't allowed to complete his sentence. It seemed that the two men did not want Stanley to speak freely in front of us. Though he had indicated to me earlier in the day that he found them ridiculous, the reality was that no one could mess with Vinay Gupta or his men.

'Stanley, as you know, we must check the apartment. Orders from the boss,' Joseph interjected – pointing firmly towards the bedroom.

They were like Siamese twins – all their actions were synchronized, as though they had been programmed beforehand.

Looking at them carefully, I said, 'We found Marian's cat locked outside. The poor thing was hot and hungry. We just gave her some milk. Please don't shut her out.' I almost added 'again'.

298

But there was no change in their expression – they nodded and gazed impassively back at us. One of them started walking towards the bedroom. There was no thought of waiting for permission from Marian's father. In fact they gestured that he should follow them.

I realized that we couldn't really help Stanley, as he would have to stay here till they found out all they needed. I wondered if they would show him the video and what would happen if they did so.

Reluctantly, I decied to leave. I needed to find out more about Marian's death and I had a few ideas who might have been involved in it. But it would be best to execute my plan while the two men were still busy in Marian's home. I didn't want them to find out about whom I planned to meet, as it could get very dangerous for all of us.

'Oh well,' I said. 'We better go. I'd be grateful if you could tell Marian we are looking for her desperately. We really need to see her to sort out our wedding plans.'

There was safety in seeming blissfully ignorant.

Getting into a taxi and speeding back to my hotel, I couldn't help worrying about Stanley. Knowing of my concern for his safety, Dennis had another brilliant idea. He seemed to be on good form today.

'I'm going to call up some of those flower children you saw the other day at Stanley's celebration and tell them the Afghan stash has been found in Marian's apartment,' said Dennis, giving me a wicked wink. 'Believe me, it will start a riot and those two guys will have to leave really fast, unless they want to get stoned. Literally. These former hippies are very dedicated to the finding of a good stash, and if we say Stanley wants everyone to share it, they will go berserk. Not even guns will deter them. So the – what did you call them? – gremlins will have to parachute out and their boss will hate them for it.'

Dennis almost chortled as he said that. Gradually I began to feel better.

He made a quick phone call to two of the best known 'Goa Freaks', Jimmy and Diane, now running a respectable restaurant in a village close by, and told them about the 'exciting' discovery, finally, of Stanley's legendary stash comprising large quantities of opium and marijuana. He said Stanley was eagerly waiting to share it with all his wonderful friends.

As Stanley expected, they were thrilled and said they would immediately spread the word and head to Marian's flat. Their excitement at recreating the old times when they used to be together for days, shooting heroin and sharing bongs, was palpable.

I watched Dennis with amazement, smiling at the sheer impudence of his plan. Marian's flat overrun with ageing white flower children scouring the apartment as they hunted for the stash would scare the gremlins out of their complacency.

'Fantastic news! The golden stash has been found! Pure Afghan! Bring out the bongs!' I could hear them sound the war cry. I finally allowed myself to laugh over what would happen to those two men in their perfectly creased trousers when a bunch of ancient hairy hippies and their dreamy women arrived at the apartment. At least Stanley would be safe in all that confusion.

And then I focused on getting in touch with that one person who could help me find out more about Liza's recent reappearance and those videos.

Finally, after a lot of introspection, and very hesitantly, I sent Vicky a message. It was a huge risk: after her behaviour at the casino, she might well betray my confidence. But I had little choice.

'*Please help. Marian has been in a serious accident, has disappeared. We really need to talk about Liza. Thanks, Simran.*'

I kept my fingers crossed that she would respond quickly, banking on her still being somewhere in the area.

And luckily she got back to me almost straight away: '*Will meet in half an hour, but I'll come to your hotel. Send me the details. Meet in the room, we must not be seen together. Please delete this message.*'

Dennis and I took a cab back to the hotel, and suddenly realized that we were both terrifically hungry. We had forgotten about lunch completely, and ordered a quick fish and chips, along with a large bottle of chilled beer.

I lit a cigarette as I sat down to absorb the events of the day. So much had happened so quickly since my morning meeting with Stanley. In just a few hours everything was topsy-turvy. Now that the adrenalin was no longer pumping through me, I felt seriously depressed over the fact that Marian was dead, and we were no closer to finding Liza, even though we had a lot of information on the possible criminal activity behind the disappearance of the two girls.

'I still don't understand why Amarjit dragged you into this,' said Dennis. 'They had all the evidence, all the videos, so why didn't they take any action? By now Vinay Gupta and those gremlins would be behind bars.'

'Don't you see, there is nothing anyone can actually accuse Vinay Gupta of. He is seen only in one video with Liza, and even though that is quite incriminating, he could claim that it was faked. Or that Liza had told him she was eighteen years old. Or that she was a prostitute. That happens often enough, and usually the men get away with it. This story needs to be pieced together and only an eyewitness can do that. These videos have shown us the way, and are crucial, but Liza is seen to have been raped for certain, only by those unidentified men. We must be very careful to get some real results.'

I took another drag of the cigarette, and got up to pace about.

'Besides, I have dealt with enough cases to know that, even when it is easy to join the dots, the moment there is a powerful politician involved, no one will lift a finger. This guy is well-connected and that's why Amarjit wanted to bypass the local police and call me in. These two men, Raman and Joseph, had been keeping an eye on Marian and she was on the run from them. I think they have also been stalking me, right from the moment Amarjit met me in Goa. They knew something was up, and their job probably is to prevent any dirt surfacing about their boss. They have to wipe out all traces of his connection with Liza, and when Marian seemed to getting out of hand – she escaped from the hotel yesterday, while they were waiting in the lobby – they most likely got nervous and eliminated her too. This morning was just an act, pretending that they had come in, just as we had, and that they merely wanted to look around. They might have wanted to wipe out any evidence of the murder, as well as checking if there was anything more to link their boss with the girls. It was just their bad luck that we were there, and so was Stanley. And by now of course, the apartment will be swarming with happy hippies.'

'Or not-so-happy ones,' interjected Dennis with a smile. 'Once they find out that there was no stash after all. But at least the gremlins won't be able to do anything to Stanley while those guys are there.'

I tried to smile too, and then went back to contemplating the case.

'Basically, it's quite clear that Gupta panicked once the videos were sent out. And then I turned up and started asking questions about Liza, everyone had forgotten about her. Gupta had probably stopped the local police from investigating Liza's disappearance for a whole year. Amarjit inadvertently started the ball rolling once these videos surfaced by asking me to step in.'

'So where do you think these videos came from? And why?' Dennis asked thoughtfully.

'I still don't know who shot them and actually sent them out. But obviously someone wants us to know, or at least think, that Liza is alive because the videos were sent from her account. If you keep putting out rumours that someone has been sighted, no one will really believe that person is dead. Most would believe that she's run away. So let's imagine the following scenario: these guys molest and intimidate Liza. She vanishes, or runs away. Then one day, she decides to come back and take revenge. And so she sends out the videos. Some of them contain incriminating or lewd shots of a senior minister. Someone in the government then gets worried and asks Amarjit to find out quietly if the girl is still alive and what has happened to her. Equally quickly, Vinay Gupta arrives in Goa to squash any inquiries. So they threaten Marian, but she doesn't give up. Then they tell her that her passport will be returned to her only if she calls off the inquiry. She falls for it, but then for some reason they panic and kill her too.

'So these are the things we still don't know: Firstly, where is Liza? Her email is being used but we still don't know if someone is just using her identity to send out those videos, or if she is really alive. Secondly, why did Marian have to die, and did the murderers take away her body? Or was it simply washed out to sea? And who killed her? Thirdly, who made these videos and why are they surfacing after a year? Except for Marian's video, which was obviously made just yesterday.'

'Unless . . . unless,' Dennis said slowly, 'they are all fake. They have been filmed with actors, by someone who wanted to let everyone know what had happened. Someone who had seen everything. And is telling us the whole story, through these videos.'

'But after a whole year? And let's not forget that some of the videos have real people in them, not actors. I have actually met Curtis D'Silva and Vicky, and we know that Vinay Gupta was in another one. As were the gremlins. No, I don't buy that. Someone had these videos for a whole year and has brought them out now. That's the important part. The clue lies in the timing.'

'But I still don't see why they couldn't get even the central bureau to investigate.'

'With a minister involved, the investigation has to be personal and discreet, which is why Amarjit was thrilled that I was here at the right time. Someone at central-government level obviously wants to make sure that Vinay Gupta is not seen to be involved in Liza's disappearance. As Amarjit told me at the start, in Scarlett Keeling's case the suspicion that politicians were involved made it all much more murky, and it affected the image of Goa. I know they should investigate this more carefully, because of the human tragedy involved, but in a high-profile case like this there are many other factors . . .

'One could be Gupta's own importance in the government. Gupta is crucial, since his party is one of the coalition partners of the government. If he gets done for rape or murder it could affect the stability of the government; after all, according to the latest reports he is headed to become the Home Minister. It's a very crucial post. He must know the secrets of every politician, and it will be dangerous if he has some skeletons in his own cupboard. He would then be open to blackmail. It is important to remove all evidence of possible transgressions. That would mean the removal of Liza and now Marian.'

Just as I lit another cigarette, there was a diffident knock at the door, and I quickly opened it, so Vicky could slip in. She walked in with a perfunctory nod, her body stiff with tension.

She removed her dark glasses and then stared at Dennis.

'You're here too?' She remembered him from our fracas aboard the *Tempest*.

'Don't worry. He's my boyfriend and everything you tell us will be in complete confidence.' I tried to sound as gentle as I could. I needed her trust.

Dennis pretended to look a little disappointed at my words. Since I had announced our marriage in the morning, he no doubt wanted to retain his superior status as my fiancé, not just boyfriend. He gave me a rueful look, as Vicky put her handbag on the bed and settled down.

I couldn't help feeling a little guilty about what would happen next.

Vicky didn't know that my laptop camera had been turned on, and everything she said would be recorded. This could be a crucial meeting, and I would need every bit of evidence to prove what had happened to both Liza and Marian.

'I have bad news.' I came straight to the point, because I thought it was best to unsettle Vicky first.

I took out my phone and played the video of Marian lying on the rocks. Her crumpled body and head wound did not make pleasant viewing at all.

Not surprisingly, Vicky lost her composure and turned visibly pale.

'Is she . . . is she . . . dead?'

'None of us know, because the body hasn't been found

307

as yet. We went to check and she seems to have disappeared. Just like Liza.'

Vicky closed her eyes in obvious distress. Perhaps this was what she feared the most.

'Do you think Vinay Gupta or his henchmen might be involved?' I asked her gently.

'Perhaps in Liza's case . . . I've suspected some involvement, but Marian's murder – I'm not sure . . .' She stumbled over her words, obviously wondering how far she should go. There was little doubt that Vinay Gupta would let loose not just the gremlins, but the hounds of hell on her if she stepped out of line.

I felt really sorry for her. This was a life from which there was no escape. Once she became Vinay Gupta's mistress and confidante that was what she would remain. All her future promotions – her whole life – revolved around him, while he maintained his image as a family man with a plump wife and three children. As a politician of prime importance. A minister.

It did not matter that Vicky was the same age as one of his daughters. Or that she went on holidays with him pretending to be his wife. Ultimately none of that mattered.

She would also have to endure all the other women who would come and go from his life.

And sometimes they wouldn't go at all.

Had Liza been one of them? A blonde, beautiful British

girl, who made no demands – unlike Vicky, with her insecurities and her parents who wanted her to remain a nice middle-class girl and marry a nice middle-class man. Perhaps Gupta had other plans for her.

Chapter 14

As the evening wore on it became clear that it had been extremely brave of Vicky to meet us. But it was obvious that she was still very frightened, though she covered it up commendably, as she told us how Liza had got involved with Curtis and Vinay Gupta.

According to her, Vinay Gupta had spotted Liza with Curtis sometime early last year and told her that he would make sure she got a nice, well-paid job. Even though she was far too young, and unqualified, she was ambitious enough to agree. Everyone around her could see the trap clearly, and Vicky said she felt sorry for the girl, but Liza genuinely seemed to believe that her future lay with Vinay Gupta. I remembered Stanley sighing as he told me how Liza wanted to go straight from Goa to Las Vegas. Somewhere along the line, to satisfy Liza's big dreams, Gupta assured her that she would travel and see the world if she worked as his employee.

Vishnu had been angry about Liza's quick seduction.

Vicky seemed to have no such emotions.

Perhaps she had become inured to such behaviour – no doubt he had managed to similarly ensnare many other women and girls.

'Vinayji is very good at spotting girls who are eager to move ahead. Usually, like me, they come from middle-class or lower-income backgrounds, so that when he gives us these fat salaries, we fall for it. And that's the trap. Once you get used to this lifestyle it is difficult to get into any other work. He buys you gifts, takes you on holidays. The perks are amazing. But of course, you have to stay on his right side, and you can't refuse him anything.'

'Does that mean sexual favours, as well?' I asked. I had tried to frame the question in a less aggressive way, but then there seemed no other way to put it.

She shot a look at Dennis, wondering how much to reveal. But her hesitation told us the whole story.

'He . . . doesn't force anyone to do anything they don't want to,' she said finally.

I was impressed at how she still tried to protect Vinay Gupta. This girl was a survivor, and even though she was trying to tell us what had happened with Liza, she was unable to forget that Gupta had paid for everything that made her who she was today. And her training and middle-class values prevented her from referring to him by any other name than the respectful 'Vinayji'.

Given that burden of gratitude and values it was extraordinary that she was before us today trying to explain Vinay Gupta's history of sexual abuse.

There was a brief silence and then I said, 'Please, carry on. Did she actually do any kind of work for him?'

'Oh, she was very keen to start work. But Vinayji felt she was still too young to do anything with real responsibility, and so he instructed his shack managers to just let her have a good time and enjoy herself for a while. Slowly we saw her change. It's like a bonanza when these kids get everything free. Free food, free booze and free drugs. As much as they want. The idea is to give them so much they will keep coming back for more and more and more. And soon nothing is ever enough.'

I could finally sense the resentment in her voice. After all, Vicky might have a special place in Vinayji's affections, but she still had to work for a living. In that case, it was hardly likely that she would want Liza around.

'Was it you who introduced her to Vinay Gupta?' I cut in swiftly.

'Not directly. I had met her on the beach and we chatted about the casino. She was very keen to take part in Curtis D'Silva's show, as a dancer, since she was too young to be a croupier. She and Curtis had planned a performance together. They would practise every evening before the casino opened.'

'On the ship?'

She nodded. 'That's how Vinayji first saw her. In a video, I was told. I never saw it, but it was something he looked at, and then he wanted to meet her.'

I looked for the video of Liza dancing with Curtis on

my phone, and played a few seconds of it for Vicky, putting it on pause before Curtis untied her halter-neck top.

'Could this be it?'

Now, knowing what we did about Liza, I felt even more sorry for her; she had probably been in a drug-daze at the time the video was shot.

How could I have not realized that the round window behind her was a ship's porthole? So this shot was aboard the *Tempest*.

Vicky watched the video expressionlessly. It occurred to me that she had seen far too many of these videos already. As a 'manager' for Vinay Gupta, there was little she did not know.

'I think there is a longer version somewhere around. Sometimes they made them for their own records, to keep track of their dance numbers. Where did you get it from?' she asked.

'That's the strange part. It seems that Liza is back and she is sending these videos out to everyone.'

Vicky looked incredulous. And more disturbed than I had seen her look all afternoon.

'That's simply not possible.'

'Why not? She's been seen around – Marian told me that a few times. And in fact that's how I got involved in the case. I was asked to come in to find out if she was back, make discreet inquiries. I think someone is very afraid that she will talk and the truth will come out about her and Vinayji.'

Vicky was still frowning in puzzlement, but nodded slowly at my words.

'He would be worried about that, for sure. If she came back. She certainly knew a lot about him, as he let her hang around all the time. I know that they spent a lot of time together, even though she was much younger. I guess he liked that,' she said finally.

'What specifically did she get to know? And was that information in any way dangerous for him – and for her?'

Vicky became even more sombre, but slightly evasive. 'Before I say anything more, there is something you need to know. The only reason I'm speaking to you is because, after this incident with Marian, I feel I've had enough. But like Liza, because I'm too close to Vinayji, I know too much, and that means I can never, ever get away. I've tried to quit many times, but I am always forced into returning, because he says he needs me. For people like me, like Liza, there can only be one way to escape. You know what I mean. Because he will hunt me down.'

She seemed harassed and anxious, much older than her years, her hands clasped nervously.

'I can't take this any more. Please, you know so many people in the government – can't you help me somehow? Help me get out. Promise me you will.'

So that was why she was here. She wanted some kind of protection.

I took out a cigarette and passed her one as well. Dennis leant over to light it for her. I got up to smoke, standing by the window. On the table nearby was my bottle of whisky and I poured us each a shot. Vicky took it gratefully and drank it in one long swallow. It obviously helped, as she closed her eyes and then opened them again to hand me the glass for a refill.

'The problem is that in this whole place, nothing is what it should be. When I came here I was even more innocent than Liza, and look at me today.' She stood in front of the mirror, and turned and twisted as though we were not there. 'Look at this skirt, this blouse, this jacket. This uniform. I hate it all. I just want to leave. Please, please, surely you can do something.'

That hunted look I had seen on her face had come back. Under the veneer of modernity and toughness she had remained a small-town girl. But now, when she wanted to return to her previous self, she found that the doors of that nice middle-class existence were closed to her. Sadly, the glamorous life she had chosen offered little security. And no love.

As soon as I poured the whisky, she took the glass from me and drank it quickly. I knew exactly what she was doing because I had been there myself. When one is staring into an abyss there is nothing like alcohol to help you jump over it. Or into it.

'Look, I'll do everything I can to help. But in return you have to tell us exactly what happened with Liza,' I said, trying to gently remind her why she was here.

'Precisely what happens to so many of the nice girls who fall into Vinayji's path. The Indian girls become managers, but the foreign ones are much more useful.'

'Because of their passports?' Dennis and I were beginning to understand where this was leading. I remembered Auntie Elizabeth's little lecture.

'So they could be used as drug mules?' I asked, at last reaching the subject which had worried me from the start.

Vicky nodded.

'That's right. It means they can come and go with impunity, and so those who agree are persuaded to carry drugs. The younger the better. Few people would suspect a schoolgirl. The anti-narcotics squad is usually on the lookout for older men and women.'

'But,' Dennis interrupted, trying not to sound shocked, 'how can a minister encourage drug smuggling? It would be very obvious, wouldn't it, because he is a public figure?'

Vicky stubbed out her cigarette.

'Vinayji doesn't do this. Drugs are usually handled by Fernando, so that if a girl gets caught the stench doesn't go all the way up. It's all very subtle and organized with careful brainwashing. Very few of the girls – sometimes boys, too – really know what's happening to them. They

316

change very quickly, especially if they get addicted to the drugs and the lifestyle.'

She paused to light another cigarette.

'Once upon a time, Goa was the place for drug consumption. Now it's become a big transit hub for sending drugs to other places, as well. Once Vinayji spotted and groomed Liza, it would have been difficult for her to escape. All his managers were given orders to give her anything she liked, free of cost. Even cash, if she wanted it. I was told to help her buy clothes if she needed them. She could come and go as she pleased. She was special. Curtis was told to keep an eye on her, soften her up.

'I tried to warn her but she wouldn't listen. Obviously if she was stoned all the time, these boys would take advantage of her. So one evening there was an incident when Curtis and some of the boys tried to have sex with her. Another boy, a local fellow who repairs computers and mobile phones, Vishnu, was very fond of her and he got into a fight with Curtis trying to protect her. The police took Vishnu away, which was terrible. But Curtis has a lot of clout.'

I nodded. 'I know he's the local MLA's son. And that's the reason the grotto got built, as a form of thanksgiving for a very macabre reason, I think. Because Curtis didn't go to jail for molestation, Vishnu did. And yet ... you seem quite fond of Curtis.'

Her face flushed, with either anger or embarrassment,

317

it was difficult to tell. I reminded myself that she was a young girl, after all. She said nothing. I poured us all some more whisky. This was a difficult story both to narrate and to hear.

'So was Vishnu in jail for a while?' Dennis asked. His intense tone would have amused me were I not so engrossed in the story myself.

'The first time, I think he was just kept overnight to teach him a lesson. But then something else happened – no one knows what – and they locked him up for nearly a year. He's actually very bright, you know – excellent with phones, computers. I used him in the casino as well – but this harassment by the police has made him very bitter. He's become a bit of a recluse. He doesn't come to the *Tempest* any more, says he hates it.'

'Did he blame Liza or Marian for what happened to him?'

'He got angry with all of us, every now and then. But he still came for the parties. He was the kid who's always around. He had a fixation for Liza, which was quite obvious, and then I remember that he once got very annoyed with Marian because she complained about this obsession of his. But he rarely said anything to Curtis. After all, he'd grown up with Curtis, and even if Curtis bullied him or beat him up, he always did whatever he wanted him to do.'

She paused.

'And then of course, one night . . . I don't quite know

what happened, Liza just vanished. She had been at a party earlier in the evening.'

The sequence of events was becoming clearer.

I showed her the video of the party and her expression changed to one of distinct anger when she saw Vinay Gupta with Liza on his lap. She had not forgotten that.

But when she spoke her voice was cool and unruffled. I had no doubt that Vicky was a very intelligent girl indeed, and if she could ever escape Vinay Gupta, I realized, she would go far. 'This might be the same night that she disappeared. There is an enclosure upstairs at Fernando's. Like at the casino, he has a VIP enclosure and he often takes his friends there, sometimes Bollywood stars, sometimes even politicians. It has a private entrance so no one sees them coming and going.'

I realized that I had not even noticed this inner sanctum when I had gone to Fernando's, it was so well hidden from public view.

'Marian says they were given drinks which were spiked, and that she has no memory of what happened after that. But that, as you said, Liza walked out of the shack and disappeared.'

Vicky sighed and said, 'Anything is possible on the beach, especially if it's late at night, or early in the morning. It depends on whom she met and what she saw. But I personally suspect whatever happened to her was probably an accident and they had to get rid of her after that.'

Her last sentence was ominous. Accident? No one had mentioned that so far. And why get rid of her? That implied that she had been killed.

I felt it like a body blow. So far I had kept hoping that Liza – against all odds – was still alive; especially after I had seen the emails sent under her name. Feeling a little sick, I stared out of the window. The sea was as calm as ever. I could see the bright orange sun diving slowly into the water. The pink-tinged clouds formed a perfect back-drop. None of it seemed real.

Just as in this story, nothing was as it seemed.

As she said the last few words, her voice slowed and became much softer. It was almost a whisper. *It was an accident and they had to get rid of her.*

'But she's back.' Dennis spoke a little hesitatingly.

Vicky got up and started gathering her things.

'I don't know anything about that. I think I'd better leave. I've told you more than enough.'

'Just take a quick look at this.'

She stood there and repeated her earlier words, looking directly at me: 'Remember, I helped you. You'll have to help me later.'

She was getting back into her sophisticated *Tempest* persona. There was even a deliberate half laugh in her voice.

But I knew how serious this could become for her. I certainly didn't want her to join the long list of 'accidental' deaths, though I had very little confidence that I could actually do anything to prevent Gupta from acting, if he made up his mind.

Feeling like a hypocrite, I nodded. 'I'll do everything I can. But there is one more thing I want you to see.'

I played the video of Liza being raped.

I could not bear to look at it.

But Vicky watched the whole thing with pain and disgust on her face. She did not seem to have seen it before. At the end of it, she frowned thoughtfully.

'I wonder if this has been staged. Just look at the way this is happening. Out in the open. No one trying to hide.'

'You might be able to analyse this better than I can. Are these the two men everyone seems to fear – Vinay Gupta's goons, Raman and Joseph?'

She did not even hesitate to answer.

'Of course it's them. And that's why I am so horrified. They raped Liza so brutally – it seems like they wanted to be seen, or simply didn't care. Though they've taken the time to get out of those silly suits and formal shirts they love to wear. Perhaps they thought it would be impossible to identify them.'

'But why would anyone want Liza to be assaulted like this?' I asked, still reeling from the fact that Liza was apparently dead.

Vicky looked at me almost pityingly.

'I just told you. There was – an incident. An accident.

Something had *already* happened to her – something that needed to be covered up; don't you understand?'

'Are you suggesting . . . that Vinay Gupta had already raped her, and these men were called in to join in the fun? A gang rape . . . but why? That sounds completely crazy,' I said, trying to make sense of her words.

'Because she was no longer useful to them and Vinayji no longer wanted her,' said Dennis. 'Had she become unreliable because she had started taking so many drugs? They could no longer risk using her? Perhaps she was not as obedient as she used to be?'

Vicky threw a look of surprise at Dennis. 'That's an intelligent guess. And yes, both of these reasons might be partly true. It's difficult to say, because I wasn't there for – any of this. Liza had simply become far too wild. But Vinayji had invested too much in her – too much time, too many drugs, too much money. So something had to be done. She had to be taught a lesson. Unfortunately, they all went too far.'

Too far. The men had not only raped Liza but had killed her.

'Just remember,' she said with ice in her voice, 'the stakes are extremely high. Vinay Gupta could be the next Home Minister. He needed an alibi, and the gang rape gives him the perfect cover. If anything happened to Liza that night, then certainly he wasn't involved. It's these two so-called unidentifiable men. Their DNA would be found on her, they would take the rap and go to jail. Not Vinay.'

She picked up her bag.

'Look, please don't forget: I took a huge risk to come here and say all this. Don't tell anyone about my involvement, even if you use the information. And try to get me out of this, please.'

On the last sentence she momentarily lost her composure once again. But then she recovered just as swiftly but for the glint of tears in her eyes.

After she left, Dennis and I stared at each other. Had this rape video really been deliberately filmed? Or had someone managed to shoot the video surreptitiously, without the knowledge of the rapists?

At every stage in this case, the probabilities were all evenly balanced.

Just when we were wondering if we would ever be able to find out what happened that night, and if Liza was still alive, a new set of photographs arrived on my phone.

Again, the screen flashed 'number withheld'.

I'd had to shut my eyes to block the rape scene; but these new pictures were impossible to view without feeling sick.

Each photograph was a close-up taken in a morgue. The little placard next to the body in the photographs read *'female, identity unknown'*.

The first one was of a girl's face, in profile, blue eyes slightly open even in death. Her cheek had been cut and roughly stitched up. The cruel black thread ran like a barbed wire across her face. The soft blonde hair lay in contrast on her cheek. They had obviously sliced through her skin to take an imprint of her teeth for identification. There was no need to be kind to a corpse, was there? Especially if it was being treated as unidentified.

The second photograph was of her pubic area, a close-up which showed an inflamed labia and bruised vaginal area. The young smooth thighs were heartbreaking. The redness of the entire area clearly indicated that she had been raped or molested very cruelly.

The third was of her shoulders, and the fragile area of her neck, where large bruises were visible, as though she had been beaten and pushed.

The fourth was of a jagged line running across her body, in between her two child-like breasts; again black stitches pulled the skin together roughly. Her body had been slashed from neck to abdomen, possibly to take samples from her organs for forensic processing, to find out the cause of death. But this surgery looked excessive even to me.

The fifth was of her hands twisted at impossible angles. The fingers were stiff and open, as though she were resisting attack.

And the sixth was of her back. There was a visible

soreness there and on her upper thighs, with angry black and red streams of congealed blood. There was little doubt that she had been sodomized, as well.

Now we knew what had happened to Liza.

And everyone on the beach must have known, as well. Near her lower abdomen was a tattoo – Veeramma's favourite. Broken hearts in a tiny daisy chain.

I called Vishnu, the only person I knew who had genuinely cared about her, to tell him that we now had the sad evidence of her death. But the phone just kept ringing.

Dennis and I decided we would have to go to the local police station and ask to look at the case files of unidentified bodies. Obviously someone had copied these photographs from somewhere.

We got up when my phone rang and my blood ran cold.

On the screen once more were the same dreaded words that had appeared a few minutes earlier: 'number withheld'.

Why was this anonymous source calling me?

Expecting another blow, I answered slowly, though my voice seemed to be coming from very far away, even to my own ears. 'Who is this?'

The soft voice at the other end was familiar. Why hadn't I guessed earlier?

Chapter 15

It was Vishnu.

The answer had been in front of me all along. But because of his appearance, his distrust of us and his fear, I had not linked him with the videos and photographs. How could such a frightened and helpless man possess this radical and subversive – and almost pornographic – material?

It seemed we were more deluded than he ever was.

With the discovery of his identity, things began to move really fast. Especially when it became clear that not only had Vishnu sent the films to us, it was he who had assiduously shot the videos of the girl he had been infatuated with. He had perfected the art of filming with a mobile phone without anyone realizing what he was up to.

But it also became obvious that, having inadvertently revealed himself by calling me back without unblocking his number, Vishnu was not entirely reluctant to share his role in this complicated mystery. In fact it did not take long to persuade him to come over to meet us. Perhaps he too realized that once his secret was out it would have been too big a risk not to tell us exactly how he had got

involved in this case and why he had planned this remark-
able exposure.

It seems that because he had been arrested a year ago,
all of those clips detailing Liza's abuse and eventual death
had lain buried under the debris of electronic gadgets in
his shop, only to be taken out when he came back from
jail. He had been filming Liza randomly and obsessively
– not quite sure what he would do with the eventual
material. Even, according to him, the rape on the beach,
was shot in the same accidental fashion.

After his brutal treatment at the hands of the police and
the threats from Vinay Gupta and Curtis, he wanted to at
last tell the truth. But initially he dared not speak up,
except anonymously.

It had taken exceptional courage from him, because if
anyone had found out about the material in his posses-
sion, who knows what might have happened? Looking at
the injuries already inflicted upon him I doubted if he
would have been allowed to survive.

Vishnu's best cover was our dismissal of him as semi-
literate and frankly, a little foolish – a view shared by his
friends on the beach. No one suspected that he had
planned the entire sequence of revenge while he had been
in jail.

And even at this stage, when it appeared he had
decided to tell us everything, he still did not reveal the
truth about one person who had helping him throughout.

Indeed that nugget of information came right at the very end. He surprised us once again with his resourcefulness and ingenuity and loyalty.

Meanwhile I told Vishnu how my hopes had risen seeing the computer in Marian's home with a live email address purporting to be Liza's.

'It was so eerie to see that. And that made me think, for just a fleeting moment, that perhaps Liza had not been killed. But,' I turned to Vishnu, 'you are a good actor; you must have known that it was a fake account. It was an excellent way to scare everyone, though, to send those videos in her name.'

Vishnu nodded, looking sheepish, as he usually did when anyone praised him.

'But who maintained the account? Was it you or Marian?'

For some reason thus far Vishnu had been very hesitant on the question of Marian.

I had always related his reluctance to the fact that he had thought Marian had got him jailed.

But he proved me wrong again.

'Madam, don't be angry, okay? I tell you something because now it is safe to tell,' he said in his usual quiet fashion.

'Out of two of us, Marian the better actor.' He gazed at us in turn, waiting for a reaction, as a smile spread over his face for the first time. Did I see a slightly self-satisfied look? Surely not!

Dennis and I stared back at him. Why was he so pleased?

'My idea, madam. They lock me up after Liza vanish. They do it once before when Curtis molest Liza. And this time she raped, they say I do it, just like before. They beat me, hit me, but I don't tell them about the video. I don't tell anything because then they will destroy it all. No one find out. When I come out from jail just one month ago I go to Marian. I share my idea with her. I show her films about Liza. She angry, want to give them to police. But I say, slowly, slowly. We need to scare Gupta and his men, make them think Liza is still alive.'

It was a brilliantly simple idea. Once he came out of jail, with Marian on board, they decided to send out the first lot of videos to everyone, including Vinay Gupta. With his Internet skills and ability to hack into computers, he could get hold of all the required email IDs. It was he who created the email identity of victoryatlast@gmail.com, putting firewalls that no one in the police had traced so far. And it was he who re-set Liza's password and started operating her account, hoping to rekindle interest in her disappearance and focus attention on those who had killed the girl he loved.

But when I asked him if he were sorry Marian had died, he said nothing, and instead handed us, almost victoriously, a clip which would probably lead the police to Gupta's doorstep. It was his way of telling us that it was time to wrap up our investigation.

But more of that later.

In our series of surreptitious conversations with Vishnu in Dennis's hotel we learnt that the first video he had sent out had created havoc for Vinay Gupta, and doubts about him grew within the government. The ripples of this were felt in Goa, as there were also a series of sightings of Liza around the beach that worried Gupta even more. He even began to wonder, just as Vishnu had wanted, if the morgue pictures were fake. When and how had Liza come back? And who had resurrected her from the dead? Had his own men been treacherous? He did not know quite what to believe.

But now we learnt that all of this was disinformation carefully placed by Marian, who also passed it to Amarjit and me. All of this together led to panic in Gupta's ranks. Not trusting the local police, he contacted Amarjit – and eventually Amarjit had asked me to make discreet inquiries. Was Liza still alive? And who was the real source of these damning videos?

Nobody knew, at that time, less than a fortnight ago, that my 'inquiries' could lead to such astonishing results. Or that I would find out that so many people could be involved in the planned disappearance of one girl, and how intricately they had worked together.

Nor, I remembered, had I known for certain at any stage that any of my suspicions were correct, until many of the missing links were provided by Vicky's information

– though piecing it all together took a few days. Days of talking to Vishnu to find out about Liza's last moments, and where her mutilated body had gone.

Throughout, I was conscious of a sense of urgency as my fear was that Vicky would lose her nerve and tell Vinay Gupta about my investigation. Or rather, 'our investigation', as Dennis had got more and more involved in it.

But the more I thought about it, the more I realized that there was nothing I could do to keep Vicky on our side. If she got nervous and spoke to Gupta I would simply have to find some way of dealing with it. But I worried that she might not be safe, either way. Which was another reason for working quickly.

Meanwhile, despite my misgivings that he had left us in the lurch, and that he might be obstructive, I called Amarjit. At this point there was no one else I could turn to. I realized that I would not be able to trust the local police because, after all, they would be very upset (to put it mildly) at some of my allegations of their acts of ommission. If they got angry with Vishnu again, I dreaded the outcome. We needed to quietly work through the evidence and protect both Vicky and Vishnu.

So when I spoke to Amarjit, let me just say that he wasn't pleased that I was still in Goa looking into the activities of a man who could well be his future boss in the next cabinet reshuffle. And especially when he,

Amarjit, had specifically apologized for having dragged me into this case and asked me to forget about it and come home.

But fortunately, despite all his other flaws, Amarjit still maintained some of the idealism with which he had entered the police service. And after he had made all his sarcastic and scathing remarks, I knew that ultimately he would do the right thing, and get justice for the two missing girls.

I also hoped that he was a little nervous about the fact that our relationship (for whatever it was worth) and our friendship would definitely be over if he showed himself to be anything less than brave this time. I had forgiven him in the past, but was unlikely to do so again.

Yet I could be shameless if I wanted something and so, even in the face of his initial reluctance and his anger, I begged him for one last favour, flattering him recklessly. I spoke in my most emollient tones: 'Please, Amarjit, this is an impossible task without your intervention.'

He was quiet at the other end of the phone line but I ploughed on. 'All we need is access to the files which catalogue the unidentified bodies at the local police station for the past year. I promise we'll be careful with all information given to us.'

He warned me that it would be a shambolic process, but I stuck to my request, bombarding him with emails till he succumbed and arranged for me to meet the local superintendent of police, Robert Gonsalves.

Thankfully, Gonsalves turned out to be quite a helpful and enthusiastic young man, equally tired of the corruption and the drug trade that Goa was becoming notorious for.

Yet even with his patient help, it took us two days of going through musty files. And that's how I found the photographs that Vishnu had messaged to me. I needed to make sure we had not been misled once more. And that Liza was really dead.

This set of photographs proved it, sadly.

Undoubtedly we would be forever grateful for Vishnu's expertise as an Internet and computer genius, which gave him legitimate and illegitimate access to all kinds of places. Even the police station, and my own laptop.

'But why did you hack into my computer?' I had finally asked him, when the penny dropped about what he had been doing that day when Durga and I stumbled upon him in our room.

He had looked contrite and said, 'Needed to check what information you send Amarjit and he send you. Also take phone number to send you videos.' It seemed the inquisitive Maggie was his cousin, who had helped him in keeping an eye on me throughout.

It also became clear that, like Marian, Vishnu sometimes had to agree to do things for the opposite camp.

And thus, I now realized that, ironically, it was he who had wiped out the videos from my phone and computer on instructions from Curtis, the day I had been 'drugged'. It was a strange double game that he had to play to survive on the beach. Something that needed very steady nerves. Vishnu was obviously braver than I was; he could bear more pain than anyone I knew.

And he was also loyal to an extreme degree.

Now in the police station we saw evidence of that, no matter how painful, he had faithfully copied all the photographs taken in the morgue of Liza's dissected and stitched body. These were photographs no one had ever seen before. And we realized that they were saved only because the body had been given another name.

In the official file it was noted that, within a few days of the discovery of an unidentified female body in a guest house off the Vagator beach, the deceased was found to be Vira Jennings, a UK resident. Her passport had been conveniently found lying in her room the next day. How it reached there no one knew, or even asked.

According to the accompanying forensic report, the cause of Vira's death was 'accidental', coupled with 'drug overdose'. The bruises on various parts of the body, and possible rape, were not mentioned. The corpse had been shipped to London twelve months ago, almost as soon it was found, and buried there by a bereaved and shocked 'fiancé', who was of Goan and Portuguese origin.

He had accompanied the corpse from Goa. That was before a missing report for Liza had been filed and there was any chance of investigating if the body might be hers.

Both Dennis and I had our suspicions who the fiancé would turn out to be.

'Curtis D'Silva. How neatly it all fits into place!' Dennis shook his head, part in anger and part in amazement.

No wonder he had wanted me out of the way as fast as possible. I had come to claim the resurrection of Liza Kay, when he had already engineered her burial.

The swift disposal of Liza's body could not have been better planned. By that time, Vishnu had been thrown in jail, falsely accused once more of molesting Liza, and a missing-person case was registered a few days later.

'No one connect with Curtis,' said Vishnu softly, as though he were telling us a children's story. 'He left very fast for London. I hear all detail in jail. The constable in charge of the morgue laughed and told his colleague he had money enough to buy villa in Paris.'

Without a body that could be examined, and no evidence of her murder, Liza's case remained that of a missing girl, and became a convenient scapegoat.

Even before Vishnu came out of jail, Marian might have been able to raise her voice about the mystery surrounding Liza, but she was facing the wrath of the police over the drugs found in her room. It had been an exhausting and humiliating run-in with the narcotics department and the police, as she had told me, after which not only was she sexually assaulted and her passport taken away, but the concocted case made it difficult for her to complain to anyone about her sister's disappearance.

Perhaps she only understood why she had been framed when it was far too late, and whatever proof might have existed about Liza's tragic rape and murder had been destroyed.

Marian's alleged drug abuse had been a masterful ploy, cooked up by her tormentors. Who would believe her now? Her reputation was in shreds.

She probably kept quiet about it all, too ashamed to even tell her mother about her own troubles and Liza's disappearance, posting emails instead about the wonderful time she was having in Goa, her career in astrology and Liza's mythical travels. Like many other women, over time, she learnt to deal with her sexual exploitation, knowing she would get very little sympathy or justice. In her case she also covered it all up by inventing another persona, 'Astrologer Anne'.

It didn't help, as she told me, that they had Stanley as a father. And the truth about Liza's disappearance was never mentioned till Vishnu returned.

Because, as Marian herself had hinted to me, to continue living on the beach, having accused or suspected someone so powerful of Liza's murder, was impossible. They simply did not have the protection or clout. Gupta was known for his wily cunning; he was, after all, someone who could eat other cabinet ministers for breakfast. What chance did Marian and Stanley have against him, or indeed of survival, when they were so dependent on local support? It was the final tragedy for Stanley – something he could never confess openly. That despite having lived his entire life in this part of Goa, when the vultures gathered and stole his daughter – he found he was still an alien.

Dennis and I were not only impressed with Vishnu's quiet execution of an almost foolproof plan, but also with the nuggets of information he communicated to us, hesitatingly and in his broken English, painting a far more authentic picture of life on the beach than we had known thus far.

I learnt from him, this boy whom we had all dismissed as being ignorant, that as the law had caught up with older methods of drug smuggling, someone designed a new and rather frightening, almost foolproof plan. It was a procedure made possible only with the complicity of the police, the forensics department and the technicians in the morgue, as well as the customs officials. And Liza, through her 'accidental death', was an ideal candidate for it, which could explain why almost her entire body had been cut open and then stitched again.

As I described later, in a note to Amarjit:

Most of her organs were removed for the so-called post mortem, in any case, and in their place, plastic bags of cocaine and heroin were packed. When her corpse reached London the apparently devastated fiancé, along with some other members of Fernando's gang, ensured that the packets were quickly removed. After that, Vira Jennings – alias Liza Kay – was buried somewhere, very quietly.

Her family might not even have been involved. Vira Jennings, a young girl who bore a fleeting resemblance to Liza, had her passport and her identity conveniently transferred to Liza's corpse, because they had been surrendered a long time back to the drug cartel in lieu of money. Or it might have been 'impounded' as Marian's had been.

Dennis wondered if the Jennings family (if there was one) was even aware of what had happened to her body. And if they knew that the wrong girl had been buried in her place?

We had no answers, and so, on Amarjit's advice, we shared the information with Robert Gonsalves, who had been so helpful in retrieving the photographs of Liza from the files.

He was understandably nervous when he learnt that a future Home Minister could be involved, but despite his fears of being sacked or demoted he tried to find out more about the case from his colleagues, as quietly as he could.

One evening, not wearing his uniform (I was reminded of Amarjit's similarly cautious approach), he invited us to a shack where we could have a private conversation. His news was not good either.

Robert poured out some tea – he had given up drinking alcohol long ago, upset by allegations that most Goan cops liked their feni a little too much. I had begun to admire Robert; he was a man of principle, and it would only be due to people like him that the police force in Goa would, one day, retrieve its reputation.

'Yes, it seems this might have happened, and still goes on, though very rarely. Since the money involved is huge, sometimes even blood relatives agree to take delivery of the body, getting a percentage of the drug sale for their silence.'

Dennis and I tried to sip our beer, but it all tasted foul. Were people really so desperate for money that they would not only kill innocent young boys and girls but then continue to exploit them after their death? It seemed like the worst form of violation.

'But surely the families raise objections. Some kind of post mortem would be conducted to find out how the person died, and they would also want to know about the state of the body. Wouldn't traces of the drugs be left behind?' I asked, astonished that such a complicated means of transporting drugs could have been conducted (if it were true) without anyone being caught. I still thought it was too macabre and fantastical.

Robert shook his head regretfully. 'I am afraid, Miss Simran, that you have a very naive view of the world. Who will bother to say anything when the stakes are so high? And remember, often these are bodies of young boys and girls who had become addicts over the years, while living in Goa. Their families usually would have lost contact with them over time or have little to do with them.'

'So you mean no one has ever asked any uncomfortable questions when these incidents have taken place, either here or in the country to whom the person belongs?' Dennis was equally taken aback. It sounded like the dead made perfect drug mules.

'Well, sir, what I have found is that in some cases there would be no demand for a post-mortem examination when the corpse was delivered back, whether in Europe or Russia or Israel, or wherever the bodies were sent. But if the family wanted one, care was taken to strike a deal with them before the body was shipped out. Sometimes the speed with which a case was forgotten was indicative of how fast a deal had been struck. It is a dangerous procedure, but with the complicity of the police and the politicians, the international drug smugglers who operate from Goa have perfected each aspect of sending these corpses back, right down to the death certificate.'

'Which is why "accidental deaths" are rarely discussed here,' I said gloomily, remembering the difficulty I had faced in trying to get statistics and information about those foreigners who had died. 'Most of the time there is so much fabrication going on. I mean, here too, they had passed off Liza's body as "unidentified female", and that is completely incorrect. Her sister and father lived here. Everyone knew her at Fernando's, Vinay Gupta knew her, as did Curtis and Vishnu. But they didn't get a single witness to identify her.'

'No,' said Robert, sipping his tea delicately, as though it were the best Earl Grey from Sri Lanka, instead of a milky brew drowned in sugary hot water. 'That is because speed is of the essence. Often a shipment of cocaine is smuggled in and needs to leave urgently. Perhaps Liza was supposed to carry it, and she was now unreliable because of her increasing addiction to drugs. It is difficult to say whether it was an accidental death or a planned murder. But once they had her body, it would have been easy for them to make the arrangements.'

One word caught my attention.

'Accident. While she was being raped they killed her accidentally. I don't think Gupta really cared one way or the other what they did with her. He just handed her over to them for disposal. She was shop soiled, unwanted. Remember what Vicky had said?' I turned to Dennis.

'She said it was an accident and they had to get rid of her.'

'They got rid of her and made millions in the process. Only poor Liza, who aspired to the good life, got nothing out of it,' Dennis said. I remembered with a shiver Stanley telling me that she had gone back to London. Perhaps he knew too about the drugs.

Shaken up, I realized from Robert's stoic demeanour that there was little he could do, apart from sharing his information with us. He knew it was unlikely any action could be taken on such an old case, especially when both the girls involved had vanished.

We had no idea what had happened with Marian's body.

Plagued by suspicion, I asked Robert to go through all the latest files to see if any recent unidentified body matched Marian's description. He even did a round of the hospitals, but found nothing. Perhaps her body had floated out to sea, after all. I just hoped that she hadn't been used in the same fashion as her sister.

Saying a silent prayer for her, I went through the video clips once more with Vishnu, with renewed vigour, hoping to find something that could nail Vinay Gupta. It was unbearable to think that, after all these ghastly misdeeds, nothing could be pinned on him or his men.

Vishnu understood my anger, and put together all the videos on a memory stick so we could view them repeatedly, trying to find anything to connect the case to Vinay Gupta.

Thankfully, he had shot many more videos than he had sent us. But despite my desire to hasten things, it would still take a long time to piece everything together. None of us noticed when the New Year was ushered in, as we didn't have the heart to participate in any of the celebrations. Apart from the rape and murders I was dealing with, even in Delhi my family had cancelled their celebrations due to the death of the young woman who had been cruelly gang-raped in a bus. She had fought valiantly to live but ultimately succumbed to her terrible injuries. The protests for justice for her carried on in Delhi. But no one had ever protested in the same way for either Scarlett Keeling or now Lisa Kay. Along with thousands– perhaps millions – of women who had been raped and molested in this country, they were dead and buried. And forgotten.

My ticket to Delhi was booked and cancelled at least four times.

We had no idea if or when we would find anything to nail the real culprits. It was a hugely depressing thought, and only the company of Dennis made it a little better for me, as we spent our spare time together, walking on the beach and dining at shacks where our conversation would not be overheard.

As we painstakingly discussed what should be presented to Amarjit, I think Vishnu finally began to trust us both. It was after a long evening of watching the videos that he finally told us the final truth about Marian.

He proved my suspicions wrong, again.

And before that he also handed me the clip which would provide the clinching evidence.

Unlike the other videos, this one had a date flashing in one corner, showing that it had been filmed on the night that Liza and Marian had been given the spiked drinks. After which Liza vanished forever.

The familiar jerky camera lens was at a safe distance as Liza walked out of Fernando's. One could hear the sound of the waves as she strolled along the beach. She was in the same clothes that she had worn in the video when she was raped. But she was not as dishevelled.

I noticed that her hair had been nicely styled and she even had a handbag on her shoulder. But her steps were a little unsteady, and she stopped to take her shoes off. As she paused, a man I could not identify came up to her and said something, pointing towards the road which was barely visible in the distance. From her lack of surprise and compliant nod, it was obvious this was a pre-planned assignation.

The camera followed her and the man up to the road, where a car was waiting. The headlights were switched off, and one of the windows was rolled down. Even from afar one could make out the familiar features of Vinay

Gupta, and that trademark moustache. So while she had been instructed to go out from the front of the shack, Vinay Gupta had taken the back exit. No one would connect the two.

The video ended when the car drove away.

The second clip which followed immediately had been shot a few hours later, early in the morning, around 2 a.m., at the same spot. Vishnu told us that he had shivered through most of the night, waiting for Gupta's car to come back. He knew it would return, because this was not the first time this had happened. He had seen it before. Both with Liza and with other girls that Gupta fancied.

So the second part of the video began when Liza almost fell out of the same car, stumbling towards the beach. Gupta was not around. The beach was deserted and according to the recorded time it was early in the morning.

Vishnu told us that she had never been in such a bad state before, and though he was fairly near to her, she had no idea of his presence. Her pupils were completely dilated, and her dress was torn, though that was not clearly visible in the clip. He also saw large bruises on her arms, while blood was trickling down one leg. She stumbled and swayed as she walked, singing to herself, apparently unaware of her pain or her condition.

She seemed to have been given so much cocaine that she didn't know what was happening to her any more. He followed her for a while, keeping away in the dark, uncertain of what she was doing. After the police complaint the last time, he had been filming her with as much stealth as possible, because he did not want her or anyone else to accuse him of molesting her again.

'I want to go near her, but I step back when I see that Raman come up to her and talk to her, and then drag her towards a shack.' His voice trailed off.

But he didn't have to say anything more. Because I had already seen this part of the video far too many times.

It was too deeply embedded in my memory. Liza's screams and then the point at which Joseph came around to put his hand on her mouth and pull her arms over her head, while Raman pushed himself between her legs.

Vishnu tried to describe how difficult it was for him to film this part, and how he had wanted to shout for them to stop. He wanted to thrash the two men. But he was kept back by the thought that they would simply kill him and then no one would know what they had done to Liza. In any case, the entire episode lasted only a few minutes, before Liza suddenly went limp. It did not stop the two men from attacking her, but if one carefully watched the video, there was a specific point at which she stopped struggling.

He did not know at that time, he said, but he suspected that she might have died in the midst of that second attack. By that time she probably had internal injuries, or she might have suffocated.

'Or,' Dennis pointed out sadly, 'the cocaine overdose coupled with the stress of the rape simply caused her body to shut down.'

Vishnu also felt that even if her death was accidental, it was possible that Gupta thought she had become a liability. He might have also realized he would be accused of raping a minor, and wanted someone else to carry the can.

Since Vishnu was present earlier the same night at Fernando's, shooting his video, he said he noticed Marian's discomfort when Gupta kissed Liza. He said she tried to censure Liza, and warned her about associating with an older man but without success. Liza might have also said something to Gupta that night which could have led to this tragic chain of events. Had either Marian or Liza threatened him with exposure for raping an underage girl?

Of course, now we could only speculate.

Even the botched post-mortem report showed that there were many more injuries on her body than could have been inflicted upon her by Raman and Joseph that night.

Liza's death, however, was probably not part of the script.

But filming it all from a safe distance, Vishnu had been confused. 'I thought she fainted. So I wait. They finish, then see her totally still. They try to shake her up, she no

wake up. Then they call someone and have long conversation. They pick her up and take her to a car that comes.
That all I see that evening.'

He waited till daybreak but no one came back. Finally
he went home and hid the phone on which he had been
shooting the videos – a fortunate decision, because,
though he did not know it then, these were his last few
hours of freedom.

By the next morning Liza had disappeared.

At last we had most of the information about Liza's
short life and painfully long death.

But one mystery remained to be cleared up.

'And what about Marian?' I asked him. 'Somehow I
don't quite believe that Gupta would risk another disappearance or murder at this time, when there has been so
much focus on Liza.'

Vishnu was intriguingly silent for a few minutes and
then sighing, spoke up, still gently.

'You right. They nothing to do with it,' he replied
slowly, still looking evasive.

Dennis patted his hand sympathetically.

'You have to tell us, Vishnu, otherwise the whole story
will not pull together.'

He looked down at the floor with that smile again.
Perhaps he delighted in the fact that he could fool us over
and over again. We, the slick city folk, were being
constantly hoaxed by an apparent village simpleton! We

had felt sorry for him – and now he no doubt felt sorry for us. He took a deep breath.

'Marian getting worried all the time. Life not safe for her, after we start sending videos. People angry. Though I am very careful and sending the video from my home, they begin to think she doing it. Then you meet Marian and they get more worried in case Marian tell you something about Liza. So she got threat from Vinay Gupta's men not to search for Liza.

'Then one day, people calling from Delhi, asking about Liza's connection with Vinay Gupta. Once the party video come out, too many people are questioning. They call her home. She worried Vinay Gupta will find out. And so she do a deal with police, and say if no complaint for Liza, she get passport back.'

That was the day she met me at the hotel.

I was puzzled about where this could be leading.

There was a tiny pause, as even Vishnu had learnt that the punch line was the most important part of the story.

'Then she was killed by Gupta's henchmen?' I asked with trepidation, half sure that this was not the correct answer.

He smiled, unable to resist the temptation of looking a little bit triumphant. 'No. Then we buy her ticket for London.'

'But too late,' I said. 'She died that night.' I wondered

349

why Vishnu was still smiling and shaking his head, as though I was being obtuse.

The irony of Marian's death, coming so close to her planned escape, was sad beyond belief.

But to my surprise, Vishnu gave another smile, and now *he* patted *my* hand. Just as Dennis had patted his a short while back.

'No, no. You don't understand. She not dead. She hide. To confuse Vinay Gupta's gang she stage her own death. That was only fake video; I film her lying on the rock, put red paint on her, and upload.'

My jaw nearly dropped out of my head.

Vishnu had that familiar uncomfortable look he seemed to get every time he spoke of Marian. Only now I had found out the real reason!

'Sorry I couldn't tell earlier, we worry she not safe, but we waiting till she reach London. She now reach there. Send email, she safe. So now I give final video to you to nail the bastard.' He looked particularly pleased saying 'bastard'.

But after a pause he added, 'But I no tell where she is.'

Underneath that misleading demeanour, Vishnu was as protective of Marian as he had been of Liza. But sometime in the future I hoped he would let me contact Marian – if for no other reason than just to apologize for what I had thought about her and how much I had misunderstood her.

Hearing his words, the burden of grief and guilt that had engulfed me ever since I had learnt about Marian's 'death' rolled away. I literally felt lighter, and perhaps even a little happier.

So that explained why she had answered the phone so promptly and met me on time on the morning of her 'death'. She was flying back that night, and that's why getting her passport back had been so important.

Perhaps prayers do get answered – and at least one sister was safe!

I looked forward to talking to Marian once again. Not as a victim, or as a renegade, but as someone who had managed to survive in the most extreme circumstances.

Vishnu now had a big smile on his face and I had to compliment the dexterity with which he had plotted Liza's revenge – and Marian's escape.

Stanley, fortunately, had made a dramatic getaway from Marian's flat, while his friends leapt into it looking for the drugs, turning it upside down, much to the consternation of Vinay Gupta's henchmen. He too was thinking of leaving Goa very soon. These days he was lounging in Dennis's room, trying not to attract anyone's attention. After learning the truth of what had happened to his daughters, he had been feeling quite disenchanted about his hippie hideout, for some time, though he had tried not to show it. Even at his anniversary celebration he said he had hidden his anguish.

He had just been waiting for Marian to leave and now that she was safe in London he was going to take a flight out very soon.

Though I had a feeling that Stanley would be homesick for Goa. After having got used to life on a sunny golden beach and under a magical banyan tree – it was unlikely he would enjoy grey city streets and underground tube stations. But first he would have to get over the trauma of losing his younger daughter – a grief he had never spoken about or discussed.

Meanwhile, much though I would have loved to acknowledge openly the real hero of this case – Vishnu – he still had to live around this beach for the rest of his life.

And so, as far as Amarjit and the world was concerned, the source of the videos would remain unknown.

He could not afford to antagonize anyone. Especially not Vinay Gupta or even Curtis. He depended on them for work and for his livelihood. And, strangely enough, for his identity.

Thus all the information and reports going to Amarjit were being routed through me and Dennis, who had turned out to be much more than a pillar of strength.

Luckily, as all of this was happening, there was a political turmoil, and the central government fell, making the persecution of corrupt ministers such as Gupta far, far easier. As elections were announced, it was a relief to think that on some file somewhere was information that would ensure that all further investment in Vinay Gupta as a leading political light would come to a halt.

But Dennis also made sure that the video of Vinay Gupta in which he had a very young-looking Liza on his lap went viral, especially in Chandigarh and the rest of his constituency. Within hours it was trending on Twitter and had a whole Facebook page dedicated to it, where people wrote and condemned it in no uncertain terms, saying it was absolutely sickening to see a senior minister behave in such an appalling fashion.

Even more humiliatingly he was slapped with a case from the National Commission for Women, and the UK government rebuked him publicly for molesting a British child. But the final reprimand came when he was taken to court for child abuse, and his passport was impounded. For a man who claimed to spend every second week in London, there couldn't be a worse punishment. As I write this, there is little doubt that he will lose his deposit in the next elections and might even spend a few nights in jail.

He must have wondered many times how a dead girl had come back to haunt him in this fashion. And wreck his career.

Actually, he deserved worse, because he was responsible for the death of two girls. Sadly, I was not able to save Vicky.

A consequence of Vinay Gupta's downfall was the

ruthless interrogation of his casino employees, to check who had been disloyal to him.

She was said to have committed suicide – leapt from the floating casino into the Mandovi River at night, according to newspaper reports.

I had insisted on confidentiality when I had sent a recording of my conversation with her to Amarjit, as it was the only account we had on record of Gupta's complicity in Liza's death and the drug trade.

I had, also, asked Amarjit to give Vicky witness protection, but the lynch mob on the beaches must have turned against her very quickly. She had broken the code of silence and had to be eliminated. Gupta himself might have ferreted out information about the recording from his moles in Amarjit's office. As she had told me, it was dangerous that she knew so much about Gupta. The only compensation was that shortly after her death, Raman and Joseph's bodies were found in a car crash not far from Panjim. The police, for once, correctly said it was a case of accidental death. What was incorrect, however, was that they had both been drinking.

But no one lodged a complaint about that case.

As I read the critical articles about Vicky and her lifestyle which flood the newspapers these days, I realize that no one can ever understand what Vinay Gupta did to her and how much she regretted giving up her life and her youth to a man who trapped her with unfulfilled promises. If only she had tried to go back to Chandigarh and settle down. Who knows, perhaps her parents would have accepted her back, and she might still be alive.

Ultimately, finding out about Liza's disappearance had been complicated and exhausting. And not everyone would face the punishment they deserved. Not Vinay Gupta and certainly not Curtis D'Silva. Perhaps one day this country would finally get better policing and a better justice system. One could only hope for that.

Quite frankly, once we had sent the last report, accompanied by the relevant videos, to Amarjit, it was a relief to finally leave the beach where I had come for a relaxed holiday and ended up fighting for my own life and for the 'life' of a dead girl, as well.

The one positive note was that Dennis and I were still together, which was unusual, given the fact that there was much we could have disagreed on, especially about Goa – the perception and the reality; but we both chose not to. Because he promised to show me the real Goa, one which I had always felt existed, away from the beaches.

So last week Dennis and I shifted to South Goa to spend some time with his family and get over the evil that we had just confronted.

Out here, in a little Goan village, where the church bells ring with regularity, I have found myself in a different world altogether. We have spent an enchanted week together and now I wait at the railway station in Margao to catch my train back to Mumbai and then onward to Delhi, planning with Dennis to meet again soon. Very soon.

And in the last week I have also been able to tell Durga that I found Liza. She does not know what happened, and so she was delighted. I did not want to focus on the pain, right now; there has been enough of that.

It was all thanks to her, I told her. It had been a very good idea of hers that I should stay on and investigate.

What she (and my mother, who was quite disappointed that I would not be returning on Amarjit's arm) does not know is that I have someone who will wait for me, quite impatiently, in Goa. Someone I want them to meet. Maybe something in my voice gives me away as I speak to Durga now from the station to tell her I will be home soon.

'So let's come back here,' I say as casually as I can manage, aware that my face is going an unnatural red, while Dennis puts an arm around me, as he bids me farewell, 'and have the holiday you missed out on.'

She says she hasn't heard of a better idea in a long time. Her voice is tinged with laughter. I have a feeling she has guessed why I want to come back to Goa.

I wonder how?

Why are children so perceptive?

Acknowledgements

This has been probably the most difficult book to write in the Simran Singh series so far. Not only did my overused laptop crash three times – as a result of which I had to rewrite almost half the book – it was also a year of excessive travel and so a lot of work happened in aeroplanes and on trains. My long-suffering editor and publisher Clare Hey was no doubt somewhat bemused by my frequent disappearances – and the fact that deadlines were sometimes missed when the internet went AWOL. I thank her, as always, for her cheery patience, support and brilliant editing.

I also thank Hannah Corbett, Rahul Srivastava, Shireen Quadri, Jennifer Bird – and the entire team at Simon & Schuster, in the UK, India and Australia, for making the whole process of writing so very enjoyable – and for keeping Simran Singh alive and investigating new problems and issues.

I also thank Caroline Michel for her sage advice and support at all times, as well as all others at PFD.

Many thanks go out to Will Atkins for his very swift editorial judgements.

ACKNOWLEDGEMENTS

The book's research would not have been complete without extremely crucial input from Vikram Varma and his wife Meenal, as well as others in his office. I would also like to thank Sujai Joshi and her legal team for her support and help. Indeed, I would like to specially extend a warm thanks to all friends in Goa, including Maria Couto, Shruti Pandit, Habiba Miranda, everyone who spent time in discussing this book with me.

I would also like to thank Malavika Rajkotia for her input.

And of course, my deepest gratitude is to my family, especially my husband, Meghnad Desai, who read a very early first draft and urged me on; my children, Gaurav and Mallika Ahluwalia, and my parents, Padam and Rajini Rosha, for giving me the love, encouragement and space to complete this book.